Stone of Destiny

by

Margaret Izard

Stones of Iona

Cover Art by *Lisa Dawn MacDonald*

The Wild Rose Press, Inc.
PO Box 708
Adams Basin, NY 14410-0708
Visit us at www.thewildrosepress.com

Publishing History
First Edition, 2026
Trade Paperback Print ISBN 978-1-5092-6388-2
Digital ISBN 978-1-5092-6389-9

Stones of Iona
Published in the United States of America

Dedication

Thank you to my husband for all the love, support, and for pretending to listen when I plot twists out loud. To my kids—thanks for letting Mom disappear into her crazy stories.

To all the creatives whose minds wander where others don't—keep chasing the dream.

The MacDougalls' journey might be over… but the story? Oh, that's just getting started.

Chapter 1

In the final chapter, is the first page.

The Fae realm shimmered around Ceallach as he stood firm in the Tuatha Dé Danann kingdom, ready to defend the maiden of the Stones of Iona in the battle that would decide the fate of all. The humans had recovered all six magical Fae stones, and the time for the prophecy had arrived. He hoped he had enough power to serve the gems and save the maiden. But most of all, he wanted to shield the one he couldn't. She wasn't a stone maiden, and he could do nothing to protect her in the coming days. He prayed to the gods to let fate keep his Kat safe.

****

Draped in a soft blue gown, Kat stood unmoving as Ewan's voice lifted into the wind to swear a love she could never claim. "I promise to love you as deeply as the ocean, with all its mystery, beauty, and power. Like the waves that crash against the shore, my love for you will be unending and unstoppable." The words of the vow were spoken softly while he held his love's hand.

His bride, Lorelei, brushed her bright red hair aside, and a soft pink glow stained her cheeks as she spoke her wedding vows. "As we stand beside the ocean tide, may our love always be as constant and unchanging as these never-ending waves that drift beneath our feet, flowing endlessly from the depths of the sea." The bride paused, the breeze blew, and everyone in attendance seemed to sigh.

The wedding event was a grand affair, all meticulously arranged by Ewan's mother, but nothing could have prepared Kat for the moment earlier when Lorelei's sisters emerged from the loch. One blink—just one—and they stepped onto the shore, unnoticed by the gathering crowd. The water shimmered around them, their sea-slicked forms shifting into human beauty as easily as breathing. Merfolk made flesh—Fae royalty in satin.

Lorelei's eleven sisters had glided forward like a painted dream. Each with long, flowing hair that shimmered with light and moved like silk underwater. Their smooth, porcelain-pale skin seemed untouched by the sun or time. While they gathered around Lorelei, they looked like stars circling the moon.

She should have been honored—standing among them as one of twelve bridesmaids. And she was proud. But that pride twisted in her chest, hard and uncomfortable, like a ribbon pulled too tight.

Kat glanced down at herself. The long and lovely pale blue dress she'd chosen and cherished, now felt plain beside the Fae gowns of pastel and organza satin. Their shimmer made hers suddenly drab and forgettable. The freckles she usually liked about herself seemed like specks of dirt against the clean canvas of her skin. Her hair appeared dull compared to their shimmering waves. As if hers had lost its blonde shine just by standing near them. Still, she lifted her chin. She wouldn't shrink in front of anyone.

Ewan laughed when Lorelei squealed and threw her arms around her sisters. That joy was real. And Kat reminded herself—she had a place here, too. Not by blood. Not by sea or spell. But by choice. And she would stand tall, even if she was the only one who didn't glow.

When Ewan glanced at her before Lorelei walked down the aisle, he'd winked, sending a mind message. *Thank ye, sister, for being here.*

His comment brought a smile even though she wasn't Ewan's sister. But he treated her like one after her brother, Doug, Ewan's best friend, decided to stay in the eighteenth century for true love. Both men had traveled back and forth between time, searching for a missing magic Iona stone. They'd not only found the Stone of Faith, but each had also found their true love.

Sister. A single word that sent her down memory lane, carrying her further into her melancholy mood. She always thought of her brother as alive in the past, not someone from the past who'd died. The mindset helped, but sometimes she missed him something awful.

Cheers from the people around her brought her out of her thoughts when Ewan bent his wife over his arm in a searing kiss, sealing their wedding vows.

The pastor chuckled and yelled, "Ewan, I said ye may kiss the bride, not devour her!" More laughter and cheers erupted. Everyone seemed so joyous today.

The guests dispersed, leaving the ship and moving to the reception in the castle yard. They'd docked the vessel at Dunstaffnage Castle, Oban Scotland, Ewan's home, near Ardachrain Priory. An old priory her mother, Marie MacArthur, refurbished into a cozy home that her da, John, loved as much as she did. Kat huffed. The place came close in size to Dunstaffnage Castle.

Lorelei's da, a tall, grey-headed, muscular man larger than Laird Mac, clapped Colin on the back. "Laird

MacDougall, thank you for the hospitality, but we—" He waved to his brood of giggling girls. "Must depart soon before the reception ends, and our time for visiting nears its conclusion." As her parents lingered with other guests, Kat took the chance to escape.

Sneaking behind another group of guests, Kat followed them towards the tables, but when she neared the old stone arch, she veered away, taking the path to the Chapel in the Woods. The one place that always reminded her of her brother. She could swear she felt closer to him when she sat inside the shadowed, peaceful interior.

As she nudged one of the heavy oak doors aside and slipped into the familiar space, she stood there for a moment, and the wind blew around the exterior. To her, it seemed the building sighed in welcome. Letting the door close, she proceeded through the space without turning on the lights. She liked the sanctuary better dimmed anyway. Today, the late afternoon sun shone through the stained-glass windows, leaving colorful patterns across the pews. She meandered past the windows depicting love, hope, and faith, before arriving at the altar.

Kat turned, facing the back, and took a deep breath as she closed her eyes. This was the one routine she did each time she came here, concentrating hard, wishing against all odds her brother, Doug, would materialize in the chapel doorway. The oak door was no ordinary entryway—it was a portal left by the good Fae, bound to the magic of the Stones of Iona. Six stones found, one still lost. She closed her eyes, hoping her brother would return. The nave seemed to pause like the earth stood still, waiting for something magical to happen. One moment passed, then another. The wind blew around the building, murmurs from the wedding drifted from a distance but nothing happened inside the chapel. After a moment of focused thought, Kat slowly opened her eyes to the sight of the closed oak doors, not her brother.

Face reality as it is, not as it was or as you wish it to be. The saying echoed in her mind. Another tear slipped free as she sank into the pew, wondering at the science of love.

Her studies reduced love to something smaller than she felt. Dr. Chu, her favorite professor, insisted no science could prove love was real, calling it mostly an illusion.

She'd never thought love illusory but knew, from past relationships, how easily selfishness masqueraded as devotion. Dr. Chu once said even platonic or altruistic love couldn't escape self-interest—no one could love what they found repulsive. That, she conceded, was true. She'd accepted bad conduct as *normal,* and a few ex-boyfriends proved that theory. Still, she couldn't help but wonder—was there any logic in love at all?

Energy thickened in the room, humming at the edges of her senses. The air felt charged, vibrating with an unseen current that prickled across her skin. It was the same taut expectancy she'd felt before a Fae appeared, like the moment before a storm split the sky, when every particle seemed to tremble in anticipation. Kat stood and turned to the door, hoping her brother would arrive. A gust of wind blew through the chapel, even though the door was closed.

As she approached the wooden doors, a familiar voice spoke from behind her. "Nice dress, Kat, but ye didn't have to dress up for my arrival."

Kat spun around and leaning on the altar was Ceallach, Aodhán's cousin from the Tuatha Dé Danann, the good Fae. His body filled out his incandescent shirt under his snug suit jacket, and his pants hugged his well-muscled legs. She had met the Fae at the wedding of Evie MacDougall and Aodhan in the Fae realm.

With him standing before her now, she almost sighed his name out loud. Kat had fallen for Ceallach at first sight. Like all her past crushes, this one should have ended quickly. Instead, her feelings lingered long after she left the Fae realm when Ceallach had vanished from her life—until today. Ever since, she'd compared every man she met to him. Not a single human measured up. That was when she'd started questioning whether love had any logic at all.

He stepped forward with a grin as he moved into a beam of sunlight shining through the stained-glass window. His long jet-black hair glistened in the rays, and the color reflected purple, matching his mother's, Morrigan—the Fae assigned to assist the Captain of the Castle, her da, John MacArthur. Being the MacArthur Fae, Morrigan also helped her and her brother navigate the duty to the magic stones.

When he shifted in the sunlight, his Fae necklace glittered. The pendant held the sign of eternity set on top of fern leaves. Over that sat a five-pointed star made of clear Fae crystal. She'd studied Evic's intently, while Evie told her how her husband Aodhán had gifted her the sacred item to save her life. The necklace was the only item a Fae could give to anyone to form a bond lasting for eternity. Evie told her it was the most powerful gem in the Fae realm—the power within held a Fae's immortality. She'd dreamt of Ceallach giving her his, if only in her dreams.

Still wearing a grin, he strode forward with confidence and a sensuality Kat had not forgotten. The man still took her breath away with one look. Ceallach arrived before her, a smile playing on his lips. As his eyes swept across her face, the expression faltered. His brows knitted together in a frown, shadowing the sudden tension in his gaze. Reaching with his finger, he lifted a tear from her cheek, gripped his fist hard, and when opened, a small, clear teardrop-shaped gemstone sat in his palm.

"Dry yer tears, sweet Kat. Yer face is much prettier without them." He took her hand and, with his other placed the gemstone in her palm. "When ye hold the gem, yer tears will fade, and happy thoughts shall fill yer heart." When the stone touched her skin, her mind cleared, and a sense of ease washed over her.

Ceallach released her hand and strode past her to the doors.

Kat turned, calling after him. "Wait, why are ye here?"

The attractive Fae stopped and turned. "Dagda sent me. I've come to meet with the guardian of the stones. All the stones have returned. The gathering and battle of good vs evil is upon us. The gods have called, and we must answer."

He opened the heavy oak doors without effort and strode through. The doors weight closed them, leaving Kat in the shadows again. She blinked, almost not believing her eyes and the truth before her. Her secret love had just casually strolled back into her life. Gripping the gem, he'd shaped from her tears, warmth washed over her. Ceallach was here. A smile crossed her face.

Ceallach was here.

Wait, he said a battle was upon them.

She pocketed her gem and ran forward, pushing hard against the doors. She had to lean against the heavy wood to shift one and wiggle through the cracked opening. When she got through, Ceallach was already halfway down the path to the castle. She ran to catch up, lifting her skirt so she wouldn't trip.

He didn't break stride when she came alongside him. "Wait, what do ye mean a battle? Evie and Ewan already battled Manix. Each separately." Manix Skene was the evil Fae who tried to make Evie his when she really loved Aodhán. They'd battled and Manix fled—an outcast from his Fae kingdom, the Fomoire. While searching for the Stone of Faith a year later, Ewan stumbled across him in the Caribbean Sea in the eighteenth century, but Manix disappeared again.

Ceallach shifted his shoulders before he marched on. "The prophecy must be fulfilled. The Stones are found. This will be the great fight I've prepared for."

Kat shoved him hard, the way she used to push her brother Doug when they fought. He stumbled back and stopped short.

She took advantage of his pause and stood blocking the path. "Wait, what do ye mean fight ye've prepared for?"

From behind her, Aodhán's voice came cheerfully. "Cousin! Welcome. Ye are just in time for the reception." Ceallach stepped around her and hugged his cousin. They stood there staring, likely doing that *mind speak* crap they did. She hated being left out of the conversation.

Kat slapped Aodhán's muscular arm, and he

flinched—not from pain, but as if her scolding landed harder than her hand. "Ouch."

She folded hers. "Ouch is only the beginning. *What is up?*"

Both men ignored her and walked on like she didn't exist. She followed while they spoke aloud.

Aodhán waved his hand. "Come enjoy the feast, try the whisky. Tomorrow, we will meet everyone who is here. Prepare while we await the arrival of the others."

Ceallach's jaw tightened, a low sound rumbling from his throat. "Ye always were one for celebration first, then business later. But aye, a drink would suit me well. And I'd like to visit with my sweet cousin, Annie, before the others arrive for the gathering." Annie was Evie and Aodhán's pride and joy—their daughter with budding Fae powers like her da.

Kat tried to shove between them and stumbled. "A gathering, a prophecy, what is this all about?"

Ceallach grabbed her arm, preventing her from tumbling. His electric white, blue eyes connected with hers as his expression hardened. "Ye are not part of this, Kathryn Marie MacArthur. Ye must stay away."

Aodhán clapped a heavy hand on his cousin's shoulder, prompting Ceallach to loosen his hard grip on her. "She's part of the family. It wouldn't hurt to allow her to be in the meetings." As the attractive Fae steadied her, Kat brushed her dress, hoping she hadn't soiled the gown in her haste, but she had to know what they spoke of and what his arrival meant. Fae gathering sounded like time travel.

They stood a moment in silence. Kat huffed when Ceallach lowered his arm, releasing her. More of that *mind speak*. She wondered if the ability was just brain waves floating between them or something spoken that she couldn't see or hear.

Aodhán nodded. "Good choice." He took her arm in his, pulling her away. "Come, Kat, we can't miss the party." As they moved on, she glanced over her shoulder at Ceallach, who frowned. For a moment, he looked like he might speak—but then his gaze dropped to the ground, jaw tight, the silence between them stretched like a thread on the verge of snapping.

She felt certain there was more to his arrival and vowed to find out what it was. If there was a gathering, maybe her brother would come home.

****

Ceallach stood rooted, eyes locked on Kat's retreating form as she slipped her arm through his cousin's. The gesture was casual, intimate, but her hand on another's sliced through him like a blade wrapped in silk.

Aodhán's mind speak came to him. *Stop standing there gaping at her. Aye, she's grown into a beautiful woman. But that's something you should know with ye spying on her ever since my wedding.*

Ceallach frowned, covering his shocked expression as the very woman they spoke of turned, glaring at him. Glaring wasn't quite right, and gazing wasn't like his Kat. No, her expression scrutinized, examined to the point of leaving him feeling naked. He shook himself. Naked was exactly what he wanted to be with her. Long strides closed the distance to his cousin and the blonde beauty striding beside him.

The enchantress shook her head, making her cascade of warm blonde strands wave at him from the back of her head. The scent of Camellia flowers wafted, soft and sweet. Which was what Kat was under all her *tart smarts*—a contradiction of intellect and her outgoing nature that wrapped in one scent representing *her*.

Kat turned slightly as they continued strolling towards the reception. "Ye will tell me what this gathering is." She stopped, yanking her arm from Aodhán. "Is my brother coming? Is he part of this?"

Ceallach didn't want to get her hopes up. Doug's decision to stay in the past wrecked Kat's life. He'd never hurt his Kat.

Drawing near till they almost touched, he said, "I wish it were so, Kat." He took a deep breath, truth always. "No, I am truly sorry. Doug is not part of the gathering." Stillness held the moment as he took in her face, pleased to stand close to her again. Her eyes roamed his, searching for the truth in what he said.

He pulled back, breaking the contact. "Ye should be glad he isn't part of this. There will be a fierce battle."

Aodhán took her hand. "Come, discussions of prophecy and battles are for tomorrow. Today is Ewan and Lorelei's day."

Ceallach grabbed her free hand, stopping their progression. "Kat, I promise there will be a day ye will see yer brother."

Her smile wavered as tears gathered again. Ceallach released her hand, which went to her pocket where the gem he'd made from her tear sat. He'd sensed the stone there when she moved close. She gripped the gem now, and he detected peace flowing over her, calming her.

They continued onto the party as Ceallach took in the crowd, sending his cousin a message. *I never thought I'd see Titan stand on two human legs*, *yet there he is.*

Aodhán chuckled out loud but replied in mind

speak. *A father would do anything for the happiness of his daughter.*

Titan turned, eyeing the three when they approached. He winked, waving to his eleven beautiful offspring. *Greetings, Ceallach, cousin to Aodhán. I still have three available daughters. Would you like to bond with one in a human wedding ceremony?*

His cousin smirked beside him. *I had forgotten Titan is well-versed in mind speak.* Aodhán came upon his wife, Evie, passing Kat off to her. Evie handed him his wiggly daughter, Annie, as they exchanged a look. Evie was half Fae and versed in mind speak to. She'd heard it all.

Ceallach's eyes followed Kat, practically ignoring Titan's address. A slight in the Tilinkis kingdom, Titan used to rule, which now his son-in-law Vinnis governed.

Aodhán shifted his daughter. *A nice offer, Titan, but I think my cousin has already given his heart away.* Ceallach ignored the men's banter while Kat pulled Evie aside, mumbling to her.

Titan smiled. *One can always try.* He stood taller as his voice boomed over the crowd. "I bid you good day. For it's not goodbye since I shall see you all again." He turned to Ewan and Lorelei. "Treat her as the gift she is, boy."

Ceallach turned to Titan while he spoke as Ceallach kept Kat in the corner of his view, wondering what she frantically whispered to her best friend and confidant, who grabbed Kat's flailing arms to calm her.

Ewan put his arm around his wife as he spoke to her father. "I shall treat her as my gift from the sea." He kissed her, sending a mind message to Titan. *And never call me boy. It's father now she's expecting.*

Titan slapped Ewan's back hard, making him stumble. "You will inform us when the babe comes." He waved to his daughters, and they strode away. The wedding guests mingled, and no one noticed that someway away, Titan and all eleven daughters waded into the water, disappearing into the sea. Ceallach smirked. Most humans were so oblivious to what was right in front of them.

When he turned back, his cousin stood grinning as he held his daughter. Annie pointed at Kat, and Evie then reached her hands out toward him. Ceallach took her into his arms sensing her emotions, something strong for a Fae so young. The tyke felt his desire for Kat and wanted them together. She squealed loudly, and her mother, Evie, turned, but Ceallach shook his head. He held the girl for a moment, reading her mind. She wanted another cookie, chocolate chip. A flick of the wrist produced the treat, delivered with a flourish that made her giggle. She nibbled the sweet, resting her head against his shoulder as satisfaction washed over her. He turned to Kat and Evic, who wore the same open-mouthed expressions, almost looking like an identical fish out of water.

His cousin whispered beside him. "They are floored by yer way with the child."

Ceallach sent Aodhán a message. *I know.*

Aodhán huffed. "They speak of your arrival."

He replied. *I know.*

Ceallach sensed the private message from Aodhán. *We are ready. The prophecy is at hand.*

He exhaled, not replying, and kept his eye on Kat and Evie, who spoke again. He leaned over, using his powers, eavesdropping where he wasn't welcome.

Evie hissed. "I know he's here, Kat."

Kat murmured back hard. "But now? And why does he have to look so damn good?" She moaned. "Dash, he even smells good." Ceallach smiled as he rested his chin on the toddler's head, who dribbled chocolate saliva onto his shirt.

Aodhán's voice echoed in his head. *It's good ye are here for a time. Maybe ye can spend time with Kat. Where she's aware ye are here with her. Not this sneakin' around ye've been about for too long.*

Ceallach huffed, then sent a harsh reply. *I am here to shield the maiden. I can't lose focus, or the evil Fae will have their sacrifice and obtain all the stones. It's happened twice before. To not shield her…*

Aodhán sighed. *Aye, but while ye are here, ye can have a little fun.*

Waving a spell, Ceallach cleaned his shirt and the toddler's mouth, hands, and chin while he kept eavesdropping on the woman as his cousin's voice echoed. *Curiosity did kill the cat ye know.*

Evie patted Kat's shoulder. "Must ye resist him?"

Kat jerked out of her friend's touch. "He isn't interested in me. This I know from yer wedding."

Aodhán's voice drifted into his mind. *Opportunity never knocks twice at any man's door. Ye won't get another chance like this to dally with yer woman.*

He turned, taking his focus from the one woman he could never resist no matter the realm. *I know my duty.* He passed Annie back to her da, who frowned.

Ceallach strode away. *Fae are not allowed to mate with humans. Ye know the law. And she's not my woman.*

Aodhán's voice chuckled as he replied. *Really? All those white roses ye left on her windowsill didn't speak of yer feelings?* He followed, skipping to catch up. *Or the many times ye visited this realm just to watch her sleep.*

Ceallach marched towards the dwelling. *They weren't roses but Camellias.*

His cousin paused. *Doesn't that flower mean destiny?*

He strode on without a reply. They did mean destiny. Giving her one meant she was his destiny. She didn't know that or where they came from. He had to keep it that way. She had to stay away from the gathering.

His nagging cousin followed. *How about the time that boy dumped her so hard ye made him trip in the mud on the way home?* Ceallach had wanted to do more but feared punishment from the Fae council. He pushed the limits with his many visits to the human realm as it was.

Aodhán's voice came to him. *What about the time…*

Ceallach's shoulders snapped rigid. He spun so fast his cousin stumbled back, clutching Annie to his chest. "Didn't ye say Mrs. A has a room for me?"

"I didn't say, but aye, she does. Here at Dunstaffnage." It was true. Aodhán hadn't said so but had thought about the needed accommodations when his cousin had arrived. He'd merely read his cousin's mind.

Ceallach strode to the stairs with purpose, mounted them, and went up to the entrance of the grand castle. At the top, he turned spying Kat with Evie among the crowd. Staying here while Kat remained at Ardchattan Priory was the right choice—yet, even that didn't feel far enough away. Kat was still in his heart, no matter the realm—but now wasn't the time for them. Evil searched for the stones, and the gathering was at hand. Ceallach had dedicated his entire existence to spells that shielded the maiden of the Iona Stones, and he couldn't fail now. The destiny of the realms rested in his hands, in his abilities. He turned his back on his one true love and entered the castle, closing his heart to love once more.

****

Later that evening Kat stumbled into her bedroom at Ardchattan Priory where she'd lived since birth. A place she gladly moved out of for college, but now after all that had happened, was a place of solace—her home.

Kat yawned loudly as she carefully removed the light blue gown, the organza catching the lamplight. She laid the garment on her desk chair, and something winked from her windowsill. As she lifted and threw her favorite sleep shirt over her head, she stepped towards the sill. The worn garment had belonged to her brother, and she'd slept in the soft material ever since he decided to stay in the past for true love. When her head popped free of the top, a white bloom sat on the ledge. The same white blossom she'd seen on her sill occasionally, no matter if she were in Edinburgh at college or home near Oban. A white flower. An item that always appeared when she needed support the most.

With a gentle hand she scooped up the bloom, marveling at the rare flower. The first few times they appeared, they looked like roses, but up close each had more petals and a lighter scent. She brought the petals to her nose and inhaled, reminded of the day she'd looked them up, curious if their appearance had a meaning. A Camellia, a white flower meaning destiny. So attracted to the scent, she'd sought out a Camellia perfume to have a daily reminder that someone out there noticed her.

Warm wood pressed against her arms as she leaned on the window frame, watching the sun sink low on a late summer night. Streaks of lavender unfurled across the sky, pale and smoky near the horizon, deepening to dusky violet where night gathered. Hints of silvered lilac shimmered at the edges of the clouds, while soft mauve bled into the folds of twilight, as if the sky wore a shawl of silk and shadow. The sight reminded her of the deep emotions folding over one another in her heart. After all that had happened, someone left her a flower. Someone out there cared.

Chapter 2

Ceallach approached the study door, intent on the first part of his duty for the Fae. He grinned, recalling the first morning in the human realm. He'd left behind the soft hush of his ma's castle, a place of mist-veiled halls and memories that lingered longer than the light. Here, warm sunlight poured in like honey, stretching across the wooden floorboards in lazy patterns. For the first time in centuries, his sleep had been undisturbed, deep, and dreamless, like sinking into the earth. No visions, restless warnings, or flickering prophecy echoes clawed at the edge of his mind.

Instead, birdsong, bright and cheerful, stirred him. He remembered blinking against the filtered yellowed light, disoriented by the soft linen beneath him and the faint smell of wildflowers carried on the breeze through the open window. The earth's slow movement, the energy of the plants, the creatures, and the building itself startled him most, not a threatening force, but a peaceful one, an energy that didn't demand anything of him.

He rose slowly, uncertain at first, expecting the illusion to break. But the solid floor under his bare feet, the warmth on his skin, and the weight of liveliness felt like safety instead of doom. Last night, he floated on air because he had. After placing the flower at Kat's window, he floated back to Dunstaffnage Castle without realizing he used his Fae powers. Even now, he hadn't quite returned to earth.

Every step felt unmoored, as if her touch still anchored him somewhere between dream and waking. He pressed a hand over his heart—steady but changed. He hadn't meant to care this much. But her warmth clung to him, impossible to shake. With the world humming softly beyond the window, his mind finally felt his own. Not as a Fae warrior or servant of ancient vows but as something new. Something almost human.

In contrast to his ease, the household's morning routine was pure chaos. Saucepans clanged, their metallic racket ricocheting through the room. They called the room a kitchen, and everyone sat around a square table sipping a morning beverage. Annie used her Fae powers to swipe a cookie from what they called *the cubby,* making the treat float across the room.

Mrs. A, the housekeeper, deftly caught the cookie midair. "Och, caught ye, ye little wee bugger!" Annie burst into wails the volume and pitch Ceallach had never experienced. He covered his ears as Mrs. A calmed the banshee with a bread roll called a rowie.

Before he could recover, Mrs. A thrust a mug beneath his nose. "Chamomile dearie. To calm those nerves." She sat him down at what she called *the bar*, a tall seat pushed up to a tall counter where she placed a plate piled high with what she called *Scots breakfast* of eggs, bacon, tomatoes, toast, and haggis. A meal she claimed would *stick to his ribs*. He hoped not.

She bustled back with a small bowl. "Yer beans. Ye must have yer beans." The scent of honeyed herbs curled round him as he eyed the meal, but his stomach rumbled something fierce. The fluffy eggs, the richness of the bacon, and the crisp toast had a bit of burned edges he found tasteful compared to the perfect brown in the Fae realm. The tomatoes added an earthy warmth and a tang. Haggis they had in the Fae realm, but this one's flavor seemed more intense.

No one said much in greeting as the agreed-upon meeting was to occur late morning in the study. Ceallach returned to his room to meditate on what was to come. He needed to gather his strength to explain the coming battle—one he'd only glimpsed through Dagda's memories.

Visions of past sacrifices flickered—maidens lost, stones stolen. He couldn't let that happen again. The first maiden's spirit lingered to this day. The second was more innocent but just as effective for the evil Fae. That was when Alex MacDougall mistook young infatuation for true love in a girl named Heather. With the death of Alex's mistaken love, Balor gained control of the Stone of Love. They faced off in a rough battle over the magic stone where Balor nearly took Alex's true love, Ivy. That time, the maiden of the stones prevailed.

Now, as he stood before the study door, Ceallach steeled his heart against the emotions raging through him, blocking all the human feelings in the room before him. The thought of losing his love, Kat, brought tears to his eyes. He shook himself. Morrigan, his ma, warned that emotions were harder to control in the human realm. She was right. He had to concentrate, not think of Kat, and focus. Shield the maiden of the stones, ensure evil didn't gain control, and complete his duty to save the realms.

He pushed open the study doors only to come face to face with Kathryn Marie MacArthur.

A low growl rumbled out while sending a message

to his cousin. *Shit Aodhán. I told ye she wasn't part of this.*

Aodhán spoke aloud while he crossed from behind the desk, handing Ceallach a glass. "Kat is family. This is a family meeting, and she's a part of the family."

Laird Colin MacDougall, guardian of the Iona Stones, sat behind his desk. "It was enough to keep Mrs. A out now that she knows so much about the stones."

Bree, Colin's wife, and Evie sat on the couch, Evie turning to glance over her shoulder. "Aye, and someone had to watch over Annie." He smirked—memories of his and his cousin's childhood antics danced through his mind, like the little tyke Annie swiping cookies just like they once had.

Marie and John stood when he entered but now held each other's hands, wearing the same hopeful expressions. He sensed their hope merged with their deepest desire that Doug would return for the gathering. Ceallach's focus shifted to the person between him and Doug's parents, Kat, who shared the same expectant look.

He sighed and gulped the golden-brown liquid in the glass. The fire hit him instantly, raw and unforgiving, bringing tears to his eyes. His grandda's favored drink was sharp with hints of peat and smoke, thick with years of aging in charred oak barrels, and carried a faint sweetness beneath the bite—like scorched honey or sun-dried fruit buried deep in the burn. As he swallowed hard, the liquid lava burned a fierce path down his throat, igniting a coughing spell that racked his chest. But even while he gasped for breath, a warmth bloomed, slow and steady, like embers catching in his belly and radiating outward, anchoring him to the moment.

Colin's chuckle filled the room. "Are ye sure ye are Dagda's grandson?" Ceallach coughed again as a soft huff sounded before him. He peeked at Kat, who covered her laugh with her hand.

Aodhán sipped his glass. "Had ye bothered to sample the whisky last night, I could have told ye few can do more than sip the drink."

Ceallach went behind Colin's desk, holding his hand over each container, searching for the one that wasn't pure alcohol as he set the first cup aside. Finding the water, he poured some into another glass and took a sip, soothing his throat, then another.

Aodhán's voice shook with a laugh as he spoke. "Ceallach ye always weren't one for the drink."

As he picked back up the fire liquid, Ceallach sent Aodhán a message. *We miss two that were here already.*

Evie replied aloud. "Ewan and Lorelei are on honeymoon. I told Ewan he has a week."

Colin huffed. "Well, at least ye finally learned I hate that mind speak ye kids do."

When Ceallach turned back, Kat stood with her parents before the chairs in front of the desk, all three wearing that same hopeful expression.

He took a deep breath. "A week may be too long, and yet may not be long enough. I can't tell."

John MacArthur nodded, his expression changing. "It's as ye told Kathryn. Doug is not part of the gathering. I can see it in yer face each time ye look at me, Ceallach. He's not coming back." Ceallach couldn't lie, not to good people like the MacArthur's, and with Kat watching him.

He swallowed the lump in his throat, telling the truth. "The gathering is for the maidens of each stone and

22

their shield, their true love. Abigail is not a maiden of a found stone, but Doug is her shield, her true love. While they serve the Stones of Iona, he will not return for the gathering."

Marie, Kat's mom, sat hard on the chair. "I had hoped." Their love for Doug outweighed Ceallach's control. He moved forward, setting his glass with fire liquid on the desk, and bent on his knee. He took Marie's hand in his, sending her images of Doug from the past. Images of his wedding day, his pride at rebuilding Portsmouth, Waitukura, and Parras, meaning paradise in Gaelic, the plantation he'd purchased. He showed her the birth of his first child, a son. Marie smiled with tears in her eyes.

Ceallach patted her hand. "His destiny lies elsewhere. Take heart, he is happy."

The room sat in silence for a moment. Each of the occupant's emotions weighed heavy on Ceallach. The MacArthur's love for the son who wouldn't come back. Bree's worry for her son and daughter and their new families. Colin's concern over his duty to the stones and what price the Fae would ask from him now. But the one whose emotions came the strongest were Kat's and her feelings for him. The draw she felt each time he was near, the love budding in her heart. He had to ignore the pull. She wasn't for him.

An emotion shifted in the room as Bree stood pacing. "Wait, a maiden of a found stone," she mumbled while she ticked off each finger. "Love, that's me. Fear, Marie." She turned to Evie. "Doubt is Evie. Faith is Lorelei. Hope is Moira." Her head came up. "Will Dom and Moira come?"

Ceallach grinned. Brigid said Bree had a sharp

mind. Allowing her time to piece the rest together, he turned to Colin, knowing the surprise on Colin's face would be worth the wait.

Bree's voice built as she spoke. "I recovered Lust, but I can't be the maiden for two stones, can I?" Her mind shifted, and her face lit up when the facts clicked into place. "Ainslie! Ainslie is Lust."

Colin stood, dropping his whisky glass and spilling the liquor on the carpet. The slack expression of shock on his face was worth all the gold in the human realm. Colin's emotions washed over Ceallach, each flickering across the man's face like sunlight shifting through leaves. First came surprise. Colin's brows lifted; eyes widened slightly like his mind struggled to catch up with what he'd heard. Then, slowly, happiness bloomed, softening the angles of his face and pulling a breathless smile to his lips. But this wasn't just joy. Wonder threaded through, quiet awe that shimmered in his gaze as he gazed at something long lost and only half-believed. His was the expression of a man glimpsing a ghost from a beloved memory, now made real.

Ceallach felt the depth of it all, the ache, the amazement, the quiet unraveling of disbelief, the past and future folding into one. A wish, written in fate, now finally coming to pass—a brother's reunion with his sister from the past was what Colin's future held.

The guardian choked out. "When?"

Ceallach gave the only answer he had. "When the time is right. I cannot say when her arrival will occur in the human realm. But aye, she and Rannick are summoned, as are Moira and Dominic. Though I suspect the pilot and archeologist will arrive first without having to travel the portals."

Bree rounded the couch, embracing Colin while Marie spoke over the murmurs of others. "Well, we may not get Doug back, but a reunion of sorts will be nice."

Ceallach moved around the desk, picking up his glass. He passed Colin and Bree as she picked up Colin's glass from the floor, handing the empty cup to her husband. Ceallach reached for the container holding the golden-brown spirits they called whisky, poured a heady amount, and lifted the brew to his lips. A hand shot out, grabbing his wrist and spilling some liquid. He felt Colin's emotions shift. But they did so quickly that he had no time to react before being grabbed.

Colin growled. "Now ye partake of a tot, the harsh *water of life*." The stone's guardian released Ceallach's wrist and shifted Bree till he sat, settling her on his lap. "The Fae don't gift us with a pleasant family visit. A reunion, like Marie claims." He huffed. "Do they, goblin?" Ceallach supposed he deserved the insult. He'd come as a friend delivering grave news that may cost them all their lives.

Ceallach gulped the whisky. Smoke-peat liquid scorched his tongue; heat pooled in his chest, steadier than any courage spell. This time, the *water of life* was a welcome burn, a fire that steadied his nerves rather than singed them. The drink settled deep in his gut, spreading heat through his chest and loosening the tightness in his shoulders, the heaviness in his heart.

He needed that warmth, that grounding. What he had to share with them all, truths of long-buried secrets heavy with consequences, clung to his bones like frost. The whisky didn't erase his burden but softened the edges, giving him a moment of courage before the storm he was about to unleash.

Aodhán's voice came to his mind. *Ye know more—more than I. This is a first.*

Ceallach sent back a reply. *I've known all along.* His gaze lifted to his cousin. *I have my entire existence.* He poured another tot and then waved his free hand, making a glass appear in each person's hand. Exclamations filled the room as each individual's favorite drink filled the glassware. He knew them all. MacDougall whisky for Colin and chardonnay for Bree. Another MacDougall whisky for John and Aodhán. Merlot for Evie and Marie. Kat sat staring at her drink, Cabernet Sauvignon.

He set his empty glass on the cart and stepped around the desk as he spoke. "The gathering is part of the prophecy."

Bree swallowed her wine. "Wait, I thought the prophecy was to save your true love by saving the Stone of Love."

Evie stood and rounded the couch, leaning on the back. "I thought it was ye must believe to have faith in true love."

Marie started to speak. "Wait, I…"

When Ceallach arrived at the window beside the *Fae Fable Book,* he held his hand up, silencing them all. In the window's reflection, each expectant face stared at him. Kat stood before her parents as he sensed her emotions dip and fear rise. He wanted to soothe her, but couldn't. He had to focus on his duty.

Aodhán's voice came to him. *They don't know what they face. There's more, isn't there?*

Ceallach took a deep breath, turned, and faced a room full of uncertainty. "Aye, each fable held its own foretelling, the prophecy of that stone. But what ye each forget is that the six stones come together to reveal the

Stone of Destiny. The one stone that makes ruling all the realms possible."

Colin stood, nearly dumping Bree on the floor. "It's here, isn't it? The Stone of Destiny."

Ceallach replied with truth. "I cannot tell ye where the stone is." He knew exactly where the magic stone sat since the gem arrived in the MacDougall's care, but he wasn't permitted to reveal the location. Not until the maidens gathered and the stones came together would the Stone of Destiny reveal itself at the time of need.

Colin chugged his whisky. When he spoke the first part, he mimicked Ceallach's calm voice. "I cannot tell." The last he bellowed. "Damn ye, goblin! Ye know where the stone is and place us all in danger!"

Bree shifted, setting her glass down, and filled her husband's again from the whisky decanter as she patted his shoulder, causing him to sit.

John rose and crossed to Bree, raising his glass for a refill. "Colin, we've faced the stone's magic before. We can do so again." Bree filled John's glass to the rim, and made an offer to Aodhán, who smiled and shook his head when Evie turned to him. The young couple paused, their silent mind speak brushing between them as they set their glasses down together.

Evie wrapped her arms around his cousin, who sent a mind message to Ceallach. *She still dreams of Manix. Will this ever end?* Manix was Balor's son, a dragon shapeshifter, and both previous kings of the evil Fae, the Fomoire who'd now turned to serving the good Fae, the Tuatha Dé Danann. Ceallach exhaled. They had so much to face and more challenges to come. He prayed to the gods he could guide them all. Kat's fear came to him again. Aye, this had to end with this battle, and he had to see all of them through this.

Ceallach waved his hand over the *Fae Fable Book*. The glass casing vanished with a simple Fae spell. He'd wondered why Evie and Ewan hadn't figured the simple hex out, having Fae powers themselves. Raising his hand, he guided the book as the tome lifted and floated across the room to many gasps. He placed the manuscript carefully on the desk before Colin, leaving the cover closed.

Colin glared at the old book. "Another tale from the Fae? Another goose chase for a fucking stone?"

Ceallach leaned on the windowsill, folding his arms and crossing his feet like Colin always did, finding the position comfortable. "Ye must open the book to find out, human," he told Colin, voice mild as spring rain. Ceallach sent a private mind message only Colin heard. *I am no goblin. And I am here to help ye more than ye know.*

Colin jolted. Seemed this was the first time he'd heard such. Strange, Evie and Ewan had inherited their powers through the MacDougall line, not as Dagda claimed were blessings from Brigid. Which was something Dagda admitted he'd said early on to ease Colin's fears, being a non-believer of a Fae's power. Ceallach searched Colin's emotions and sensed his trepidation at opening the book. Looked like his position as a non-believer had changed over the years.

Colin grumbled. "More games the Fae play with the humans. What price will it be this time, goblin?" He pounded his fist on the desk, jostling the book, which opened on its own to the page Colin needed to read. Ceallach felt the book sigh, knowing this was the last task, here at least.

Ceallach waved to the book. "Ye must read."

Bree leaned over Colin's shoulder. "The Stone of Destiny." She set her glass down. "A new fable."

Colin slammed the book shut, not taking his eyes from Ceallach. "No, ye can't read it yet. He hasn't said the price to the humans."

Ceallach breathed. "I don't know the price."

Colin rose, rounding the desk and pointing at Ceallach. "But ye do know the fable, the outcome."

The others in the room gasped. When Ceallach turned back to the desk, they all stood around the book. Kat remained before the desk outside the circle.

Bree sat in Colin's chair before the opened *Fae Fable Book*. "Colin, the book opened on its own." She bent, reading from the tome silently. Colin turned and glared at Ceallach, then returned, completing the circle of people responsible for the outcome of the coming battle. All but Kat, who stood outside where she needed to stay.

Bree read from the book. "*A great Fae warrior was assigned to guard the Stone of Destiny for all the realms. So great was his responsibility, the Fae gifted him with extra magic and skill. The tale tells how his roses of hope, faith, and love wooed a logic-bound mortal.*"

Her recitation of the fable faded, and Ceallach rose from the sill and moved toward Kat. The closer he came, the clearer her tears became. He sensed her sorrow, the feeling of being left out. She wasn't part of the gathering and certainly wouldn't be near the stones if Ceallach had anything to say. When he stood before her, she lifted her gaze to his, and a tear escaped. His finger rose and caught the drop.

He gripped the wetness, making a gem, and took her

29

free hand as he had the day before. "Dry yer tears, Kat. Remember, yer face is much prettier without them." He dropped the gem in her hand, knowing the stone would make her feel better.

Yet, her smile faltered. "Will ye take each tear I shed and make it a gem?"

He held her hands in his. "If that's what it takes to make ye happy."

She huffed. "I'm left behind again. Lost to the adventure of the stones."

Ceallach's voice hardened. "Ye will stay away, Kat. This battle is no place for ye."

Aodhán's mind speak drifted to Ceallach. *Cousin, something is wrong.* Ceallach blinked. As he dropped her hands, the heavy emotions for Kat faded, making him step back.

He turned, and his cousin glared at him. *The fable's ending can't be right.*

Ceallach spoke aloud. "What do ye mean the fable isn't right? The story ends with the maiden saving the shield, her true love, and the Stones of Iona kept safe for all mankind."

Colin growled from behind Bree as he lifted and turned the book around. "Read the words for yerself, gnome. It's a Fae trick ye gift us with again." The heavy book thumped when he dropped it but didn't switch pages. The book needed him to read what was there.

Ceallach nudged forward, catching certain parts of the story while cold washed over him. He read on, mumbling aloud. "The stones, the maiden, the shield. The story's all the same. He declares his love and gifts her with roses. But wait." With the next sentence, his heart dropped. "She rejects him over logic?" He turned the pages, examining the back, searching for other words, not finding them.

Aodhán's voice spoke aloud. "The story's changed? How? We must know."

Ceallach read on as he lifted the book a little, rounding the desk so the rest could read with him. "The tale's all the same so far."

"*The Fae, wanting to show his love to her, brought her roses and secretly left them on her windowsill. He stayed till she found the bloom, wanting to know if she loved him.*

She rejects his offering, saying. "Red? One knows the most beautiful roses are yellow."

He searched and found a yellow, only to have her throw the rose out the window.

She said, "Only blue roses smell the best."

He travels and gets her a sky-blue rose. He traveled back and left the flower on the windowsill for her.

She enjoyed the rose for some time, then threw the flower out the window, barking out, "Only the purest of love is found in a white rose."

He traveled the world three times and caught the attention of a wicked, evil Fae who followed him, curious about what the good Fae was doing while searching the human realm, thinking he was after the magic Iona Stones.

The good Fae found his perfect white rose and left the bud on the windowsill for his love.

The evil Fae barked a laugh, "True love. What a silly waste of time. Power is more valuable than love."

"Even this part is the same." Ceallach read on, caught up in the tale as this was the first time he'd read this version. "*Three times she scorned his roses—red,*

31

yellow, then sky-blue—dismissing each as illogical." Kat gasped. When his gaze rose, she sat hard and gulped her wine. The tale echoed her own life in ways that felt unnervingly precise, as though fate had etched her story into its lines. She didn't know his part in this, but he carried the weight of his role—and far more.

He shook himself. *Focus on yer duty, the gathering.*

Pulling his eyes from hers, he read on, needing to find where the tale drifted from the original Dagda had shown him. *"The evil Fae came upon them. "Enough of this foolishness with true love." He shot a power into the good Fae, hurting him.*

The good Fae thrust the Stone of Destiny into the woman's hands. "Hold the gem to your chest. Protect the magic stone, the Stone of Destiny, for me. If he possesses the stone, he will ruin the realms."

The evil Fae laughed. "Perfect, another maiden's sacrifice for the Stones of Iona."

Ceallach silently read ahead a bit. "When she rejects him. That's what's different." He spoke aloud. Each person involved in the gathering needed to know what had changed. *"She held the Stone of Destiny and felt nothing. To her, emotions were not logical. She glared at the stone and back at the good Fae. "Faith and hope leading to love? That makes no sense. Love is not something I can wish it to be."*

The evil Fae growled as he reached for the Stone of Destiny. "Foolish Fae, falling for a human. They will do nothing more than disappoint." The Stone of Destiny flew from the maiden's hands to the evil Fae. With a flick of the evil Fae's wrist, a bolt shot out from the stone, hitting the maiden and killing her. The good Fae rushed to her side. "Why? Faith is the substance of things hoped for, the evidence of things not seen." He pulled her to float beside him.

The evil Fae held the Stone of Destiny to his chest, and all the Stones of Iona flew to him, the red Stone of Love, followed by the purple Stone of Faith, then all the others flashed by in brilliant streaks of color, each absorbing in the chest of the evil Fae. "The Stones of Iona have their maiden's sacrifice. Now evil shall rule the land."

After reading the last, he rocked back. "No!" He flipped the pages. "This is not what Dagda showed me!"

Colin roared, his voice slicing through the air like a blade. "What does this mean?"

Ceallach pushed back, blinking, not believing the fable had changed, but the tale had. "She rejects his love. The evil Fae kills the maiden, taking all seven stones, controlling the realms, casting us all into dark times."

****

A jolt shot up Kat's legs, stiffening them as if the ground itself had grabbed hold. *Flowers to his love.* She had flowers that occasionally appeared, but she wasn't part of this. Ceallach told her so. Kat tipped her drink, finding an empty glass as the people around the desk argued over the book and the story within. All she wanted was her brother back, her family once again. Not all this confusion of the stones.

Bree's voice rose above them all. "The maiden's sacrifice. Will we ever be rid of her, or is this a curse?"

Colin's voice swelled, carrying his frustration across the room. "Bree, ye will not worry over the fable. I changed the outcome before, and I will do so again."

But wait, if she was the one getting flowers, then wasn't she the maiden? Kat rose and crossed to the fireplace, staring inside. No fire burned today—it was summer, after all—but a chill clung to her skin anyway, the kind that no sun could banish. *Flowers for a maiden.*

Her professor's voice echoed. "How can metaphysics, physics, or any other more or less scientific structured thinking prove what I feel or don't feel, and why I do so?"

Structured thought is logic.

Aodhán's voice rose over the rest. "No, no! The prophecy is 'The grandson born with the greatest Fae powers of all would take his place as king over the Tuatha Dé Danann and oust the latest and most evil ruler of the Fomoire Fae, their new king.' " The clash of voices swelled, sharp and jagged, each arguing over the prophecies.

Ceallach's firm reply stopped all from speaking. "No, cousin, there are two prophecies, one from the good Fae. 'Each king, one with the greatest Fae powers serving good, one the latest, most evil ruler, will come together in battle, marking the end of the human guardianship. In the end, the evil Fae's spawn will safely guard the stones.' Then, one from the evil the new king of the Fomoire shared to help us all united for good. 'With a human sacrifice, the lone stone's guardian shall rise from the ashes of a great battle. Once joined again, the stones will reside in a pure heart forever kept from the evils of the realms.' "

All eyes stayed on Ceallach as John spoke. "Which one is it?"

Ceallach shrugged. "Only time will tell."

Colin slammed the book shut. "Figures!" He bellowed. "Brigid!"

Bree placed her hand on his arm. "Yelling for your

Fae will not help." She waved to Aodhán and Ceallach. "There are two Fae before you, and you have the same answers."

Aodhán rolled his eyes. "She can't come anyway. She's busy with the dragons."

Marie chewed on her nail, something Kat's ma did often. "What is it with the dragons always needing her?"

Kat didn't know. But all this prophecy, fables, stones, and magic. She stood outside the circle around the desk—uninvited, unnoticed—while the people who meant the most to her leaned in without her. The only thing she wanted was for everyone to be together again, including Doug and Ainslie, the MacArthurs and MacDougalls—a family again.

Ceallach moved from the circle while the rest in the room carried on about the fable. Their voices faded as he neared her, his presence consuming her.

He took her hand in his. "The gem. Ye lost it already?"

She smiled, pulling the stone from her pocket. "No. And before ye ask, I have the one from last night, too." She sighed. "I want to be part of the gathering, of the duty."

His hand tightened on hers. "Kat, ye cannot. Too many things change. The gathering is too dangerous, especially since ye are not part of the stones. Ye do not have a shield." His statement hit her hard. No shield meant she had no true love, making his statement mean he didn't love her. She pulled the hand he held away, huffing, but he gripped her hard. His gaze intent on hers.

Colin yelled over the din of voices. "Stop yer guessing. Ye only fret and cause the women to worry."

John nodded. "Aye, we must be practical about

this." He turned to Ceallach. "Advice from the goblin?" Kat grinned at the previous insult, repeated, intended as a jest. At least her da hadn't made any reference to rock jokes. Still, Ceallach was nothing like what they pictured as a fairy: light, small, and weak. No, he was more of a hardened warrior.

Aodhán spoke as his eyes traveled over them, stopping at their clasped hands. "We must wait for the gathering. Maybe the fable will change once we are all together, giving us more answers than questions."

Evie smirked when her focus landed on Ceallach and Kat before the fireplace. "In the meantime, how about Kat showing Ceallach around? He's not spent much time in the human realm."

Colin picked up the *Fae Fable Book* and marched to the book's place in the wall. "Aye, a fine idea." He placed the tome on the shelf. The glass case appeared slowly, covering the book again. Colin flinched, then caught himself and simply nodded at the book in agreement.

Ceallach squeezed her hand once. "What will ye show me?" Kat's heart sped up. A day with Ceallach, she'd never spent a whole day with him. The thought warmed her heart more than his teardrop gems. She smiled, and he patted her hand. Waiting may not be so bad after all.

Chapter 3

Ceallach dropped Kat's hand, catching himself. He should not encourage anything between them, but the thought of exploring the human realm with her as his guide sounded too good to be true. A temptation he should decline. His focus should remain on the gathering.

Marie, Kat's ma, took her husband's hand. "Kat, that sounds like a lovely idea."

John, her da, pulled her ma towards the door. "Aye, maybe a picnic at the priory by the loch."

She stopped smiling at her da. "What a lovely idea! I'd love to! Maybe we can get Mrs. A to pack lunch before we leave." Her da's response became muffled when they moved out the study door.

Evie went to her ma, Bree. "Can ye believe this? We'll get to see Ainslie! Oh, I hope she brings Rannick. I want to meet him."

Bree's response faded as Aodhán's voice came to him in a private message. *Ye aren't going to tell them, are ye?*

Kat stood beside him, fidgeting. He patted her shoulder, sending comforting energy, and she sighed, relaxing her hands.

Aodhán's voice became harder. *Ignoring me isn't going to help them. The quote in Fae ink that humans cannot see.*

Ceallach replied softly. *Like Colin said, ye only fret and cause the women to worry.* His eyes flitted to his cousins. *With the discovery of true love, its power will give you the desire of your heart and make all your plans succeed.* He huffed aloud. *There's no telling who the quote refers to. Is Bree the maiden, or is it another stone's maiden?*

Aodhán barked a laugh and quieted when Evie stopped speaking, eyeing him. His voice came again. *Ye know damn well it's ye and Kat. Roses left for his love. What of the evil Fae?*

Ceallach took Kat's hand in his. "Kat, let's head outside, and ye can tell me what ye plan for today." She nodded and led him towards the door. He sensed her mind ran frantically through options, settling on her grandma's home, Granny Mac, and the village first.

As Ceallach followed Kat through the door, Aodhán's voice became harsher. *The evil Fae?*

Passing through the doorway, Ceallach offered his reply. *The evil Fae will show themselves in due time. They cannot resist it. Evil will falter as it always has, and we will be ready.*

Aodhán's response came faintly the farther away Ceallach walked. *I'm not so sure this time.*

****

Kat led Ceallach out the castle doors, down the steps into the porte-cochere where she'd hastily parked her car for their meeting. Her parents had come earlier to speak with Bree and Colin privately, leaving her to drive on her own. Each step of the way, Ceallach's presence exuded a certain electromagnetism that pulsed behind her, drawing her to him. Getting closer to the car, she rounded the vehicle and opened the driver's side. When she glanced up, Ceallach still stood on the last step. She paused, taking in his immense figure that sent shivers over her till she got to his face. His lips pressed thin, as though the contraption reeked of sorcery best left untouched.

She leaned on the car door. "Come on, Ceallach, I'll drive ye into the village of Dunbeg, show ye around." His eyes traveled over her car, a small, bright red sedan. She liked to imagine the red vehicle was a luxurious sports car, but she only had a four-cylinder engine versus an eight one that reached higher speeds quicker.

His focus moved quickly to hers. "I'll not place myself in a metal box and allow ye to fling me through space." He shivered. "We might hit another racing box."

Kat snickered. "The metal box is called a car." She tilted her head. "Don't ye fly, as in *fling* yerself at fast speeds through space?"

Ceallach stepped off the last stair and slowly proceeded to the vehicle. "Aye, but I control where and how fast I go by visualizing my destination." When he arrived at the opposite side, he placed his hands on the top and ran one down the side, almost like someone might examine a horse.

Kat climbed into the driver's seat. "Come on, I drive and control this. Plus, I know where we go. Ye will be fine." She started the car. When the engine revved, Ceallach jumped back.

She reached over, opening the passenger side door. He bent over, glaring at her from the outside. His hair shifted aside, uncovering his pointed ear and the Fae immortality necklace resting just below. Light fractured across a slim silver chain that lay against his collarbone. Her eyes stared for a moment, the necklace she dreamed he'd give her one day glittered.

A breath to steady her—then she locked her gaze on his face and waved her hand, summoning him in with a silent command. "Come on, try something new."

He placed his foot on the floorboard and the car shifted as he bent to squeeze his long, large frame into the seat. Kat had to stifle a laugh. He looked bent in half. She'd never minded the small car, being so short herself.

He grumbled. "I am bowed, like a dew fairy curled into her flower."

Ceallach sat staring ahead and Kat nudged him. When he didn't move, she pulled on her seat belt as she gave him a look. He rolled his eyes as he wiggled in the cramped space and grabbed the belt buckling it in place.

Kat put the car in gear and pulled out of the area as Ceallach mumbled. "The box hums like caged lightning, fascinating." They drove along for a bit as the countryside flew past.

Ceallach stared out the window and seemed to relax within a few minutes in his seat. "This is not much different than flying." A car pulled out in front of them.

Kat swerved to miss them, hitting the horn. "Look out ye son of a…"

Ceallach twirled his hands fast, and energy filled the car. He thrust them to the sides, and Kat sensed they had lifted and suspended in midair. She blinked, stunned by what had just happened. The engine still purred beneath them, but the world tilted—as if they hovered weightless, suspended between seconds.

She patted his arm. "Ceallach, we are fine. Please release the car from whatever that is ye hold over us."

A flick of his wrist sent the car skidding back to the ground, swerving down the road and forcing Kat to adjust the steering wheel again.

He blew a breath out and then another. "Damn near scared the life from me, Kat." He breathed once more. "I put a shield around us in case the other box hit us."

Gravel crunched under the tires as a grin tugged at Kat's lips, and she eased the car down the lane. "Scared the life from ye, eh? Here I thought ye were immortal."

He folded his arms. "I am. Everything's all so different here."

Kat steered down the winding road easily as they headed down the cliff. The tang of the sea air blew through the car windows. Ceallach breathed in, seeming to relax. From the cliff's point, the view of Loch Etive always took Kat's breath away. Farther beyond, the shadows of the mountainous landscape stretched on in the distance.

Ceallach hummed before he spoke. "The mountains. Hills rose and fell in endless green waves, their reflections stitched perfectly into the loch's surface—a mirror too calm to trust, as though it remembered things the air had long forgotten." He rolled his shoulders. "Reminds me of Boremere, home."

Once at the bottom Kat pulled into a car park near the town square and turned off the engine. "See, we are here. No more moving vehicle." He reached for the door handle, and Kat stopped him with a hand on his arm. "Ceallach, ye um…need to change a bit."

He turned to her, tilting his head to the side as his pointed ear peeked out again.

She pressed her lips together and decided it was best to be out with it. "Ye need to look less, Fae." She eyed his suit, the iridescent fabric that people would think him a fairy, not the Fae kind, but the kind who liked men. Her

41

focus went to his ears as they poked from his long hair. He needed jeans, a tee, trendy boots, and most of all, lose the pointed ears.

Grumbling, Ceallach waved a hand over his body. His form wavered, and when he came back into a clear view, he'd changed to precisely what she'd pictured.

Kat blinked. "Did ye just read my mind?" He opened the car door and unfolded his body, stretching himself to his height. Mouth open, she gaped at him.

He bent down, staring at her with a smile. "Yer mind is an open book lovely Kat. Come, show me yer little town."

She closed her mouth with a click, gathered her backpack and keys, and stepped out of the car. When she stood up, Ceallach was beside her, holding the door. He grinned and closed the door for her.

She shoved past him. "I'd appreciate it if ye didn't go reading my mind without permission. That's an invasion of privacy." She walked on toward the square and the center of Dunbeg. "Plus, I thought ye Fae couldn't read everyone's thoughts, only the weak-minded." She turned to him as he strolled beside her. "At least that's what Ewan, Evie, and Aodhán tell me. Neither of them has been able to read my mind."

Stopping, she placed her hands on her hips, and he bent his head, hiding a grin. "My powers differ." He glanced to the side. "Sometimes I wish I could turn them off, but the best I can do is muffle them." He took her hand in his, patting the back. "For ye, Kat, I will try to respect yer privacy."

She returned his smile. "Thank ye." She turned to cross the street. "Now up here…"

Ceallach yanked her back into his arms as a car

whizzed past where she'd tried to step out.

Kat tightly gripped his shoulders. "That car. Did ye see it coming?"

His arms tightened, the steady press of his body telling her she wasn't going anywhere. "Something like that." Kat froze. She'd dreamed of being held in his arms like this. Her petite frame pressed and held against his broad chest. The feeling was like she had imagined— exciting and comforting, all-consuming of her senses. Their gazes connected. Close like this, his bright blue eyes had flecks of silver, making them glisten. She would be foolish to think he returned her affections.

Kat pulled from his grasp and shook herself. "This way down the lane is my grandma's house. I want to show it to ye." She started to step into the crosswalk, stopped, glanced back at him, and he took her hand in his, guiding her across the street. They strolled on, with her hand on Ceallach's arm, almost like a husband and wife. Kat grinned, liking that image.

His voice brushed the air, low and gentle. "Ye know, this isn't much different than the Fae realm. Each house set neatly in a row." He huffed. "Some even have gardens like yers do here." Her toe caught on an uneven cobblestone.

Ceallach caught her before she tilted into a fall, making him huff. "Well, in the Fae realm, our city sits on clouds not land." Holding her hand, they continued for a bit as Kat enjoyed walking hand in hand with him. The simple act seemed so comfortable.

He stopped and turned them to face a house. Kat glanced around, enjoying the beauty, the sun, the light wind, and a bird chirping nearby. Fresh flowers wafted in the breeze. Ceallach cleared his throat and waved to

the house they stood before. Sure enough, they stood before her grandma's house.

Kat turned to him. "Did ye read my mind again?"

A slow shake of his head dismissed the thought before it fully settled. "No. Granny Mac, as ye call her, she lingers." Kat drew in a breath. Evie saw ghosts, but only the kind that never rested. She glanced around, searching for her grandma, whom she'd only seen in photos, the lively little woman with a wicked grin. Kat swore when she got older, that's what she'd be like.

A light pat touched her hand. "Please don't worry. She is at rest but sometimes visits her fond memories. She likes ye a lot." They stood there before the house. Kat tried to detect her grandma's spirit but couldn't. A woman walked her dog toward them, and they had to step aside to allow her to pass. When they did so, Ceallach turned her back to the square, crossing the street and placing himself on the side where he'd protect her from cars. She bent her head and grinned at his manners.

When they arrived at the main square, he led her to the gardened area and a bench. She sat, dropped her pack, and he followed. First, the car trick, then the mind reading, and now he saw ghosts like Evie. No matter how she turned it over, she couldn't piece together the full reach of his powers. The ability of brain waves to do such a thing, all those powers. Her logical mind had difficulty reconciling it all.

He leaned back, stretched his long legs out, and rested his arm on the back of the bench. Kat opened her mouth and closed it, having trouble deciding what to ask first. The bubble around the car, how he floated, or read minds.

He chuckled. "Start with the simplest first Kat. Ye

may ask me anything, and I will always answer truthfully."

She lightly slapped his leg. "Stop reading my mind."

A burst of laughter shot from him, his body jerking under her playful slap. "All I had to do is watch yer face, Kat. Yer thoughts are all in yer expressions."

With the arm from the back of the bench, he pulled her to him till she nestled in the crook of his embrace. She leaned over till she lay against his side, rotating a little till she stared at the sky. The clouds slowly drifted by while the breeze tickled her hair.

His chest expanded, and then he released a breath. "Better to ask away to clear that mind of yers that runs faster than the thing ye call a car."

She smiled at his banter, his ease at merging the unknown human with his world, the Fae. "I always wondered what it was like for Evie to have powers like the Fae." She sighed. "I wished to have Fae powers, wanted them so badly."

Ceallach's chest rose with a deep breath. "Being Fae is a heavy responsibility that comes with great powers, Kat. They aren't so easily carried or kept." He whispered. "Sometimes I wish I never had them."

A quick nod answered, her thoughts already spinning ahead. "Evie said the same about her being able to see ghosts. Said they weren't always nice or easy to deal with."

He shifted beside her, maybe a nod? "Aye. Ye grandma, for instance, is a flitting spirit that floats by but returns to her rest. Kind of like yer mind, never in one place at once."

A wisp of cloud drifted past, its shape curling into something like a heart. "Visiting the ones she loved? So,

45

with ghosts, it's like ghost hunters claim they can detect electric fields generated by ghosts. Their theory explains that living organisms produce low-level electrical currents due to metabolic processes. So, the energy lingers in the spirit as they move in the realms then?"

He shifted a little till he laid back, giving her the perfect cushion against which to lounge. "Energy, aye, that's what our power is."

Swinging her legs up, Kat stretched out along the bench, claiming it as her perch. "Evie tried to describe her powers once, saying her energy revolves around people and objects, like the power around them, but Ewan's centers on people's minds. But yers it seems, is all energy." His fingers drew lines along her arm, causing her to shiver even on a warm day. He curved an arm around her waist and gently drew her until she pressed to his side.

His chest warmed, chasing the chill away. "A person's body has an abundance of energy. The human brain only uses a fraction of its mass and capability. The Fae have so much more capacity. The traditional way a human dies is the body releases energy into the environment. Either as warmth from the body's decay—carried off by creatures that feed on it—or as sustenance drawn in by the roots of growing plants. When humans consume plants and animals, they absorb and convert their energy through digestion and metabolic processes, primarily heat and chemical energy, rather than a mystical electromagnetic energy."

A sharp breath puffed from Kat, her frustration slipping free. "I get that, but what about the spirits that linger, the energy they hold? And the Fae who use power in spells?"

Ceallach hummed and then sat for a moment before he spoke. "Well, that's a little different. There is energy surrounding ye and I. Then ye add the force of the plants, items around ye, even the hard part of the street holds form of energy."

She blew out a breath, half amused. "Cement, ye mean cement."

His words stalled, a beat of silence stretching before he spoke again. "The clouds, the sky, yer planet spinning. Energy surrounds us, linking us together. Gathering that energy is the force a Fae uses. What our talents and capabilities entail dictates what we can or cannot do with that energy."

Kat blinked at the passing clouds, not seeing them, but in her mind's eye, she envisioned the swirling of energy around each object. A flow that stirred like when Ewan swirled his arms. Gathering energy was what he said he did each time. In her mind, it was like smoke moving through the air to see the pattern.

She tilted her head, looking up at him. "But for ye, ye seem not to have just one ability." She ticked off her fingers listing them. "Ye traveled the portal. Ye turned water to a gem, ye read minds, ye placed some forcefield around the car…"

He grabbed her hands, staring down at her upturned face. "There are many powers I have." His stomach rumbled loudly. "Yet, I don't have the ability to know the best place to find dinner in the human realm." He grinned. "So, what's a guy got to do to get a good meal in this little town?"

Kat sat up, noting the sun sat farther in the sky. "Oh, we wasted the day away. I'd planned on taking ye to the priory, my home."

She bent, grabbing her bag while Ceallach stood. "We'll add that to the list tomorrow. For now, the human realm has made me very hungry."

He pulled her to her feet, and Kat stumbled as she stood, falling into his arms. "Whew, I guess I got a little too comfortable." When she lifted her head, his face followed close to hers like they might kiss. Her gaze locked with his, and in that endless pull, nothing else in the world seemed to matter—only him, only now.

He set her away from him, brushing his legs. "Dinner. Where's a good place for dinner, Kat?" Set away from him, the distance reminded her of all the differences between them. How far-fetched her dream of them together was.

A quick nod answered him before she turned, eyes finding the parked car close by as she started towards the vehicle. "Dunstaffnage Marina Pub. Hamish serves the best beer and burgers in town."

He came to the passenger side with a sigh. "I do like flying better than cars."

Chapter 4

Sharp pops of gravel marked his steps as Ceallach followed Kat towards the large brown and white building. His legs turned to mush after that last car ride from the square to the pub beside the loch, but his hunger won over his nerves from traveling in the *death mobile*. He grinned at the name. *Death mobile* perfectly suited the metal square she called a car.

Kat pulled hard on the heavy wooden doors, and they barely nudged. Ceallach reached around her easily, opening the large door and holding it for her.

She walked past him, and a skinny, red-headed man behind the counter called out. "Whoa, lookie there! My favorite physicist is back for dinner!"

Ceallach followed closely, placing his hand on her back and glaring at the tall man skirting around the bar. "And looks like ye brought yer bodyguard with ye." The man's thoughts flipped through Ceallach's mind. Hamish was the owner, and his curiosity at Ceallach's relationship with Kat burned.

As Hamish flipped his towel over his arm he bowed. "This way, milady." He escorted them through the main area filled with patrons into an empty room near the back and sat them at a table before floor-to-ceiling windows overlooking the boats and loch. Hamish held a chair out for Kat, then one for Ceallach, who sensed the man's questions before he expertly weaved them into conversation.

"Yer parents favored table, away from the band playing tonight." Hamish pulled documents from the centerpiece and handed one to Kat and then to him.

Hamish shifted toward Kat, his attention settling on her. "Ye usual, beer? Stout?"

She grinned in agreement, but it was Ceallach who replied. "She only drinks the beer since it's her da's favorite outside of whisky. She'll have Cabernet Sauvignon, the bottle, please." His hand skimmed the document, and each item pictured in his mind was from Hamish's memory, including each taste. "I'll have the stout, room temperature."

Hamish rocked back on his feet, then his gaze moved to Kat's, whose cheeks turned a warm shade of pink as he spoke. "Yer new friend then? Introduce me, please."

Ceallach dropped the document which he now knew was a menu. His gaze connected with hers while the pink coloring her cheeks deepened. "Hamish, this is Ceallach, Aodhán's cousin." She stopped, eyes wide stumbling on the reason why he visited.

Picking up where she faltered, Ceallach completed the introduction. "Visiting the family for a time." He smiled at her. "Kat has agreed to show me around the town, and she's done a marvelous job on her first day."

A low chuckle rumbled from Hamish. "Good, that is. Kat yer usual?" The image of a juicy beef hamburger with all the fixings and chips flashed in Ceallach's mind from Kat's.

Her grin stretched, and Ceallach caught the flicker of hunger in her thoughts. "Aye, I'm so hungry I'd eat the whole cow."

The tall man turned, expectant, his stare weighing Ceallach for an answer. "I'll have the same."

Hamish plucked the menus away. "Well, it seems Kat has herself a new *bràmair, boyfriend.* Wait till I tell the wife! She'll be so happy for ye!"

As the man chuckled and turned Kat raised her hand. "But he's only a friend." She spoke to Hamish's retreating back.

She turned back, a shrug lifting her shoulders as if the answer hardly mattered. "Ye didn't even know what I ordered. Ye read my mind again."

It was Ceallach's turn to shrug. "Yer thoughts about that juicy cheeseburger came so strong I couldn't ignore them, and I like burgers as well." He pictured a burger appearing in the meal bin in the Fae realm, and his stomach growled, anticipating the juicy delicacy.

Kat sat back when a young man delivered their drinks. "I'm Hamish Jr." He set the beer down, plucked the wine from the tray, opened the bottle, and deftly poured, filling a quarter of the stemmed glass.

He set the glass and then the bottle on the table. "My da's teaching me the business."

A smile tugged at Kat's lips, playful and quick. "Ye are doing better. Ye didn't spill my drink this time." The young man picked up his tray and grinned from ear to ear as he backed away, bumping into the table behind him. He turned and made a fast getaway, the backs of his ears turning red.

A soft giggle slipped from Kat, light as a breeze. "He's had a crush on me for some time, but he's too young."

Ceallach sipped his beer, enjoying the heady flavor. "Aye, he *is* too young." He nearly threw a spell at the boy just to shove him into the arms of another woman—anything to pry him off a Kat obsession. His grip tightening before a grunt broke free and he forced his hand to ease. Kat was a temptation he didn't need right now. Duty demanded his focus, no matter how his thoughts strayed. Silence stretched between them, punctuated only by the soft clink of her glass against the table. The bottle caught her eye once her glass emptied, and she reached for it without a word.

His hand stopped hers as he picked up the bottle filling her cup halfway. "The wine tastes better if it breathes a little."

Kat leaned back, a smile playing on her lips as she watched him. Ceallach's gaze stayed steady, but beneath his skin, something restless clawed for escape every time Kat moved. Her small, effortless smile unraveled something tightly bound in his chest. Wanting a human like this the Fae forbid. Yet, there she was, radiant in her quiet confidence, and he couldn't look away. In a way, something about Kat just fit—like a memory he hadn't known he'd lost, finally slipping back into place. Nothing in his endless existence ever had. Dangerous, yes. Disarming. But necessary, somehow, like she was the thread that might either bind him to the mortal world, or unravel him completely.

The youth Hamish Jr. staggered under the large tray, disrupting his thoughts. The youth clanged it on the table beside them, but the food remained undisturbed. He served Kat first, turning her plate till the chips and burger sat side by side. Then repeated the same for Ceallach. He bowed as he backed away.

Ceallach, impressed with the youth, smiled at him. "Jr. ye do yer job well, thank you." The boy beamed, picked up the large tray, and strode from the room.

Kat cut her burger in half, set the knife aside, grabbed the ketchup, and made a little dollop next to her chips. She picked up half her burger with both hands, kept her elbows out of the way by sticking them out to the sides, and tried to take a large bite with her tiny mouth, only biting the corner.

Smiling at her routine, Ceallach waited till she took her first bite before he lifted his with one hand and bit into the morsel, easily eating a fourth of the burger. The juice from the beef burst into his mouth as the slightly burnt edges of the meat teased his taste buds. The bread was almost better than the beef, all soft and fluffy. The vegetables had a fresh, earthy taste that the Fae realm's food lacked. He chewed, marveling at the multiple flavors rolling around his mouth.

When he swallowed, he caught Kat's stare. "Is our food that much different than in the Fae realm?"

The burger hovered midair, forgotten for a beat as his eyes flicked back to her. "Aye, 'tis. There's an earthly taste underwriting all the others, and yer food is so much more flavorful."

He took another large bite, and Kat huffed. "Yer second bite and the burger is over half gone. Shall I order ye another?"

A rough swallow came first, then he tipped his beer back, chasing down whatever stuck in his throat. "No, this will do." He nodded to her. "Finished yer meal, Kat." She offered a faint smile, then focused on her meal, the hush between them deepening with each bite. Hamish Jr came again and got Ceallach two more beers not stopping when he set them on the table "I must oversee the band's setup. Da will put the meal on yer parent's tab." The youth trotting away as his satisfaction of a job well done flickered to Ceallach. The air fractured under a storm of blows, each one pounding in jagged rhythm, the echoes shrieking wild and crooked, like sound itself had lost its balance. Like a rising siren weaving between the noise like a warning threaded through the wind.

Ceallach tilted his head. "Is that music?"

Kat barked a laugh. "Rock and roll. But not the music. They warm up, so the instruments sound bad now, but later they won't."

His gaze caught on the gentle heave of boats drifting on the loch, but his mind stayed anchored in darker waters.

Kat stood, picking up the wine bottle and emptying the last into her glass. "Come outside. The band will start soon, and I suspect ye will find them noisy."

****

Kat elbowed her way out the back door, keeping her glass in hand, and Ceallach gulped the last of his beer. She glanced back while he grabbed the second untouched bottle and followed, easing the recently closed door with one finger to step out to the deck outside. She meandered down the dock, passing several vessels. Sensing his heat behind her, she kept strolling until she came to the last one, a large antique sailboat from the nineteen hundreds named *Mo Chridhe, my heart*. The boat was no stranger—she'd stepped onto its deck more times than she could count. The ship belonged to the MacDougalls. One of Colin's and Ewan's joys was sailing the grand ship which prompted them to purchase Ewan's beloved vessel, *The Faithful*. A quick scan of the pier revealed nothing but ropes and shadows—no plank to help her aboard.

Ceallach stood behind her as he sipped his beer, then lightly belched. "This boat, ye know it." He made a statement, not a question.

Over her shoulder, Kat replied. "Aye, and stop reading my mind."

Both hands lifted in surrender. "Habit. But when they're such lively thoughts, the temptation is hard to resist."

Drawing closer, he brought a calming presence to Kat. "When Ewan first bought his replica galleon, Doug and Ewan used to take Evie and me sailing a lot." The wind blew a little, ruffling her hair. "I loved the feeling sailing gave me. To be out on the ocean sailing the Western Isles." She wrapped her arms around her, taking another sip of wine. "I miss that. Being with my brother and our friends. We were family."

The air stirred around her, salt-tinged and restless, and she angled her head as if savoring its touch. "The galleon is with Doug now. Ewan's bought himself a newer frigate, but he takes Lorelei out sailing these days."

A chill rippled through her, and she folded in on herself, hands gripping her sides. "I would like to sail the open waters again. Feel the wind in my hair, see the sight of the isles once more."

Ceallach moved closer, his warmth welcome against her back. "Sailing seems so freeing." As she turned to face him fully, warm streaks of amber, sienna, and rose bled across the sky, casting him in a glow that made him look carved from the last light of day.

She drank from her wine, needing to steady her nerves. "Sailing, aye, it is freeing." She tilted her head to the side and imagined him flying as Morrigan, his ma, did sometimes. "Ye fly, don't ye?"

He smirked, gulping the last of his beer, and set the bottle on a crate. He shivered his shoulders a bit, and blueish green wings popped out from his back. He seemed to stretch after they did, like he'd kept them folded in, hidden. Ceallach's wings stretched behind him in a quiet display of power, their span casting shadows that flickered like dancing flame against the forest light. Unlike his mother, Morrigan's, gossamer, iridescent butterfly wings, which were delicate and dazzling, his were rougher and wilder. The leathery surface shimmered with a blueish-green sheen like moonlight skimming the surface of deep water.

Each membrane stretched between dark, sinewy veins that flexed with subtle motion, giving them the appearance of ancient parchment inked by the night sky. They were bat-like in structure—predatory, primal—but elegant in their own right, the edges tipped in faint silver where magic bled through. Kat tilted her head, studying them, struck by the contrast. Where Morrigan's wings whispered beauty and illusion, Ceallach's spoke of shadows, storm winds, and truths too ancient to be kind.

He rolled his shoulders, and they flapped till he lifted a bit as his arms stretched to the sides. Kat glanced around, worried someone would catch him in his Fae form.

When her gaze came back to him, he floated before her. "I don't know if flying is the same. Come and tell me."

Kat backed away. "We'll get caught." She held her wine glass up. "I have my wine to finish." Ceallach floated closer and tipped her wine glass to her mouth. Like under a spell, she obeyed his command and willingly drank the rest. With a flick of his wrist, the glass disappeared. She stepped back and would have taken a dunk in the loch if Ceallach had not swooped her into his arms and held her close. His wings beat an even pace. They rose, floating above the marina, making Kat squirm and squeak, and she grabbed his shoulders.

Ceallach squeezed her once. "Stop moving, I have ye." He spun them in fast circles as dizziness overcame her. The world tilted, and her stomach lurched. Then he blew gently against her cheek, and the nausea slipped away like mist in the wind.

She peered at him. "What was that?"

He smirked. "Cloaking, so the humans cannot see us."

His wings beat a fast rhythm, and they floated around the marina. Kat giggled, and that seemed to be the only encouragement Ceallach needed. He dipped, and they took off fast, flying toward Dunstaffnage Castle. The wind blew hard, chilling Kat immediately. With her shiver, his chest heated, warning her.

At Dunstaffnage Castle, he pulled up above the ancient stones, and they hovered, suspended between space and time. The setting sun over the mountain range appeared as a large molten disk spilling streaks of honey gold and burnt umber that set the horizon aflame.

Ceallach hummed while gazing at her. "So, tell me, Kat, is flying like sailing?"

Laughter shot from her throat before she could stop it, sharp and sudden. "No! Nothing like it."

He swept her hair aside, his fingers trailing where the wind had tossed it across her eyes. "What was flying like?"

Air rushed into her lungs, and the words tumbled

out, one chasing the next before her thoughts could scatter. "Dash, where to begin. The flight was faster. The turn around the marina is like sailing; smooth and steady but sometimes goes fast." She sighed. "The cloaking, that was weird." She jolted. "Wait, yer chest warmed. Ye did that earlier as well, didn't ye?"

Heat stirred from him, as he gave a slow nod. "Ye were chilled." He kept them suspended while he gazed at her.

Warmth crept up her cheeks, and another thought hit her. "My cheek, ye blew on my cheek, and I felt better."

A flicker curved his mouth, the smile quiet but sure. "To make yer stomach better from the side effects of cloaking." His eyes traveled to her face, then her hair. "I do not possess the same healing power the dragons have for their soul mates, but I can alleviate some discomfort."

She hummed. "A nice skill to have. Do all Fae possess these skills?"

"Some, aye," he said as he shook his head slowly.

Her hair blew on her face, and he brushed the strand away again. "Now that I've taken ye flying, will ye take me sailing, *bruadarach, dreamer*?"

Kat's face warmed under the endearment, "Ye call me a dreamer. I'm far from someone who daydreams. I am more practical."

A low breath escaped him along with a slow shake of his head. "Ah, *mo bruadarach*, ye are the source of dreams."

"If I am the dreamer, ye are the *buisneac, wizard*."

He frowned, moving closer till their lips brushed once. "Wizards are evil, Kat. I am the *tionac, shield*." He kissed her softly at first. As his hand moved to cup her head, he deepened the kiss. She opened her mouth in a sigh, and his tongue delved in, swirling with hers, making her dizzy all over again in a delightful way.

As he brushed a kiss on her cheek, she whispered. "Are ye my *tionac*?"

His head came up so swiftly that hers fell forward. When she lifted her gaze to his, she met a stern expression. They tilted hard, and a wave of dizziness engulfed her. Her world spun, tipping until up and down traded places and nothing held steady. The motion all happened too fast; she held on to him, praying for land. All the movement stopped like she hit a wall of force. Kat opened her eyes, her hands gripped the steering wheel, and she sat in her car.

Ceallach's voice came from her left. "Go home, Kat. Forget about flying."

She turned and he stood outside the car. "But how did we?"

Long strides carried him off, his parting words tossed over a shoulder, which had no wings. "I won't explain. Go home."

Tears gathered. "Ceallach?"

He was beside her car in a blink. "Don't make me cast a spell forcing ye to forget." He turned, striding away. "Go home, Kathryn." She glanced at her steering wheel, then turned to Ceallach, and he had gone. She twisted this way and that, trying to find him. He'd vanished in the night.

For a moment, stillness anchored her, giving space for the night's chaos to settle. What started as a nice night out had turned so fast. A quick pull of the seatbelt, a solid click, and she turned the ignition, the dashboard lighting up in a soft glow. Darkness swallowed the last trace of dusk, and she flicked on the headlights, their beams slicing through the night. She pulled out and sighed while she drove the short route home. Not recalling getting out of the car or into the house, Kat meandered up the stairs. In her room, she mindlessly changed. When she pulled her brother's shirt over her head, she had tears covering her face. Wiping them with her shirt, she went to the window to open it wider, and a white flower sat on the sill. A Camella placed precisely like the ones before.

They always seemed to come when she needed them most, and today was no exception. She sat smelling the sweet scent while the night replayed in her mind. Her secret love kissed her for the first time, and when she mentioned him as her shield, her true love, he'd dropped her like some hot potato. They all did, the men. The minute she'd opened her mouth, and they realized how smart she was, they ghosted her. She turned, placing the flower on her nightstand, and crawled into bed, praying sleep would soon consume her and that she'd fall into the dreamer Ceallach thought she was.

Sleep came fitfully for Kat, not the dreamland she'd imagined. Blurred images came and went. Evil chased her no matter where she turned. She tried to call out for Ceallach, but nothing. A restless shift, a flutter of breath, then the heavy pull of sleep caught her again, deep and unrelenting. Something sharp filled her nose, a scent of deep, heady musk she'd not smelled the likes of before.

A laugh came low, deep, resonating in her soul. "What is it that, given one, you'll have either two or none?"

Kat stopped speaking aloud. "A riddle?"

The only reply she got was a deep chuckle. Her mind raced as she turned over the riddle. *Given one, you'll have either two or none.*

The man yelled, "Move on, the riddle will seek the end!" The chase started again. Turn after turn, she could never find her way out. The musk smell came again with a man's voice when she came to a turn. "Shall ye choose ye answer or take the turn?" His mocking tone answered easily.

She shouted. "A choice." And took the right turn, running towards the promised end.

The man's voice chased her as the musk scent hung in the air. "The gems, I want the stones." He chased her again, left, then right, to a dead end. She turned, and a black cloud churned before her.

His deep voice came harder. "The stones, get me the stones." Kat didn't know what he meant. She had no gems, no stones. Wait, she had Ceallach's tear gems. One appeared in her hand, and she held the glittering stone out to him. The black cloud consumed her hand, chilling her until ice locked her joints and stole the breath from her lungs.

The man chuckled as evil washed over her. "Tears? Ye bring me tears when I want the power." The icy sting forced her to yank her hand back, tucking it beneath her arm as warmth slowly seeped back in. She opened her mouth to yell, but nothing came out. Air refused to come, her chest locked tight as if clamped by invisible hands. The black cloud swirled around her, and she spun, falling into a bottomless abyss. A sharp jolt shot through her, limbs flailing until the sheets wrapped tight around her legs. Whipping her head one way and the other, she tried to make sense of where she was.

Her room—safe in her room. She breathed out once, then took a deep breath and blew air out to expel the evil from the dream. A cold breeze blew from her open window, and she pulled the covers up. When she started to lie back, a woman floated at the end of her bed, dressed in older clothing, looking like one of the portraits in Dunstaffnage outside Evie's childhood bedroom. Kat sat up, focusing on the woman as the apparition slowly rose and fell like a light wind. Her eyes roamed the figure again, and no sense of evil like in her dream came to her. No, a feeling of ease filled her heart, and she allowed her gaze to travel to the woman again.

Before her stood a figure awash in green light, its shape too solid to be air yet too ethereal to be flesh. This wasn't an ordinary ghost. This was the Green Lady of Dunstaffnage Castle, the ghost who haunted the castle and foretold the future of the MacDougalls. Crying meant bad, and smiling meant good. Kat sat staring at her hands, holding one to the right, thinking about why the ghost would be at the abbey, not the castle. Then held her other hand to the left with the following thought: *why has the ghost come to me? I'm not a MacDougall*. Her gaze snapped to the ghost's face, who smiled. The apparition's face wavered, and the face of a crying woman appeared. Kat drew in a breath and tried to scream, but like in her dream, nothing came. A sharp inhale was all she managed before the ghost struck, a cold weight hurling her onto the bed, sheets crumpling beneath her. The wind blew her curtains and out the window with a howl. All fell still and silent.

Kat lay there for a moment, forcing her breaths to steady, though each one dragged hard and uneven, trying to keep her racing heart still. The Green Lady had visited and cried, meaning something bad was in her future. Kat stayed there wide awake, reasoning about the ramifications of the ghost sighting against the reality of what she'd seen. Memories of her dream flashed, and her mind dipped into the scientific logic that ghosts do not exist and that this merely had been a bad dream. Her mind raced between the three thoughts: logic, ghosts, or her own fears. Each battling reason out till the early rays of dawn streaked the sky. She took a deep breath, knowing she could not tell anyone.

Chapter 5

Kat peeked into the playroom at Dunstaffnage Castle, finding her BFF, Evie, playing with her daughter. Evie wore loose jeans and a soft button down, much better than her all-black goth look she favored years before. Their play filled the space with warmth and noise, and for a fleeting moment, she pictured herself in their place—cradling a babe, its weight and wonder entirely hers. Annie turned, squealing at her with a wide grin.

Evie followed her daughter's stare and smiled. "Well, Annie, it looks like we have a visitor."

Kat strode in, bellyflopping onto the couch longways. Her slim denim jeans hugged her form as her crop top allowed air to cool her. She lay there briefly, allowing her body to sink into the comfort of the familiar seat.

Annie toddled over, stopping near Kat's face and aligning her eyes with hers.

Kat grinned at the small, sweet face. "Hello, wee one." Annie giggled and waddled on, apparently satisfied with the attention paid to her. Evie huffed from her place on the floor, making Kat roll over to stare at the ceiling.

A low, frustrated sound rumbled from Evie's throat. "I know that look." Kat didn't look her way, leaving the unspoken questions open.

Evie crawled over and leaned against the couch. "That's the lovesick look." It was Kat's turn to huff. Kat couldn't resist glancing her friend's way.

When their gazes connected, Evie lifted an eyebrow. "Tell me why ye are here and not showing Ceallach about?"

Kat folded her arms. "I wasn't aware he needed a guide every day."

The soft thump of Evie's head hitting the couch back was answer enough, her smirk widening. "Snapping like a turtle. Oh, it must be bad." Kat let the silence stretch, rotating her head back and staring at the ceiling. The cornice pattern really was unique in this room. With the sunlight shining across the ceiling, the shadows made the design look larger.

Her friend huffed a low, breathy laugh, the sound light but teasing. "Ye know avoiding the subject isn't going to help. What happened?"

A stinging built behind her eyes, and she threw an arm over them to hide the tears wanting to come. "Nothing's changed. Ceallach is like he's always been." She moved her arm away, wiping the moisture so her friend wouldn't see. Evie held her arms out as Annie toddled back but turned to Kat, falling then catching herself on the couch by Kat's head.

Kat turned, peeking at the tyke. "Hello, ye." The child drooled, grabbing some of Kat's hair and pulling the strands. Kat had to shift, sit, and remove her hair from the toddler's grip. Annie pounded the couch, letting out a squeal.

With a playful grunt, Evie scooped her daughter into her arms, the child's laughter bubbling up instantly. "I agree, Annie. Kat needs to explain what happened.

Yesterday, she and Ceallach looked happy, and today they aren't." Annie gurgled in reply. Kat smiled at the pair. Mother and daughter seemed so happy together. She always wanted a family.

Evie lifted Annie overhead, the little girl's delighted squeal ringing out as her arms stretched like wings. "Do ye still get the flowers?'

Her face heated. "Aye."

"Last night?"

"And the night before," Kat remembered the dream, the terrifying chase, and that laugh. She rubbed her nose as the heady musk scent lingered as she shivered. "Evie, can ye still see the Green Lady?

The little girl twisted in Evie's embrace, but Evie held fast, pressing a playful kiss to her cheek. "Aye, but I haven't seen her in some time."

Kat blinked back tears. "Ye think she's still around?"

Her friend paused, tilting her head as if hearing something. "For sure, I sense her near the Chapel."

Another squeal burst from Annie just as Evie pulled her close, laughter bubbling between them. Light caught Evie's Fae necklace, the one Aodhán gave her that saved Evie's life—the necklace worn by each Fae that held their immortality. Ceallach's necklace had shone in the light like Evie's.

Kat stared as the stone glittered again. "Your Fae necklace. Tell me again about the feeling when Aodhán gave ye immortality?"

Evie held a calmer Annie close, rubbing her lips against the tot's hair. "The moment I cannot recall being almost dead. But his sacrifice, not staying a Fae and taking his place as King over the kingdom of the Tuatha

Dé Danann favoring a mortal life with me makes my heart melt." She sighed. "But when we exchanged Fae necklaces at our wedding." The slight tremor in her friend's words tightened Kat's chest. "Aye, that was magical."

They sat in silence. The previous night echoed like it had left fingerprints on her soul. Ceallach hadn't asked when he lifted her, just scooped her into his arms as they took off in flight. The first jolt of flight stole her breath, her arms instinctively wrapped around his neck, her cheek brushing against the curve where his shoulder met the base of those massive, bat-like wings. She had expected coldness, maybe a little fear. Instead, steady warmth wrapped around her, and the rhythmic, thunderous beat of wings rose—not just built for flying, but for carrying.

They soared above the loch, then the marina, making the trees pass in a blur of silver and green below. When he stopped hovering midair, the stars hung close enough to touch. And by the way he held her—strong, certain—everything settled. She wasn't a burden. She belonged.

She had turned to look at him as his wings beat behind him as that soft shimmer of blue-green caught starlight, his hair tousled from the wind, and a softness in her eyes she didn't think anyone else had ever seen. He hadn't taken her on just a flight. With him, it was *freedom*. It was *trust*. And something that might have been the beginning of falling in love.

Someone tapped her arm, shifting her focus to Evie, who lifted her brow again.

Kat pushed forward, the couch sinking beneath her hands as she sat up. "There's nothing to say. Nothing's changed. His disdain for me is the same as it's always been."

Her friend shook her head, her voice firm. "I disagree."

Kat sank into the couch, letting its cushions catch her weight. "It doesn't matter."

Evie sat Annie on her lap, allowing the tot to bounce witha giggle while she held her. "My Da always said start from the beginning. Tell me about yer night. Then we'll see what the issue is."

Kat stared but didn't see the ornate ceiling anymore. Ceallach's smile filled her vision, blocking out everything else. She rubbed her eyes.

Start at the beginning. "We started in my car."

A sharp breath caught in Evie's throat, her expression widening. "He rode in one. He never has, claims he's afraid of them."

A sharp laugh burst from Kat, catching even her by surprise. "Yea, well, he is. Threw some force around us in the middle of the road."

Evie laughed, her smile threaded within the sound. "That's not new; my husband did the same on his first car ride." She paused, then her voice softened. "But that's not where the evening went sour, is it?"

A low groan slipped free. "No, it's not." The memory of them flying flashed in her mind—the light feeling of soaring. Her heartbeat had raced when Ceallach held her in his arms.

Evie's sudden shout snapped Kat upright, her pulse jumping. "Aha! Ye beam. Ye had a good time. Spill it. Details girl!"

Heat flushed up Kat's cheeks, blooming faster than she could stop it. "He took me flying." The words came out almost a sigh. She couldn't help herself and didn't want to.

Excitement laced the one word, the kind Kat could feel without glancing her way. "And?"

Kat's lips still tingled with the memory of Ceallach's kiss. Her fingers rose to trace the lingering warmth as if by touching her lips, she could summon the moment back, electrifying and leaving her breathless.

A slap on the couch came before Evie's outburst. "I knew it! He kissed ye, didn't he."

Her body jerked as her fingers yanked away. "So?"

Evie set a wiggly Annie on the floor, who took off crawling as she leaned over. "A Fae's kiss lingers. Kind of like a little shock."

She gave her friend a slight shrug. "It does? I wouldn't know."

"Liar. Tell me where the night went wrong."

A soft moan escaped as she spoke. "Everywhere." Then she shook herself. "Doesn't matter. It's like he said. Forget it. He's here on a mission and needs to focus on that."

"Mission, bah. He likes ye."

Tears welled again. The scene replayed too easily—him walking away, the weight of his question about being her shield heavier than the slam of the car door. Would she ever find love?

Someone tapped her arm. "One day, aye, ye will."

She pulled free with a jerk. "Ye said ye can't read my mind."

Evie took her hand in hers. "I didn't have to."

Kat blinked hard, the sting behind her eyes deepening as the warmth of tears gathered along her lashes, heavy and close to falling. "I asked if he was my shield, and he said no."

Her friend shifted until she sat near her, holding Kat's hand. "All the stones have a shield. They've all returned. He said he had to shield us all. That's why he can't be yer shield, but I don't think that means he doesn't like ye." Evie patted Kat's hand. "Give it time."

Kat stared at their hands. "He's traveled the portal to the future. Ye know there's a rule about time allowed shortening." She exhaled. "I don't think he has much time here."

Evie shook her head. "Ceallach is Fae. He has all the time he wants."

****

The floorboards creaked under his cousin's steps, each turn before the grand fireplace like a shadow of old councils in the Fae realm. Ceallach lingered behind the couch, the weight of memory pressing in—this was how Dagda paced, heavy with decisions that shaped kingdoms. He huffed—this was one meeting his grandda demanded Ceallach hold.

Aodhán spoke each word with each step. "The fable had another ending."

Of course this would come up. Ceallach launched into the tale just as his grandda had taught him, word for word. "The woman gripped the Stone of Destiny, her love for the kind Fae overpowering her fear. She raised it high and cried, 'Begone!' The evil Fae shattered, his remains scattering into the bloom of white rose bushes across the land.

"The good Fae turned to her. 'You see me as I truly am. Your belief gave me the strength to find faith, hope, and love—both in myself and another. I had to believe first to see.'

"He took the stone and reached for her hand. 'Now faith is the substance of things hoped for, the evidence of things not seen.' Lifting her to float beside him, he smiled. 'True love shall no longer require a maiden's sacrifice for evil.' She took his hand, love igniting within—and they lived happily ever after."

Aodhán waved one hand. "She kills the evil Fae." Then the other. "Saves the stone for the good Fae." He stared at his cousin. "Happily ever after?" He huffed. "That's so cliché. No real Fae fable ends that way."

A soft mutter passed between his lips in a tone barely above a breath. "It's part of the gathering."

Aodhán stopped. "A gathering. All of us?"

Planting his feet wide, Ceallach crossed his arms, bracing for the conversation ahead. For certain, the gathering's purpose would surprise his cousin as much as it had shocked him. His reply was a solemn nod.

His cousin resumed his pacing. "All the women, the maidens." He turned, waving his arm as if all the women stood before the fireplace. "And each man, as the shield, must protect them."

Ceallach gave the same nod.

Aodhán turned, striding the other way. "Why? Why the shield and the maiden?"

Without a shift or glance, Ceallach echoed the words his grandda once used when asked the same. "The shield is to protect the maiden for the transfer."

Rather than easing, his cousin's glare grew heavier, each second thick with unspoken tension. "Transfer? Of the stones?"

Ceallach nodded once.

The reply tore from Aodhán, pitched just short of a full shout. "To whom?"

71

A simple shrug was all Ceallach gave, though his grandda's answer echoed with something colder. *Ye will see when she arrives.* But he'd not share that information with his cousin, which would yield more questions than he had answers for.

His cousin's steps restarted, sharp and uneven, as if the motion could shake loose his frustration. "Transfer. How the hell will we do that?"

Ceallach needed his cousin's help in the coming days, not just his guidance but also his Fae powers. "The shield must protect the maiden. The stones will only change guardians through the maiden."

Aodhán ran his finger through his hair, then flipped the long lengths over his shoulder. "Change guardians? Ye mean we do more than transfer?"

His voice dropped low as he spoke, "Aye, the time of the MacDougall guardianship has ended."

With an impatient sweep, his hands cut through the air, as if the motion alone could vent his irritation. "Ended. I thought this was the final resting place, the Chapel in the Woods."

He couldn't share all Dagda had told him and had shown him from his visions of memory—the battles with the evil Fae, the Fomoire. Too much information could risk the mission, his duty to the Fae, and the realms.

Taking a deep breath, he spoke. "I only know what Grandda has shared. But I need yer help. Yer counsel, confidence, and most importantly, yer powers. Each shield cannot fail. If the shield fails, the stones become vulnerable to the evil Fae."

His cousin rounded the couch, patting his shoulder. "Aye, I will be there for ye always." His grip tightened as he gave a sly grin. "Care to share what happened last night? I cannot help but notice ye are without a guide today."

Ceallach's focus moved away from his cousin's scrutiny as he focused on the fireplace, masking his emotions. "Nothing. She drove us around; we saw the town and had dinner."

With a swift pull, Aodhán stepped back, his expression locked and measuring. "Nothing? Ye block yer emotions from me, yet that's nothing new. Ye always were closed off." He rounded the couch to resume his pacing before the fireplace. "Drove? Did ye ride in a car?"

Ceallach turned his head to the side, not wanting to admit a weakness to his cousin. They'd competed at everything since their youth, Aodhán usually winning, being the next heir, King to the Tuatha Dé Danann.

His cousin's chuckle filled the room. "I don't have to read yer thoughts. I see it in yer face. Ye got into one of those tin boxes, and it scared ye shitless!"

Ceallach rolled his shoulders. "Did not."

The sharpness faded from his cousin's voice, leaving something gentler in its place. "It did me, too, when I first got in one. Threw a bubble spell encasing us from any impact."

His mouth curved despite himself—too many fears, too many failures bound them closer than blood ever could. "Well, it wasn't me who was scared shitless, but Kat nearly lost it when I threw a bubble spell surrounding us. She doesn't know her way around magic or spells."

Aodhán nodded. "She wouldn't. She's not had much exposure not being a maiden." They stood there for a moment, each still in this silence.

His cousin's voice came at a near whisper. "What

went wrong? With her?"

Ceallach unfolded his arms, running one hand through his hair, smoothing the length. "Nothing."

There was a smirk in his cousin's sly reply. "Liar. Yer first moment alone with her that she's aware of, and ye both come away pricklier than a thistle."

His cousin was right, as usual, but he'd never admit as much. He bent his head, wondering for the millionth time what a life with Kat would be like. His heart replied. Paradise.

The energy shifted, indicating someone new approached the castle. A grin came when Ceallach sensed who had arrived. His head came up, and his cousin lifted his head, grinning. He'd felt it, too. Bree's retired special ops, Airforce pilot teacher, anthropologist wife, and daughter had arrived. The fourth Iona stone maiden and shield, Hope. Time passed faster than Ceallach anticipated. Time, he needed more time.

The castle doors burst open, and greeting sounds filled the entryway down the hall from the Great Room.

A heavy breath slipped from him, his chest sinking with the weight of it. "So, it begins."

He closed his eyes for a moment, letting the voices echo through the stone walls like a warning. The start of the end—he'd known this would come, though he'd hoped for more time. Every arrival marked another thread pulled loose from the world he'd sworn to protect. Soon, there would be no turning back. The Iona Stones would find their new protector, and the balance between darkness and light could shift forever, only his failure stood in the way.

Bree came from the hall into the Great Room, walking sideways as she spoke to someone behind her.

"Dom, I am so happy about the visit! And you brought your daughter Olivia!"

Dominic followed into the room. "Yes, and she's natural at flying. She didn't get ill or throw a fit. Sat and watched the clouds fly by."

His wife, Moira, followed. "It only figures you held her the entire time, telling her of each action the plane took and why." She carried the young toddler who hugged her mom's shoulder.

Colin followed Moira in, taking his wife, Bree, in his arms. "Well, a visit was in the making, and here we all are."

As Moira stood rocking them back and forth, Bree eyed the child. "Dom, I love that you named your daughter after our mom."

Dominic smiled as he stared at his wife and daughter. "Seemed only natural." He rounded the couch, falling into its softness. "We have arrived. Imagine my shock when Dagda popped into my study announcing I had a calling."

His wife slid into the seat beside him, still holding the content youth. "Your anger was more over the fact the man drank all your MacDougall whisky. His instant appearance, announcement, and abrupt departure was your shock."

Dominic huffed. "Calling on a person like that? Dropping mysterious news, then vanishing. Who the hell does that?"

Aodhán rounded the couch and leaned on the mantel. "My grandda, that's who." He waved to his cousin. "Ceallach, my cousin."

Dom nodded. "Greetings, Dagda mentioned you. You do resemble your mother."

The air shifted, the faint buzz beneath his skin telling him Kat and Evie were near before he caught their voices.

His gaze rose to Aodhán's, who raised an eyebrow. *Kat comes with Evie. Ye really should try to work out whatever happened last night.*

Ceallach huffed, crossing his arms and ignoring his cousin when the two women entered the room. He had to focus on something, anything other than Kat's intoxicating scent, her allure. He took a deep breath, enjoying its pull of light Camellia scent, then blocked the smell, calling himself a fool.

Evie beamed, leading Kat inside. "I told ye, Moira and Dom arrived." Evie carried Annie, who pitched herself sideways almost out of her mom's arms when she saw her cousin, Olivia. Olivia wiggled from Moira's arms, sliding from the couch, and crawled toward her cousin. Annie, who Evie set on the floor, which was more like landed on the floor, wobbled and then beat an unstable march to her cousin. Once reunited, both sat before the fireplace, chatting away in gibberish. Annie's making more sense; a word here and there being recognizable.

When Kat flashed a smile and then ducked her head, Ceallach's focus drew to the children both holding a conversation, of sorts. Annie was happy to see her close friend from afar, and Olivia tried, using her broken words, to convey her excitement at being in the sky.

The conversation floated around the room, focusing on the calling, the gathering, and the stones. Each person tried to reason out the why of it all. The answers burned on Ceallach's tongue, but he couldn't share a single one. Not till the time was upon them.

Aodhán's voice came into his mind. *Can't ye give some answers? The women worry.*

Ceallach sent a reply. *Not until all the shields and maidens have assembled.*

A sharp breath flared from his cousin. *Well, that's the first thing ye've said that makes any sense.* Aodhán nodded to Kat, who leaned on the couch's arm beside the girls as she watched the toddlers play. *Ye both ignore one another. Was yer night that bad?*

Ceallach's reply came with an edge of magical command. *Leave off.*

Power stirred, warping the air until it rippled, his pulse quickening as if his body sensed what his mind hadn't caught yet. The flame tore free from the fire, searing a path striking Olivia's arm. She screamed as the blaze snapped past her shoulder in a searing arc, the heat brushing Kat's cheek. Annie grabbed Olivia's arm, cradling her. Moira moved, but it was Evie who reached the child first. A heady musk scent filled the room, thick and cloying.

Aodhán's voice came fast and hard. *I detect it, evil. And what's that smell?*

Ceallach didn't know the source, but the smell and the sudden surge of energy put him on edge. The flame had moved with a will of its own, arcing straight toward Kat. No power outside of the Fae could conjure such a force.

Moira took her daughter into her arms, which reduced the howl to a sniffle. "Bree, a first aid kit?"

Bree nodded, directing the woman out. "Mrs. A has one in the kitchen." Both women filed out, with Dominic following. Colin stood at the end of the couch, crossing his arms like Ceallach, a man ready to accept ill-fated news.

Annie whimpered, and Evie took her daughter in her arms. She sent a mind message to both Ceallach and Aodhán. *Explain what is happening now. That wasn't some spark. The flame reached out, nearly grabbing the child's arm. And how did the flame moved on its own to Kat?* She shifted Annie in her arms. *The scent seems familiar, but not.*

Colin's gruff command had all jolting. "Stop the mind crap. Answers now."

Ceallach stilled, his gaze sweeping the room, weighing each face in turn, gleaning any and all emotions. Colin looked ready to thrash them all. Evie held Annie as Aodhán, who'd taken his wife in his arms, soothed both wife and daughter. Kat's breath hitched. The musky tang—dry husk and heated stone—seeped across the room. Her pupils dilated, then stilled, as though she'd stepped behind frosted glass. Ceallach brushed the edge of her mind and found only polished obsidian: no crack, no echo, no entry. The silence tasted wrong, borrowed, as if someone else's shadow stood between them. Strange, she'd not been able to block him, ever.

Aodhán was the first to break the silence. "Colin, I have no answers."

Evie rubbed her daughter's back. "Honest Da, that was as much a surprise to us as to ye."

Colin's regard slid to Ceallach, who had to give some response. "Be on guard. The evil Fae seems alerted to the gathering."

Ceallach's gaze drifted back to Kat. She hadn't moved. The vacant stillness in her eyes clawed at something deep inside him. If the flame had shifted an inch, it would have taken her.

A dull ache pressed behind his ribs. She was never meant to stand this close to the heart of it all. Yet here she was—marked by the same darkness he'd fought his whole life to contain. He'd planned to focus every scrap of his will on the gathering, on keeping the Stones from falling into the wrong hands. But if Kat had become a target, the entire balance would change. Protecting her while guarding the Stones would border on impossible. He swallowed, the taste of ash lingering in his throat.

Duty demanded he keep the maiden safe—the one foretold in the fables was Bree but with the Stone of Destiny fable, the girl with flowers, which one did the evil target? But what if Kat was *her*? What if every legend, every whispered warning, pointed straight to the woman now staring blankly past him?

He'd sworn an oath to shield the chosen at any cost, to place the gathering above all else. But Kat wasn't meant to be part of this. Or—gods help him—was she?

Colin barked. "That's it?"

Focusing back on the conversation in the room, Ceallach bent his head, replying softly. "That's all I have." When he lifted it, his gaze landed on Kat, who looked like she'd seen a ghost.

Bree called from the kitchen. "Colin?"

He stormed from the room, calling as he left. "Answers! The moment ye get them, answers ye will give."

The room seemed to sigh when all the energy from the people left. Ceallach focused on Kat, searching for what scared her so much. The black wall had disappeared and all he got was her relief as she moved beside Evie.

Aodhán's voice came brightly. "Well, I think

today's events call for some fresh air. Evie, a walk?"

Evie nodded as they both sauntered to the doorway. "Aye, Kat, how about ye show Ceallach the abbey? Maybe a picnic like yer parents like." Kat made a face at her friend but hid her expression when Ceallach caught her.

Aodhán sent a message when they cleared the doorway. *Fresh air, cousin. The abbey has such nice views. Ye'll need to tell Mrs. A to pack a meal.*

Ceallach huffed. *I can't fall for her. It's forbidden. Plus, I have my duty to the stones.* Though as he sent the thought, being near Kat again tempted him in ways he couldn't deny—and didn't want to. With the threat possibly circling her now, he told himself he needed an excuse to stay close. Perhaps protecting her would demand he spend more time with her. At least, that was the reason he'd let himself believe.

Aodhán and Evie did not answer as his eyes met Kat's as her playful comment lifted his spirits. "The abbey? We'll have to go in the car." Her teasing pleasure washed over him.

Ceallach allowed a small smile, relief warming his chest as he sensed her ease. "I can manage the *death mobile* if ye show me what a picnic is."

Chapter 6

Kat beamed as they approached Ardchattan Priory from her family's private garage. Her eyes roamed the familiar building, and that sense of ease washed over her. *Home.* The grounds lay in an idyllic location overlooking Loch Etive. Years had passed since the first remodel, and with each year, her ma, Marie, had found a new project. Something else that needed updating. The old abbey had been her ma's lifelong dream, to remodel a historic religious structure. Marie had helped Bree remodel the chapel at Dunstaffnage. Her ma said the Priory was in the worst condition of the two, but no one could tell today.

She glanced at Ceallach, who seemed more at ease now that they were out of the *death mobile*. While he hadn't put a force field around the car like yesterday, he had gripped the dash during the short drive from Dunstaffnage Castle to her home. Today, he wore snug jeans, a tank with a button-down over it, and sturdy boots to complete his look. His hair he'd styled like a photo of a model she'd seen in a magazine. In the car, his masculine scent had nearly driven her to distraction. He rolled his shoulders for the umpteenth time as Kat hid a smile.

Ceallach growled. "Laugh all ye want, Kat. Cars are dangerous."

She came up short. "Reading my mind? I thought

we had a deal."

He stepped closer, and his finger brushed her cheek. "I didn't read yer mind. Yer smirk gave it away."

Kat held her breath as his finger tickled a path down the side of her face. As she stared into his near-white, blue eyes, Kat held her breath as his finger traced her cheek. For a heartbeat, she thought he might kiss her. Then his gaze hardened, and he stepped away.

His voice became harsh. "Ye said ye'd show me the grounds." Last night, he'd said to forget them, and maybe she should but today he was here, and she'd take the chance, hoping it meant he wasn't ready to walk away after all.

Shaking herself, she pushed past him. "This way, then."

Kat led them around the main building. The rear area opened into the garden with a picturesque view of Loch Etive. Beyond the loch, layers of green highlands folded over one another. Ben Cruachan's Mountain range stretched for eons as the range's shadows slipped into the loch, reflecting like a mirror in its tranquil waters.

She sighed. "The sight of this familiar view always eases me." Today, she seemed to need it. Ceallach moved behind her, brushing her back, then tensed and pulled away. They stood there for a moment as the sounds of the loch's waves lapped lightly. The call of a bird sounded overhead while the clouds drifted slowly by.

Ceallach took a breath and let it out, seeming at ease. "The range resembles Mount Broemere in the Tuatha Dé Danann realm." His voice softened. "The view's only missing the castle."

Kat glanced over her shoulder. "I knew ye'd like this."

Ceallach's gaze traveled over her face, and when their eyes connected, he smiled. "Aye, this feels like home."

They continued along the garden paths as Kat shared her ma's work. "Each garden path is named in honor of its monastic origins." She pointed to the sign. "This one is Monk's Walk, which crosses Priory's Walk." She led them along next to the main house area. "Ma revamped this rock garden and extended the herbaceous and rose borders." She pointed along the border, which also ran out to the excellent view of Loch Etive, a path she ran many times as a child. When they rounded the west of the house, rows of shrubs lined the walkways, surrounded by a wild garden of roses and other floral areas, each a perfect display of native plants.

Midstep, she angled toward him. "My ma planned the garden honoring the abbey's original design." Loving the gardens, Kat stopped to take in the view as Ceallach stopped a short distance away. His constant distance reminded her how alone she was in his company. Kat glanced at him and then shrugged, turning to lead them farther along the path until they reached the primary display marker—the one she'd read countless times before.

She leaned against the cold rock, not needing to see the inscriptions to recite the words. "So, the MacDougalls built and developed the property years ago. They founded this entire area of Scotland with my family alongside."

Ceallach read the text from the marker aloud. "Duncan MacDougall, Lord of Lorne and builder of

Dunstaffnage Castle near Oban, founded the priory dedicated to St. Modan in Twelve hundred thirty-one. Kings of Scotland and Norway fought to control Argyll and the Inner Hebrides. Robert the Bruce held a parliament here in thirteen hundred and nine."

Kat moved beside him, reciting the rest. "The MacDougalls' dominated the priory throughout most of its existence. Indeed, by the end of the fifteenth century, the family monopolized the prior position."

Steps light, she wandered into the chapel ruin, her finger gliding along the weathered piscina with its trio of stone-carved bowls near the altar. "My ma claims she can detect the people who made the old stone when she touches it." She pulled her hand away from the cold stone. "Says she feels closer to the monks who worked here centuries ago." Kat ambled past each marker, running her fingers over each one, trying to sense something, anything. "I can't feel them like her."

Ceallach nudged behind her, grabbing her hand. "The people who built this place." She spun, stopping as he took a deep breath and brought her hand to his chest. "They appreciate what yer family does here. Restoring the property's history to share with the people."

He pulled her along the path, crossing to areas of the chapel yard where the monks had crammed the tombs into burial rows. Kat had to keep her feet parallel while he easily led them between the graves.

Ceallach stopped mid-way, taking both her hands in his. "So many." He closed his eyes as his hands warmed. "*Mo bruadarach.* They all wish to thank ye."

Her lashes flickered, a quick flutter as her mind caught up. "They, ye mean the people here?"

He nodded as he opened his eyes. "Everyone

entombed here for all time is happy with what yer family has done."

Kat stood immobile, his gaze locked on hers, a twinkle in his expression revealing the power he carried within. She'd been with Evie when she saw ghosts, but when she held Ceallach's hands like this when he used his powers, the warmth and energy flowed between them. The connection pulsed through her—raw, electric, and startlingly real, unlike anything she'd ever known.

From the corner of her eye, Kat caught a couple meandering by. Chastising herself, she pulled her hands from his. While the main abbey, her home, remained closed to the public, the grounds were open and managed by the Historic Environment Scotland. She often forgot the public roamed parts of her home as well.

She proceeded toward the crosses, intent on showing Ceallach the MacDougall cross. The one cross her parents claimed they'd saved each other in front of while in the past. As Kat strode from the grave area, Ceallach appeared before her, stretched his hand out, and helped her. Kat stopped, glancing behind her and then back towards Ceallach.

Ceallach tilted his head, a teasing lilt in his voice. "Temporal displacement," he said, like it should've been obvious. He held his hand out to help her over the graves. "A gentleman always helps a lady." She blinked. He'd done this before, appeared before her without moving.

He cleared his throat, and she took his hand as he helped her up and over a large grave slab. "Time displacement in sociology refers to the idea that new activities may replace older ones. New activities that cause time displacement are usually technology-based…" When she stepped up, she stumbled, falling into his arms.

Steadying her against his chest, he rasped. "I got ye, Kat." For a breath, neither moved, their gazes locked as if the rest of the world had fallen away. Ceallach lifted her from the stone, turned them, and allowed her to slide down his body. Kat's body molded against him, every bump and crevice imprinting along her skin as if the earth itself pressed into her. When he set her on her feet, she became breathless and stumbled a little.

Ceallach held her close, his breath brushing her ear. "Careful, Kat." When she strengthened, he shifted back and took her hand, guiding them to the other side of the ruins. In this area, the old grave markers sat upright so visitors could look closer. Kat blinked. Ceallach had led them, stopping before the MacDougall cross, her intended destination.

She turned, glaring at him. "We agreed no mind reading."

He squeezed her hand once. "I couldn't resist. Plus, I know the story of yer parents and this cross from my ma."

Their fingers laced together, shoulders nearly brushing as they faced the cross in quiet unity. Kat imagined this must have been the same way her parents had stood before the cross in the fifteenth century.

Next to the display sat the large cross with portions of the design cracked off. Kat knew the design, or the lack of completion, having examined the relic hundreds of times as a youth. "My ma said, 'Cromwell's Clearances is probably responsible for the damage.' On one side, the cross bears a crucifixion scene. On the other side is an incomplete image of the Virgin and Child."

Kat moved toward the marker. "She drew the

completed design from the memory of seeing the cross whole. That was when it was new." Ceallach didn't release her hand as she pointed to the sign. "She told the historic environment she'd found a damaged scroll. Had studied the roll before it fell to dust." Kat sighed. "She lied, but the fib explained how she knew the original design without any documentation to support her claim." Bright and freshly painted, the sign stood out among the others. "Before they went back in time, the ghost of a nun haunted the priory ruins. This used to say she was the lover of a monk, and hid beneath the floor of his room so that she could visit her lover at night. But the prior found her and, as punishment for her sins, buried her alive." An icy ripple coursed through her whenever she remembered the story. She shivered, reaching to rub her arms.

His presence swept in close, arms encircling her, and she let herself lean into the steady strength of him. "I know the story well. In the past, yer grandda tricked and fooled the priest who'd kidnapped yer ma in the future before dragging her to the past to search for a magic Iona Stone." His body warmed, chasing her chill. "It was the priest they'd buried in the past for his transgressions against yer ma. In the future, Colin and John had the priest's grave relocated far away before yer parents moved in."

Kat shivered again as Ceallach's breath brushed her ear. "I cannot sense his spirit. Ye truly have nothing to fear."

She twisted within his hold, the brush of his warmth never leaving her skin. "Really? For so long, I feared I felt him near."

He kissed her forehead. "I promise, his spirit is at

rest and not here."

A couple strolled into the area, looking over the markers, making Kat jolt, but Ceallach held her tightly to him. "Hungry yet?" Kat shook her head as her stomach rumbled.

Warm breath skimmed her ear. "Now, I don't need to read yer mind to know yer belly complains." He stepped back, taking her hand in his. "Come, show me what this picnicking is."

She bit back a wider smile, the flush already blooming across her face. "Aye, I'll take ye to my family's favored spot." She led them to the grassy area near the loch around the back side of the house, out of the public areas.

With a quick pivot, she released his hand. "Ye, wait here. I'll get the picnic basket. Mrs. A packed our lunch, and I am certain what she's picked will not disappoint." She strode past him. "It's in the car. I'll be right back."

A chuckle rumbled from Ceallach, rough and brief as a wave of energy flowed behind her. She turned. "What's so funny?" When she faced Ceallach, he held the large basket in both hands. The wind ruffled his hair as a smile rose on his face. A fluttering grew in her chest as she took a breath, struck again by how handsome he was.

Her regard went from his face to the basket he held before him. "One of these days yer going to get caught doing all that magic and have to explain yerself to a human." Ceallach set the basket down, waving his hand as the MacArthur plaid spread itself in the same position her da always set it—a perfect view overlooking both Loch Etive and the priory.

Ceallach tipped his head toward the open tartan, a

flick of his hand in invitation. "Ye'd be surprised what humans take for granted." He snorted. "And they say seeing is believing."

Kat sat on the fabric beside the basket as she dug inside. "Evie always said faith is believing without seeing."

He stepped around the plaid, easily lounging beside her. "Those who will believe without seeing for themselves are uniquely blessed."

Movement halted, her focus narrowing until he was all she could see. "Do ye truly believe that?"

A slow curve tugged at Ceallach's lips, his gaze steady on her. "I truly know it." Silence lingered as Kat sat there for a moment, absorbing his statement. What exactly had Ceallach seen in his years or eons in existence? Kat didn't know exactly how long Ceallach had lived. He'd been born after her parents married but before she came along—a detail she'd clung to ever since their first meeting, hungry to piece together who he was. And as a Fae, they aged quicker.

His fingers drummed lightly against her hand, a playful rhythm in the contact. "Yer stomach growled again, Kat. Better unpack the food soon before ye expire from hunger."

Brought out of her thoughts by his touch, she blinked and reached for the basket, laying out sandwiches and fruit to fill the silence. Next, she lifted a large bottle of beer, then another with wine, berating herself for becoming lost in Ceallach again.

Setting down the beer, she held up the wine bottle. "Oh, Cabernet Sauvignon, my favorite. How did she know?" Kat lowered the bottle, leveling her eyes on Ceallach. "Did ye do something, like to her mind?"

Ceallach barked a laugh. "To Mrs. A? No one can tell Mrs. A what to do." He picked at the blanket's edge. "I may have spoken with her about what to pack when ye got the *death mobile*." He glanced up with a smirk. "She can be easily manipulated when it comes to what she calls *love birds*."

Kat dug into the basket, producing the wine opener. "Love birds. Ha! She's always into everybody's business." She fumbled with the corkscrew and then dropped it. "Love, such a fickle emotion."

The bottle glinted in the sun as Kat reached for the opener, just as Ceallach sat up and took the wine from her. "Tell me, Kat. Why is it at times ye find such fault with love?" He sat back and waved his hand over the bottle, the stopper lifting into his hand. She reached for the wine glass, and he beat her to it, easily handling the cork and glass as he poured a measure. "Sometimes, ye seem to embrace the emotion. Other times, ye seem to push it away, not believing." He handed her the glass with a raised eyebrow. "Must one see to believe, Kat? Ye can't see love, can ye?" The first sip was casual, but the second came heavier as her thoughts circled back to what Ceallach had said. Ceallach corked the wine and set it aside.

He picked up the beer, screwed the lid open, took a long pull, and settled back on his elbow. "Kat, can ye prove love?"

Her scientific mind argued with her heart, forcing her to blurt out the answer. "Love? Proven? Scholars have proven it to be an object phenomenon in people's behavior. Attraction of one to another." She grabbed a sandwich, bit into it, and then waved the snack while Ceallach ate two stacked as one. Thoughts raced ahead, leaving her mouth scrambling to keep up. "Attraction is a metaphysical concept exhibited in a few different forms. Magnets, in gravity, people, other stuff that sticks together, adhesion."

Ceallach picked up a melon piece, waving the fruit in the air. "People stuck together. Like glue?"

She took another gulp of her wine. "Yes! It may fall under metaphysics since attraction acts as a fundamental force of nature expressed in various forms. It is a metaphysical concept even though it has physical manifestations."

He pulled on his beer again before sighing. "Kat, love isn't like glue. While I agree with yer metaphysical analysis, there is something more to attraction."

The sweetness hit first when she drew the juice from the watermelon, mind turning even as she ate. She picked another piece and took a bite, her thoughts rushing while she spoke around her chewing. "Attraction must be metaphysical because it is a concept that transcends physical examples into the domain of ideas, as in thought, certain ideas attract others." She swallowed and reached for another piece of fruit. When her hand returned to the bowl, Ceallach caught her wrist. He brought it to his mouth, sucking the juice from her fingers. His free hand waved, and her glass and his bottle disappeared.

The space between them held her attention, and in the next blink, the food was gone. "What if I was still hungry?"

He slid closer, taking her into his arms. "Food is for later. Now ye only need to feel." She caught the glimmer in his eyes, those silver flecks that sparkled when she came close. He brushed his lips over hers softly. Once, then again. A sharp breath stole her lungs, her heart thundering beneath the weight of his nearness.

Ceallach's hands pushed her back, bringing them together as his every hard and soft spot aligned perfectly with hers—as if God made each for the other. His gaze roamed her face and then settled on her lips. He kissed her again, and she opened up to him, desperately wanting more. His tongue delved in and danced with hers till she grew dizzy. He hovered above her, and she melted beneath him, savoring the way his kiss devoured her with unrelenting hunger. Ceallach's hand slid from her hip to her chest, gripping her while his kiss deepened. A moan escaped her lips when he cupped her breasts, teasing them until they ached with need.

Kat wiggled, drawn to the heat of his body. Ceallach lifted his head, and the teasing grin on his lips coaxed a smile from her. His hand drifted from her chest to the ache between her thighs, each stroke igniting sparks even through the barrier of her jeans. Her eyes fluttered shut, head tilting back to offer her neck, where his lips traced featherlight kisses that trailed lower, dipping into the valley between her breasts.

Fingers threaded through his hair—she held him there, anchoring herself as much as claiming him. Each sweep of his tongue moved with purpose, slow and firm, circling her like he knew exactly how to pull her apart. His rhythm matched the motion of his hand—steady, insistent—and the heat inside her bloomed with every deliberate stroke. It wasn't just pleasure, this was possession, growing thick and molten, spreading through her limbs like fire licking up dry wood.

She breathed his name, barely audible, like a secret slipping from her lips. Her thighs trembled, tightening around him, drawing him closer, needing more, needing *everything*. Her hips moved on their own, caught in the pull of his rhythm, meeting him with desperate urgency. The wave rose slowly, curling higher with each pass of his mouth, each curl of his fingers, building a pressure so exquisite it blurred the edges of her thoughts.

When he found that perfect place, the one she hadn't even realized she ached for, her breath hitched, and her body jolted—arched—offering him all of her. Her hands clutched at him, no longer steady but frantic, as if letting go would shatter her completely. A cry tore from her throat, ragged and raw, as sensation broke over her in a rush, her body unraveling in a cascade of heat and light. She wasn't thinking anymore. She was only feeling— *him*, in every way she'd ever craved and never dared say aloud.

Ceallach eased the movement of his fingers, then brushed a gentle kiss across her lips. She panted, breath shallow, needing a moment to return to herself.

And gods, she had just climaxed—fully clothed.

Breath shuddered from her, soft and spent, as warmth pulsed through every limb. "I've not felt that before."

Ceallach kissed her again with a smile on his lips. "The sensations overtake yer body, consuming ye, right?" Kat could only manage a nod.

His fingers found her hip, grounding her in the moment while his mouth claimed hers again. "*Mo bruadarach.* Love does not need to be proven, Kat. Ye either feel it, or not, as a conscious being."

Kat grinned, using his earlier comment, enjoying the banter. "Seeing is believing *tionac, shield*."

Ceallach replied as his fingers brushed her cheek.

"Evie always said faith is believing without seeing."

Her body moved before her mind caught up, a slow retreat to shake off the pull he always carried. "Blind faith? Ceallach, each woman has a shield, their true love. Ye said Abigail is not a maiden of a found stone, but Doug is her shield, her true love. Why can this not be for us?"

Ceallach tore himself from her embrace, the sudden absence of his warmth making her sway. His hands trembled at his sides, jaw tight like he braced for a blow. "I am not yer shield, Kat."

The words hit her like a slap—but it was the break in his voice that made her breath catch. Not anger. Not rejection. Fear.

His gaze flicked away from hers, as if he couldn't bear to see her believe in him.

The denial cracked out again, hoarse and raw, aimed at her but echoing back on him.

"I can't be."

She didn't move. Didn't breathe. Because she saw what he couldn't hide. The strain in his voice didn't push her away—it drew her in. He didn't want to say it. He needed to. Like someone clinging to a lie they had to believe to survive. But he was wrong.

He raked a hand through his hair, pacing a short, jagged line before her. When he looked up, something raw flickered in his eyes—want and regret, tangled so tightly she couldn't pull them apart.

"I have to protect the maiden." He swallowed, his throat working around the words. "It's—" He turned sharply, the motion sending the basket tumbling onto its side, food spilling out.

"This is impossible." His jaw clenched. He wouldn't

meet her gaze. "Go home, Kat. Just…go."

She pushed herself upright, hand stretching toward him before she could think better of it. "But…"

Ceallach twisted his shoulders, and his figure wavered, then vanished, leaving Kat reaching for air. "I am, but this doesn't feel like my home anymore."

Kat sat back, tucking her knees to her chest and hugging herself. Why was love so hard and disappointing?

Dr Chu's voice echoed in her head again. "Love is an overused and often misused concept that applies to mostly selfish desires and attachment to all kinds of illusory things of the world." Kat sat staring at Loch Etive. Was love truly a selfish desire that led to imaginary diversions? She grabbed the wine, unstopped the cork, and drank straight from the bottle. Was her lot in life to be the spinster who had too smart a mind to feel love? She tipped the bottle, taking a long drink. The fire burned down her chest, not warming her chilled heart. She sat for a while, turning over everything that had happened in the last day. So much in so little time. She sat longer as the day turned to dusk, and burnt sienna plum hues lit the sky.

Upending the bottle, Kat muttered, only to find the bottle empty. "Those who will believe without seeing for themselves will be uniquely blessed or doubly cursed."

Chapter 7

Ceallach stood off the side, cloaked so Kat wouldn't see him. He hated leaving her so abruptly. Had he stayed, the evening would have taken them to her bedroom. He chastised himself a million times for being a fool, losing his heart when he needed to focus on his mission, the gathering.

Kat tipped the wine, trying to drink from the empty bottle again as she gazed at the fading sunset. Time slipped by while she sat motionless, silent tears carving paths down her pretty face. She deserved so much more—more than he could offer. With dusk disappearing and darkness consuming the land, she knelt, picked up the basket, and loaded the empty bottle and food inside. Rising while lifting the basket, she fumbled and fell over, spilling the contents.

Yelling, Kat slammed her hand on the blanket. "Damn it!" Ceallach moved towards her but stopped short. The urge to bolt clawed at him, but he melted deeper into the shadows even though he'd remained fully cloaked.

Kat sat on her knees, bent over, soft sobs shaking her shoulders. Ceallach's chest ached with the need to gather her close, to crush her against him and kiss away every tear. To promise he'd never let anything touch her again.

But he couldn't.

The mission weighed on him like a curse. The maiden of the Stones needed his full devotion—nothing less. If he faltered, even for his mate, the evil Fae would seize the chance to strike. To kill the maiden. To claim the magic Iona Stones and bend every realm to darkness.

Fists clenched at his sides, the ache in his chest tightening with every breath. Gods, he wanted to choose her—*Kat.* To cast aside everything else and reach for the one thing that made his world feel right. But duty chained him, cold and unyielding. He couldn't look away from her, couldn't let her walk into danger alone. Not when every instinct screamed to protect her. How was he meant to guard her—*the* maiden, the evil Fae's target—complete his mission, and not lose himself in the fire of wanting her?

A sniffle came, then another. Kat rose, picking up the basket and sweeping the MacArthur tartan while she stood. "Serves me right! Falling for a Fae." She threw the blanket over her arm, swiping each side of her face and wiping her tears away. "I should have known better." She stood taller. "Face reality as it is, not as it was or as you wish it to be." She shook herself. "Right, Dr. Chu?"

That familiar, stubborn stride carried her toward the abbey, her home. "If wishes were horses, beggars would ride." Ceallach followed while she stomped a few more steps, then stopped waving her free hand when she spoke. "If turnips were watches, I'd wear one by my side." It was a poem her ma had spoken to her as a child. He'd heard her recite the prose often when faced with hard times.

Kat shook her head and beat a quick pace to the house. "If *ifs* and *ands* were pots and pans…" The door flew open with her hard yank, banging it against the wall.

97

"There'd be no work for tinkers' hands." Her hand flung the door wide, and she disappeared through it, allowing it to close in Ceallach's face. His heart went out to her. Too many *ifs and onlys*. Usually, the poem lifted her spirits, but that wasn't the case tonight.

He faded through the door and floated into the kitchen, where Kat set the basket on the counter, then turned and wandered up the stairs. He followed while sniffles filled the stairway. Kat stumbled into her room and fell flat on her belly into her bed. Only the bedside table lamp lit the room, casting odd shapes on the walls. Ceallach floated into a shadow.

She rolled over, flinging her arm over her eyes. "God, why me? And why does it hurt?" She lay on the bed as more sniffles filled the room.

He should leave, quit this torment to his soul, but he couldn't leave his Kat hurt. He flicked a wrist, and a Camellia flower, white as snow, appeared. He floated over, setting the bloom on her windowsill. He glanced over his shoulder, and she still lay with her arm over her face. She needed to see, see that someone cared. He tapped the window lightly as if a tree's branch swayed in the wind. Kat sat up so abruptly he jolted but remained cloaked while he leaned against the wall.

A low grumble rumbled from her throat to the empty room. "A fly on the wall."

He smirked, then sobered, recalling the rest of the idiom. *When the right man comes along.* Why was fate so cruel?

Kat rose and crossed to the window, picking up the flower. "How? The windows closed." She brought the bloom to her nose and inhaled a deep breath. "They come when I need them most." She crushed the flower in her hand. "But die like all my other dreams."

Petals scattered like confetti. As if on a war march, Kat stomped on them on her way to the bath and let the sharp clatter of objects crashing fill the room.

Ceallach bent, picking up the pieces as he whispered. "I am here for ye, Kat." He waved a hand, made the flower whole again, then set the bud on the sill and backed against the wall.

Kat shoved into the room with her favored nightshirt on and turned the bedside lamp off, casting the room into the blue glow of night. The white flower sat on the sill, almost glowing, but Kat kept her back to the window while more sniffles came from her.

Drifting to her, he brushed his fingers near her face, catching her tears then gripped his hand hard, made teardrop gems, and set them on her bedside table. He would have put them in her hand, allowing the gem's power to heal her hurt, but the sensation of someone touching her who wasn't there might have been too much. Setting them on her bedside table, he had to be content that she'd find them in the morning.

Without a sound, he floated to the window, pausing before fading through it as he thought. *Kat, if only I could share my heart now the way I want.* He passed through the window mentally, swearing off *if only* he whispered. "I swear, when this ends…I will find a way to make us right."

****

Kat drifted in and out of a restless, feverish sleep. Her eyes, swollen and scorched from relentless tears, fluttered shut only to snap open again. A burn clawed her throat, each swallow choking down the cries she refused to let free. She twisted beneath the sheets, tangled in the ghosts of her torment, each breath shallow, uneven.

Then, the darkness took her.

It wasn't sleep—but a plunge, a merciless descent into an abyss that swallowed her whole. As she fell, air ripped from her lungs, weightless yet suffocating, lost in the void. Shadows clawed at her, whispering her name, pulling her deeper. There was no ground, no end, only the endless drop, a freefall into oblivion.

She woke sitting on the ground, and the menacing voice from her dreams returned. "Back again, Kitty?"

Her body twisted sharp and fast. "Don't call me that!"

Before her, the maze appeared again, and the cloying musk scent returned. "Care to play a game?" She'd come to the same place, a large turn with forks going off in four different directions.

Kat pushed to her feet, her back meeting cold stone as she edged away. "No, not with ye!"

A deep chuckle filled her head. "Not even for yer brother?"

Her steps cut forward with a stumble. "What do ye know of Doug? Is he here?" The pause in the silence deafened her, her own breath roaring in her ears. She took another step, and a turn in the way appeared.

The voice slipped through the air again, low and curling. "Right or left? Which way shall she go?"

Every word sent a shiver down her spine, but her feet stayed planted. "I'm not doing shit till ye tell me about my brother!" Icy wind blew hard on her body, but she stood firmly, wanting to know about Doug.

The man's light chuckle came again. "A riddle, dearie." The walls shifted before her until a single hall was the only direction. "Come, Kat, let's play."

One step, then another carried her forward before his voice curled through the air once more. "Tell me, what can go through glass without breaking it?" Kat walked quicker, knowing the answer. Solving the riddle promised the end.

The word tore from her, sharp and certain. "Water!"

Black smoke engulfed her, blinding her. She waved her arms about as the man's voice replied. "Not right." When the cloud faded, she faced the fork in the path again.

"Right or left, dearie?"

Her voice burst out, raw and loud. "Where's Doug?" Silence was the answer she got. Kat turned right, mumbling. "Men go left because women are always right."

The chuckle came again. "Smart lass." He sighed. "Tell me, what can go through glass without breaking it?"

Kat walked on. The answer led to the end. She must see this through. *Riddles were typically easier than the mind thought. Free yer thoughts, Kat. What can go through glass without breaking it?*

The answer slammed into her mind, halting her mid-step, breath caught tight in her chest. "Air!"

A force blasted into her, making her stumble as the man's voice yelled. "The stones, where are my stones?"

Kat took off at a run, yelling. "They aren't yers!" She ran flat into a wall and fell hard on her rear end.

"The stones, bitch!" Time cracked around her, a jolt that left her sprawled and breathless, as if the world itself had yanked her backward. She shifted, disoriented, trying to make sense of the space around her—a vast nothingness that swallowed sound and shape alike. She had to try, get up, and find Doug. He needed her. A shaft of light came from her right. Bright like sunlight. A beacon in the darkness, coming regardless of what stood in its way.

A raw shout tore from the man. "Get my stones!"

Kat rolled over, screaming the right answer. "Light!"

Light pierced her eyelids, and she shot upright, breath catching as the dawn pressed against her face. Kat scrambled only to find herself tangled in her bedcovers. Flailing, she fell on the floor, covers and all, and lay there panting, still half in her dream. Her mind tried to replay the nightmare, but the only thought that came was the riddle… *what can go through glass without breaking it*? She rolled over into the beam of sunlight.

Light.

Kat took a deep breath and then another. The dream haunted her in the day as much as it had in her sleep.

Untangling herself from the covers, she grabbed the bedside table and pulled herself up only to encounter three small teardrop gems identical to the ones Ceallach had made from her tears days ago. She stood fully and marched to her jewelry box, flipping the lid open to find the two made before. Her focus flew back to the gems on the table, and sure enough, they sat there winking at her in the sun's light. Why?

Bundling the bedding over her arm she flung the mass on the bed, hoping a shower would clear her head. Passing the window on the way to the bath, she spied the whole white flower. Her gaze moved to the three gems, then back to the flower. Had Ceallach been there? certainly not after dumping her. Maybe a day spent with her bestie shopping was in order. She weaved into her bath, stripped her clothing, and flicked on the shower. As Kat stood under the cold stream, she tried to knock out the emotions thinking of Ceallach being there brought up in her.

Kat finished washing in the cold, dried off, and left her hair wet to dry in the warm summer sun. She dressed in a flip skirt, short tee, and sneakers and applied light makeup. A girl always felt better after a shower and a good primp. Blowing a kiss to her reflection, she turned and headed to the door. Along the way, she picked up the flower, smelled the petals, and then put the bloom in the special box on her bedside table. Then she scooped up the three gems, pocketing them, feeling better about her day, and headed to the stairs.

Feeling lighter, she did her typical skip down the stairs like when she was a child. Two at a time, in a syncopated rhythm that lifted her heart. At the bottom, Kat grinned, thinking of how Doug had always teased her about her *dance down the stairs*.

When she entered the kitchen, her ma rose from the table. "Kat dear, ye look like ye haven't slept a wink." She moved to the kettle. "Tea?"

Kat pulled a cup from the cupboard and held it out as her ma poured steaming water. Setting the cup aside, she placed a tea bag inside. Lifting the mug to her nose, the familiar bite of black Scottish tea wafted, her morning favorite.

As her ma bustled about the kitchen, she picked up bread and placed it in the toaster. "Dr. Chu called and left a message."

Kat swirled her tea bag until the water turned dark. She lifted it, ringing out the excess, not missing a drop. "I know. I got a text."

Her ma leaned on the counter, eyeing her da. From the corner of her view, Kat caught his raised brow. She turned, facing the kitchen window and the garden outside as she sipped her tea.

Beside her, her ma leaned in with a subtle nudge. "He mentioned a new lecture."

Her da cleared his throat. "On time travel. Invited ye to attend at the university in Edinburgh."

Kat sipped her tea again, liking the dark brew. She didn't face her parents, their goal was obvious to her, trying to get her to leave with the gathering happened soon. She wanted to be here with them all.

The toast popped, making her ma jolt like she always did. "Does it to me every time." Plating the toast, her ma added a dollop of butter, and jam then pulled Kat's arm, and situated her at the table to break her fast. Kat did like toast and jam, especially strawberries. There was comfort in the familiar rhythm of eating breakfast at home with her family the quiet joy of buttering the warm slice and spreading a thick layer of her favorite jam across it.

Her ma slid into the seat beside her. "Kat, dear." Oh lord, *Kat dear* meant a lecture. She bit into the toast twice, filling her mouth, hoping to avoid having to answer. The sweetness of the jam mixed with the creaminess of the butter on the wheat bread hit her hunger spot as it always did.

"The Fae boy. Should ye spend so much time with him?" Her ma wasn't letting anything go easily. Kat chewed and shrugged. She tried to swallow her food, and the mound got stuck. She coughed and had to gulp hot tea to wash it down. She opened her mouth, allowing cool air in, hoping she hadn't burned her tongue.

Her da sat forward. "Kat, we worry. Ye know the Fae play with humans." He sat back, nodding. "Yer grandda knew all too well."

Kat bit into the next piece, chewing. She'd heard all too many times about her grandda, who bargained with a Fae to spend time with his dead wife, who the Fae made alive in the past. In the end, he'd tricked the MacArthur Fae, Morrigan, Ceallach's ma, but the whole ordeal had still taken his and his wife's life. But maybe that was meant to be. Both were in the past, escaping the mortality within their future—a bargain with a Fae to outwit their destiny.

He da huffed. "He may have won, but the deed still cost him his life."

Her ma shot him *the look*, which meant *shut it*.

Marie turned back, patting her arm. "Maybe not spend so much time with him, eh?"

Kat ate the last of her toast while speaking around her bite. "Well, ye won't have to worry. He dumped me like all the others." She finished off her tea. "I'm off to see Evie. Maybe go shopping."

Her ma sat up, grinning. "Shopping is a great way to pass the time."

Her da huffed. "Did you hear about the drunk geologist?" She paused, knowing he couldn't wait for the punchline. With a laugh, he spat out, "He finally hit *rock bottom*."

She stood. "Da…" saying it in two syllables like when she was young. His jokes were the corniest in existence, but they still comforted her.

He grinned wide. "I've got rock puns ye won't take for *granite*."

As he barked a laugh, she strode away from the

table. "I'm off. Don't wait up."

Her ma called out. "Power to the pebble!" Both her parents broke into gales of laughter. Kat huffed. To be that happy and in love must be nice.

When she strode past her da, he caught her arm. "Kat, we are pleased ye are home. We just *lava* ye so much." Her da offered his wide cheesy grin that he did with all his jokes. She teared up a bit, knowing he only wanted to show her his love.

She bent, kissing his cheek, giving the same response she had since childhood. "I know Da, I lava ye too." She headed out to her car, hoping she'd catch Evie for a day of escape. Passing through the main door, she slipped her hand into her pocket, fingers brushing the gems. Her heart lifted, the weight she'd carried easing with each step. Escape sounded perfect.

Chapter 8

That shopping day got canceled, and the next two as well. Evie had dodged her for the last three days, but having Moira and Dom's tot, Olivia, plus her own Annie to look after, Kat supposed the children took up most of Evie's time. Kat strolled through the Dunstaffnage Marina's parking lot. Evie had finally asked to meet her this afternoon. Kat smiled. Evie loved being a mom, and Kat enjoyed being an honorable aunt.

Today, she'd donned loose-fitting pants with a loose-fitting crop top she loved and found comfortable. She'd selected her white sneakers for comfort on a day that promised much walking. Dunbeg village had blocks of shops she hadn't been to for a while, and she looked forward to a day of window shopping, maybe splurging on something too.

When she came to the pub door, Hamish pushed his way out. "There she is, my favorite customer. They're waitin' for ye at the dock." Kat strode past him to go around the building as Hamish called over his shoulder. "Ye have a good time and be careful of the winds today!"

She wondered what he'd meant by that. They'd only planned the postponed shopping trip. When she rounded the building, the wind hit her, blowing her hair all different ways. She reached up, gathering the mass into a ponytail and securing her locks with the band she usually kept on her wrist since sudden windy days were frequent in Scotland.

Kat stood for a moment alone, wondering where Evie was. The boats bobbed as the lapping of the water soothed her. She closed her eyes, allowing the sound to ease her troubled mind. Her dreams had seemed to intensify recently. The chasing became increasingly powerful, and each new night brought another riddle. She crossed her arms, and last night still nagged in her mind.

The evil man had chased her again, but this time, she recognized the twists and turns, seeming able to navigate the maze without running into a dead end. The black mist had encircled her again, demanding an answer to that night's mystery. One that promised she'd see her brother if she solved the riddle. She'd been unable to think through the riddle and ended up tangled in her sheets on the floor of her bedroom again with no answers.

She whispered the riddle, hoping the answer would come to her. "I am something people celebrate or resist. I change people's thoughts and lives. I am obvious to some, but to others, I am a mystery. What am I?"

"It seems like ages since I've seen ye." Ceallach's voice startled her from her daze. She stumbled a bit, and he was beside her, holding her after standing far away. "Careful, *bruadarach*. Ye almost took a dip in the loch." He'd flashed from one place to the other in a blink and held her in his arms, once again preventing her from falling into the water.

She shifted in his embrace, and he released her. "I'm to meet Evie. Have ye seen her?"

Ceallach stepped back, leaning on a crate. "Aye, I have. She's back at the castle."

Kat's grin faded. At the castle? So, Evie bailed on

her again.

He cleared his throat. "But she's been busy." He stood offering his hand to her. "Come, let me show ye."

Ceallach settled her hand on his arm. Today, he wore loose slacks with a button-down shirt and carried a jacket. He'd even opted for sneakers she hadn't seen him wear before. They strolled toward the edge of the dock, each step echoing like a whispered reminder of the past. It was the same path they had walked that night, the night Ceallach had first joined them. The night that had changed everything.

The memory surged through her like a breath of wind against her skin. That first flight was weightless and exhilarating, the world shrinking beneath her as she soared. She could almost feel the sensations again, the rush of air tangling in her hair, the thrill of Ceallach's steady arms holding her aloft, the impossible magic of it all. A smile ghosted across her lips, unbidden, unstoppable. Even now, standing firmly on wooden planks, her soul still longed for the sky.

They strolled on a bit, and Ceallach leaned ever. "So, Kat, what have ye been doing to keep yerself busy?"

Her face heated as she half lied. "Oh, I've had so much reading for the university. They recently presented a new theory on time travel. Dr. Chu sent it over for me." She'd missed the lecture but read the paper. She tried to, but her mind kept wandering back to the man casually strolling beside her. She peeked at him while they walked on, and strolling wasn't how she would describe his walk. Smooth, graceful, and with purpose. His gait was more like a panther stalking prey than some casual stroll.

At the end of the dock, he stopped them before the

MacDougall's large antique sailboat from the nineteen hundreds named *Mo chridhe, my heart.* Kat's eyes traveled the deck as the feeling of nostalgia overcame her. She loved that boat and the memories the vessel held for her.

Ceallach let out a low huff, making Kat glance his way. "Ye said Evie's been working on something. She hasn't been working on this boat, has she? Hamish keeps the MacDougall's ship in perfect order for Laird Mac. He and his wife sail it most of the summer."

A smirk tugged at Ceallach's mouth, his gaze fixed on her. "Not that one." He rotated them to the right and shifted behind her, holding her shoulders while he rocked them, almost waltzing them to the rear of the large vessel. As the larger boat passed near the stern, another sailboat appeared, hidden behind the larger ship.

Stopping at the bow, Kat recognized the small sailboat immediately. The vessel was one Hamish had up for sale for the past few months. Smaller than Laird Mac's but one large enough to have its own kitchenette and bunk for two. She'd wanted to purchase it, but as an unemployed recent college graduate, she lacked the funds.

The name *Lochan Legend* gleamed from the front. She'd dreamed of buying the vessel and naming it *Fairy's Wish* but never told anyone.

Ceallach's body moved closer to her back, warming her while his arm reached around, waving before her. "Evie's project."

She tipped her head, suspicion blooming. "She bought *Lochan Legend* for herself?"

His breath grazed her ear, warm and quick with his huff. "Not exactly."

Hamish Jr.'s head popped up from the hatch. "Thought I heard someone about." He climbed out, dusting his hands. "She's all ready for ye like Evie wanted." He grabbed the jib line and swung onto the dock, landing firm like he'd been born on a boat, which made her grin because he had. Hamish and his wife were on a sail when she entered labor. His birth was one of Hamish's favorite tales to tell. He'd tried to sail back but claimed the Fae wouldn't have it. Hamish boasted that the Fae wanted his son to be born on the sea. Like a Selkie Fae, another of Hamish's favored tales.

Ceallach stepped around her, patting Hamish Jr. on the shoulder. "Thank ye, Jr. Ye've done a great job as always." Hamish beamed, then turned, walking tall down the dock towards the marina pub. Kat had to smile at how Ceallach complimented Hamish Jr., giving the youth an extra boost of confidence.

When she turned back, his gaze focused on hers. "Now, I believe ye have a bargain with a Fae to keep."

Kat crossed her arms immediately on guard. Her grandda had bargained with the Fae and lost his life. Her da constantly reminded her never to bargain with the Fae. Ceallach approached her in that stalking walk that now made her feel like a worm on the end of a hook.

She lifted her chin, ready for a fight. "I made no bargain with a Fae."

Standing before her, Ceallach gave her a grin she'd never seen before, which looked nearly devilish. "Oh, I do believe ye have, Kat." He bent down till their eyes came even, making her breath catch. Those silver flecks glinted as his smile widened, and his white teeth showed. Under his gaze, heat curled through her—like a naughty woman caught in the sights of the big bad wolf, ready to be devoured.

His voice came out like silk. "Ye promised me a sailing trip if I took ye flying." Those Fae eyes glinted, sharp and unyielding, pinning her in place as if his stare alone held her captive. He stood up, breaking the spell. "Evie set this up and said we are to sail today."

A playful grunt slipped from Kat as she leaned her weight against the nearness of him, then pushed back. "Sailing! With ye! It would take weeks to teach ye proper, and from the looks of it, they've left us alone." She flung her arms wide, a playful flourish that showcased the empty dock with mock offense. "Two to sail the boat, one not knowing what he's doing. We'll get stuck!"

Ceallach turned, and without warning, swept her into his arms. "Come, Kat," he murmured, his voice low against her ear. "How hard can it be?"

Before she could argue—or remind him precisely how challenging sailing with *him* could be—he bent and brushed his lips over hers. The gentle heat of that touch scattered every sensible thought.

His mouth moved again, more insistent, and when his tongue slipped in to tease hers, her knees nearly gave way. She clutched the front of his shirt, dizzy with the taste of him, the feel of his strength closing around her.

Somewhere in the back of her mind, the memory tugged, the boat had a motor in case of emergencies. But truly—being stranded anywhere with Ceallach wouldn't be an emergency at all. It would be exactly where she wanted to be.

The thought had her gasp, and he took advantage, thrusting his tongue inside, swirling with hers as her world tilted and her head spun. He deepened the kiss when he danced, turning them. When he finished the kiss, he blew on her face, and her dizziness receded. She stayed with her eyes closed, wrapped in his arms, savoring this same moment she'd dreamed of since his last kiss.

A low chuckle vibrated against her, the warmth of his kiss still lingering on her lips. "Open yer eyes, Kat." When she did, his grin was the first sight to greet her. He turned them, and the view of Loch Etive met her.

The deck rocked a bit, and she squeaked, grabbing him. "We are on the boat?"

His breath brushed her ear, making her shiver while he spoke. "Sailing. Ye will teach me sailing. A bargain made is a bargain kept, Kat."

Stepping out of his embrace, Kat strode past him toward the steering wheel. "Well, my grandda would disagree." She glanced at the mooring lines, noting someone pulled them in. Had Ceallach managed that during their magical transfer? Either way, the boat was free from the dock to set sail.

Ceallach folded his arms as he leaned against the keelson box. "Yer grandda wanted something beyond his reach, which came with a price. One he was aware of." He shook his head. "Ye know he knew the outcome when he made the bargain. That he'd find an Iona stone and save his son."

She froze before the ship's wheel, unsure what to make of Ceallach's statement. *Grandda knew?*

The small nod came, firm and certain. "Aye, Kat. Ye'd be surprised the trials a parent would go through for their child." Enough about the past—what mattered now was the future. And hers, at least for the afternoon, involved a sail. The thought thrilled her. The open water, the wind at her back... freedom. She relished it.

Even if her so-called assistant had no idea what he was doing. Especially since he happened to be distractingly good-looking. Too good, really. And far too close for her to pretend she hadn't noticed.

She grinned as she started the engine causing Ceallach to jolt. "I thought sailing didn't use a motor." Just as she thought, her attractive assistant didn't know boats had death mobile motors. Watching him flinch only made it better.

Kat smirked as she steered the sloop away from the larger boat. "Aye, it does, but we must motor out till we clear the marina, then we cut the engine, loose the sails, and that's when the magic happens."

Ceallach shrugged, folded his arms, and positioned his legs apart, seeming to find his sea legs easily. "Magic? Kat, ye are no Fae."

Kat nodded, and she turned out of the marina's area and into the central lane of Loch Etive. "Aye, but humans can create our magic of sorts."

A short puff of air escaped him, and she caught the trace of amusement shining in his gaze. "This I shall like to see." Her fingers tightened on the wheel, steadying the boat even as her thoughts drifted dangerously toward him. Magic didn't have to shimmer or spark—it could be breathless laughter under the stars, the brush of his fingers on her skin, the way he looked at her like she was the only thing tethering him to this world. And God help her, she wanted to make that kind of magic with him.

Once clear of the marina traffic, Kat cut the engine, and they free-floated for a bit. That lifting feeling when the boat glided across the water was one of her favorite parts of sailing—the second was to face off with Mother

Nature. As they drifted, Ceallach's stern expression eased. He unfolded his arms and rolled his shoulders.

Tugging the rope tight around the wheel, a grunt slipped from her, more from effort than frustration. "No relaxing just yet. Ye must have a lesson on sailing, and I'll need yer help with the lines. It takes two to sail this thing." She moved past him and leaned on the keelson box. "In a sailboat, we play a bit with Mother Nature, as a far more active role in harnessing the energy that propels us forward. We can get stuck in *neutral*, with no wind in the sails—or we could even capsize, which would dunk us in the loch."

The crease between his brows deepened, a flicker of frustration she didn't miss. "I have no desire to take another bath today, Kat."

"Good, then ye will do some work before we can relax into sailing."

Kat turned, pointing to another sailboat as it glided past them. "It's easy to see how a boat can sail when the vessel goes in the same direction as the wind. The sails, those white triangles, catch the wind, which pushes the boat forward." They stood in silence while the boat passed them. The ease at which the sails took on the wind made Kat anticipate an excellent trip today. She glanced at Ceallach, if her assistant could catch on quickly enough. She waved her hand into the wind blowing across the stern like a wave. "The wind blows across the sails, creating an aerodynamic lift, like an airplane wing."

The huff came quickly and sharp. "Ye mean those metal tubes ye fly in?" A faint shiver caught his frame, visible even from where she stood. "Worse than cars if ye ask me."

Kat folded her arms, her voice wry. "Aye, well, I am not fond of flying like Uncle Dom, but it is a fast way to travel."

Ceallach shook his head, a hint of mockery threading his tone. "I disagree, but we are in the human realm, and what is it ye humans say? *We shall do as the locals do?*"

The sky caught her eye, and with it came the memory of wind in her hair and salt spray on her skin. "Something like that, aye. In the Western Isles of Scotland, we sail."

With a quick rise, she waved him on while she strode alongside the mainsail. "Ye must help me untie them. Thank goodness Hamish Jr. already took the covers off." She untied one, and Ceallach followed her lead. Moving on to the jib, Ceallach followed her, untying the fabric.

When she reached to untie another, he brushed her hand away. "I have it, Kat. Ye go on to the lines to release them."

Kat placed her hands on her hips. "Ye promised no mind reading."

After untying another, Ceallach leaned over and kissed her puckered lips. "Aye, I did. But this *work part* is not the best part, is it, Kat?" The kiss tingled as she stood absorbing the shock.

Shaking herself, she proceeded to the mainsail line and tugged the metal lever, unlocking the line. "Well, aye, but my da always said part of the enjoyment is the reward after hard work."

Ceallach moved to the handle for the jib line, grasping the device, unlocking and rotating the line while he grinned. "True, but the sailing part is yer favorite, so let's get on with it." He proceeded to the mainsail line, unlocked the crank, and rotated it, unfurling the mainsail.

Kat turned to the jib, losing the sail. She quickly strode past Ceallach, and he turned, allowing her to pass. The sails flapped in the wind, filling them when Kat reached the steering wheel, untying the rope. It jerked at first, but she gripped the wheel hard, loving the power the wind pulled in the vessel. She steered into the wind, allowing the breeze to cross the boat, causing them to lean to the left as they headed toward the gorgeous sight of the glen and mountains.

Ceallach moved till he stood beside her and sighed, making Kat smile. "Aye, I love this view as well."

She took his hand, placing it on the wheel. "Take it, but don't lose yer grip." He did so, and the helm pulled a little till he tightened it back.

He glanced at her, then the sails. "The sails have energy."

A grin tugged at her lips, the spark of mischief lighting her eyes. "Aye, but not from the motor. From wind, nature." Ceallach shifted till he had a comfortable stance. The wind blew his hair, and his shoulders relaxed while he eased into controlling the boat. Kat stood beside him, guiding him occasionally, keeping them in the wind.

They sailed up Loch Etive towards the Munros range that framed the Loch Ben Cruachan, Ben Trilleachan, and Ben Starav mountains. Her favorite was Ben Cruachan, the largest of the three. Passing under Connel Bridge, they came upon the Falls of Lora. She reached over and gripped the wheel turning the boat away from the rapids, being careful of the current.

Her voice lifted, sharp with command. "Ceallach, can ye…"

He beat a hasty step to the mainsail, pulling the tack, keeping the sail tight and full of wind.

The lock snapped shut, his gaze rising with it, and when his eyes found hers, his smile came quick and warm. "I got it. Loch Etive is hemmed in here by the narrow gap and a shallow underwater cill making the rapids we must avoid."

Returning to the helm, he moved behind her, wrapping her in his arms as he gripped the wheel on either side of her. "Can we steer it together?" His breath skimmed her ear, sending waves of awareness through her. She could only manage a nod.

Soon, Ardchattan Priory appeared on the right. Ceallach strode to the mainsail and pulled it in. Afterward, he waved his hand, and the jib came in without help. The boat slowed, and Kat turned it a little till it free-floated again.

When Ceallach returned to embrace her, she huffed. "Ye cheated using Fae power."

His lips brushed her ear, sending a spark that danced along her skin. "I allowed ye to enjoy the view of yer home without interruption." She let a purr spill free, a soft vibration that carried her agreement in its tone, as if her body answered before her lips could.

Kat tied off the wheel and strode aft, intent on sending over the anchor so they might stay a bit. Before reaching the rope, the anchor lifted, floated over the side, and splashed into the water. She turned, placing her hands on her hips as Ceallach emerged from the hatch carrying pillows and blankets. She marched toward him intent on a lecture about reaping the rewards of hard work, but when she arrived, he'd set up a cozy little sitting area before the keelson box he casually leaned on. "For ye *bruadarach.*"

At first, Kat thought this was only a short trip, but the promise of getting to view her favorite landscape from Loch Etive was something she could not resist—and to do so in Ceallach's arms. What girl wouldn't want to spend the afternoon in the arms of her secret love?

Chapter 9

As Kat moved to the cozy nest he'd set up, her thoughts kept drifting to him, and damn him for a fool, he didn't block them. In her mind, she just called him her *secret love*. All this time, had she pined for him as much as he had for her? He'd only ever popped in to see her, never spending enough time to read her mind. Evie and Aodhán had encouraged this outing, no, manipulated to be exact.

Only two days ago, he'd peeked into the kitchen, hoping to have missed the morning chaos, and found Evie and Aodhán at the table relaxing after breaking their fast.

Aodhán had risen and retrieved a covered dish, setting it before a seat. "Mrs. A left this for ye." Ceallach sat beside Evie, who held a napping Annie. She grinned and uncovered the plate to reveal a full Scots breakfast, which had become his norm: eggs, bacon, tomatoes, toast, and haggis. A meal Mrs. A had claimed would *stick to his ribs*. He'd grown to like it.

Ceallach shoved the first bite and asked around, chewing. "What day is it?"

Aodhán raised his hand, all five fingers up. "Thursday, day five in the human realm." Ceallach let out a half a scoff, before Aodhán spoke. "Aye, time travels slower here."

Evie eyed her husband, then turned toward Ceallach.

"Ye should have Kat take ye out. Maybe the mountains? Ye have time. We only wait on Ewan, who isn't due till Sunday."

Aodhán smirked. "Sailing, she promised him a sailing trip. Right cousin?"

Ceallach's shoulders had climbed a bit, and he focused on his food. "Maybe." He glanced at his cousin as he pushed his food around his plate. "We wait on more, and it doesn't matter. I must focus on the gathering. Kat is human, forbidden." The words tasted like ash.

Sure, she was. Human. Off-limits. Not his to want, let alone protect. Still, he checked on her each evening— just in case. To be sure no evil Fae had marked her, no mistaking her for the maiden. That's what he told himself. But it wasn't just duty. It was her. Always her.

He had to stay away. He *had* to. But gods, he already knew he wouldn't.

Aodhán's laughter cracked out, sudden and sharp. "Since when has that law written too long ago had anything to do with the Fae now?" Ceallach shoved food in his mouth, trying not to reply. His cousin was right, too many Fae found love with humans, a race so closely connected to theirs.

Evie sat up, her thoughts flying into his mind. As she spoke them, he formulated his rejection.

"Kat's wanted Hamish's sailboat he has for sale. The one named *Lochan Legend*. If ye ask, Hamish would allow ye to take the boat for a trip. Better yet Kat's wanted to buy it for some time. A surprise?"

Ceallach had his denial ready. "Impossible. If I dally with a human, our ma's will come, take me for a punishment. Throw in the labyrinth, like they did when we were young."

Aodhán's chuckle rumbled low, amusement curling at the edges. "Aye, that was a trail for ye cousin. It took ye days to figure out the maze and me, moments."

The fork rose, aimed squarely at his cousin in silent warning. "Ye cheated. Used Fae powers that the maze had blocked, but ye secretly overroad."

Aodhán put his hands behind his head, rocking back in his chair. "It's not my fault I had stronger powers than ye." Evie hit her husband's stomach, causing him to bend over. "Well, used to. I have fewer now that I'm mortal."

Evie swayed Annie a bit. "Brigid and Morrigan haven't come, and ye have seen Kat a couple of times. What would one afternoon…" She leaned over, winking. "Or a night—hurt?" A whole night with Kat. The thought slammed into him like a punch to the chest. One night—just one—where he didn't have to watch her from a distance, didn't have to bite back the words building in his throat or chain the hunger clawing at his chest.

A night where he could memorize the shape of her laugh, trace the freckles across her shoulders with his mouth, and let her fall asleep in his arms without fear stealing the moment away.

What would that cost him? Everything.

But he'd trade the weight of a dozen missions for one night that belonged only to them. No shadows. No Fae. No fate clawing between them. Just Kat. Just him. A breath of something real in a world full of lies. Gods help him… he wanted it more than he wanted air

Interest stirred sharp and sudden, and without thinking, he broke his silence. "Kat did make a promise with a Fae. Sailing, ye could arrange this?"

Evie sat back, patting Annie's back. "Consider it

done."

Thinking of time alone with Kat, he'd relented regardless of Fae law. For so long, he'd observed her from afar. Along with her, he experienced her trials and tribulations, her successes and joys. Today, he wanted nothing more than to make her happy—with him.

The rustle of her settling stirred his awareness, yanking his thoughts from where they'd wandered. Kat settled herself, bringing his mind to the present. Ceallach started to sit. Damn it, he'd forgotten the refreshments. Ceallach waved his hand, calling the items from the hold and moving them to the deck beside him. A bottle of Cabernet Sauvignon with a glass and a couple of large beers in an ice bucket as he slid beside her.

A sharp breath caught in her throat, her eyes wide. "Ye really should stop using so much magic here. Someone is bound to catch ye."

He waved, and the cork popped off the wine, then he manually poured her the ruby drink. "Nonsense. As I said, humans see what they want, not what is before them." He handed it to her and rested the bottle beside him.

A twist and a pop released the beer's seal, the moment easy between them as Kat sipped her wine, leaning into him. "I must admit. Yer Fae powers make life easier." Ceallach wrapped one arm around her as he tipped the beer back, gulping twice, enjoying the cold brew in his throat.

Lowering the bottle, he stared at the bubbles inside. "Sometimes, aye, it can make life easier, but the burden of some powers is hard to bear."

Kat sipped again, then sighed. "Well, yer powers do differ. The mind reading seems to be stronger than with

Evie and Ewan. More than even yer cousin."

The taste of the beer faded under the heavier thought: which powers to confess, and which to keep close.

He decided to stick to the parts only Kat had brought up, those that only she had seen. "The mind reading is constant for me, unlike Aodhán. If I do not focus, it invades my mind unwillingly." He pulled her closer. "Yet it is very convenient when an evil Fae is nearby. I can sense them before my cousin." He took another chug of his beer, allowing the bold taste to numb his throat. "That is if the evil Fae hasn't blocked me."

Kat emptied her wine and sat forward, reaching over him. "Block ye? They can do that?"

He opted for the manual task of grabbing the wine bottle, opening the cork with his hand, and holding his beer while he poured her a full glass. "Aye, they can block us, and we, them."

She breathed, and he set the bottle aside, replying before her question came. "Aye, ye can too. But for a human, it takes an immense amount of focus. The human must be open to the hidden powers within to know how to use them."

Kat sat back, sipping her wine again, seemingly content nestled in his embrace. He emptied his beer, set the bottle aside with a soft clink, and reached for another, its chill misting in the smooth air. They sat quietly as the afternoon unfurled around them, the silence between them comfortable, unhurried.

The light over the loch began to stretch and soften, shifting from the golden warmth of late afternoon to a cooler hue. Shadows lengthened over the rippling water, silver and slate catching the shifting breeze. The old priory, her home, stood in a quiet silhouette, its weathered stones glowing briefly while the sun dipped lower. Ivy clung to its walls like a living tapestry, and the ancient stone walls cast a long, crooked shadow over the rocky shore.

Beyond it, the Scottish mountains rose in layers—first in muted greens, then dusky blue, and finally a deepening violet as the evening crept in, their peaks softened by a gauzy haze, kissed by the fading sun, then slowly swallowed by the oncoming dusk. A few clouds hovered above the highest ridges, their edges lit with the last flare of sunlight.

The loch, so lively with sparkle earlier, stilled with the cooling air. It mirrored the deepening sky now, a dusky rose that melted into indigo, punctuated only by the occasional ripple of a bird's wing or the distant plunk of water against rock. It was a slow, quiet shift but somehow profound, like the landscape drew a long breath, settling in for the night. The human realm's energy and nature's wonders left him curious about the raw naturalness. While the human realm looked similar to the Fae, they differed in many ways.

A wave hit the boat, shifting the vessel and sending it closer to the shore.

Kat set her wine on the keelson box and jumped up. "Whoa, I can't let the boat get too close to shore. The keel will run aground, and we'll be in one hell of a spot." She nearly ran to the vessel's rear, hopping ropes and grabbing the anchor line, leaning over the side.

Ceallach sat back, and her knowledge and expertise came to him. She moved with purpose—it would only take a minute, and she'd done it a hundred times before. The wave shifted harder this time as a heady musk scent came to him, the same scent that had wafted when the flames leaped out at little Olivia days before. His Fae senses went on alert, but nothing notable was close. His focus shot to Kat, and a wave rose over her body. Without further thought, he transported to her, covering her with his body and a force shield. The wave crashed against his shield, rocking them and the boat. Kat screamed but held onto the anchor's rope while Ceallach held her tightly to him. The wave vanished into the calm loch waters as fast as it had appeared. Releasing the shield around them, he held her to his chest. She took a deep breath, then another.

His hands found hers, still clenched hard around the rope, his touch gentle but firm, coaxing her fingers loose. The pulse beneath her skin beat wild against his, and he held on—not just to steady her, but because letting go wasn't an option. "Ye can let go, Kat, I have ye."

She jolted and released the rope, turning in his embrace. "I… I've not been on the loch when it's been that rough." Her thoughts flashed to him, jumbled. She feared something greatly, but a void appeared when he searched for what it was.

He leaned on the vessel's side, still holding her. "Kat, that wasn't just the loch. Did ye catch the smell?"

A small dip of her chin answered, the motion quick but sure. "The same as the day the fire hurt Olivia." He sensed that the deep musk stirred something in her recognition flickered in her expression, though the source remained just out of reach.

Ceallach shifted till she lifted her head, and their eyes met. "Kat, are there other things happening? Something I must know about?" She pulled from his embrace, but he held her close. She shook her head

126

without meeting his gaze. Her mind closed to him.

Strands of her hair whipped across her face, and he swept them aside, his fingers lingering longer than they should. His eyes searched hers, hungry to catch whatever storm still flickered there, only finding a blank. "Kat, there is some…strife in ye?"

She tugged back, and Ceallach released her, sensing her frustration with him, his powers invading her privacy.

"It's nothing. And *stop* reading my mind." Her sneakers thudded against the deck, each step sharp with annoyance. "I moved the anchor so we'd face the mountains and the setting sun. The tide comes in, and the water splashed up, that's all." She grabbed her wine and gulped it all in one tilt. She uncorked the bottle and filled her glass again. Ceallach strode toward her, knowing that was no mere splash. With the threat gone with the scent, he let it slide for now. Evie had planned an entire evening for them, and he wanted to savor what little time he had with Kat. Troubles were for another day. Tonight was theirs.

When she gulped half of her glass, he grinned, glad Evie had insisted they pack two bottles, claiming when it came to wine, Kat could drink Dagda, his grandda, under the table. Arriving before her, he grabbed the beer he'd set on the box and took a long pull. He put it behind her, using the motion as an excuse to wrap her in his arms.

She sighed, leaning into the embrace and resting her head on his shoulder. "I don't want tonight to end, but it's getting late."

Ceallach smirked, savoring the secret of Evie's plans while Kat remained in the dark. "No one said tonight was ending just yet, Kat."

Her head popped up, and her expectant gaze met his, so he let her in on the part of the plan. "Evie planned supper as well."

She moved toward the hatch opening, and he pulled her back into his embrace, not wanting the surprise of later being spoiled too soon. He couldn't let her see what Evie had set up in the cabin.

Ceallach turned them with a shuffle like a dance again and pushed her down till she sat back in their cozy nest. "Ye will wait here while I do the labor so we can savor the rewards."

Kat giggled while he moved away and disappeared into the hatch. The ice chest with the meal sat where Evie had placed it. Ceallach gathered the assorted plastic bins filled with another of Kat's favored dishes. His mind ran through the wave incident only moments before. There had to be more to the two events with the heady musk scent, but he couldn't place it. He couldn't leave Kat to consult with his ma, Morrigan, but he needed to remember everything and ask her about it. He couldn't detect it, but he feared evil was close. He'd proceed with tonight but keep his senses alert. Ceallach had dreamed of tonight for so long, and he wanted to take advantage of Evie and Aodhán's prodding and planning. With his arms full of their meal, he stifled the temptation to flash onto the deck and took the steps, careful not to drop any containers.

His head cleared the opening just as he turned to find Kat tipping the bottle as a few drops fell into her wine glass. As he moved toward her, he blinked, and the empty wine bottle faded, but a full one appeared already open.

Kat gasped, almost dropping the heavy bottle. "Ye could warn a girl before ye do that! I almost dropped it, wasting the wine." Ceallach chuckled as he arranged the containers around her.

She reached for one, and he tapped her hand, "Ah, ah. Ye must wait until the reveal."

He waved, and full ones replaced his empty beer bottles. He opened one and nested beside an excited Kat. She should be. When Mrs. A heard what Evie had planned, she'd rushed to the market, insisting she hand-pick each item on the menu for the *love birds*. He sat back, upending his beer, taking his time. Kat turned, glaring at him. The fresh scent of boiled seafood wafted to him. The faint sound of Kat's stomach growling filled the air, forcing Ceallach to relent. He reached over, manually opening each container. The first was boiled shrimp, the extra-large ones, according to Evie. The next revealed fresh crab and steamed vegetables; the last, which Evie swore was one of Kat's favorites, was lobster.

Kat pushed upright onto her knees, the movement quick. "Seafood boil? I love seafood boil!" She set her glass aside, reaching for the shrimp, easily peeling it. Ceallach opened the small container filled with what Evie said were dunking sauces. The butter was familiar, comforting in its smooth richness—but the tangy red one hit his tongue with a jolt of something entirely new. Without pausing, Kat reached over and picked up some vegetables with her fingers, eating them and licking her fingers. Ceallach grunted as he waved a hand, and the paper towel roll from below appeared before Kat, one in her hand.

She wiped the juice from her chin and grabbed a

wipe. "Okay, yer powers are handy."

A lopsided grin tugged at his lips before he could stop it, her antics far too easy to enjoy. "Care for a fork?"

She grabbed a crab, breaking it in half. "No, the fun of a seafood boil is eating it with yer hands."

Grunting, he set his beer aside. "It is?" She handed him a part of her crab, and he ate it, savoring the fresh, light flavor. He grabbed a shrimp and bit into it, hitting the hard shell and making a face at the bitter taste.

Kat burst into laughter. "Ye must peel it."

She took one, peeled it, dunked it into the red sauce, and then offered the morsel to him. He wrapped his lips around her fingers, sucking them as the tangy flavor of the red sauce matched its scent, tomato sauce with deep tart spicy undertones.

His jaw worked slowly over the morsel, savoring the bite with measured ease. "I like steak better, but fish does have its appeal."

They ate together. Kat peeled his shrimp, and he ate two to three at once. The crab she harvested for him. That was the only way he could describe how she picked the meat from the shell. The lobster was like a large shrimp, so he could get to the meat alone, liking the fish in butter. Throughout the meal, Kat consumed nearly as much as he did, making him smile. He sensed she was comfortable and content.

She wiped her hands on the towel, leaned back, and exhaled deeply, only to punctuate the quiet with a low, unabashed belch. A grin tugged at her lips, unbothered by decorum. Beside her, Ceallach cleaned his hands with unhurried ease, then settled in close. He reached for his beer and her wine, handing the glass to her with an effortless familiarity. Their fingers brushed, gently and fleeting, but enough to send warmth curling through his chest.

They lay there, side by side, the silence stretching between them like a lazy river. The sky blazed in hues of gold and crimson, the sun sinking into the horizon. She hummed softly, contentedly, as the evening wrapped around them like a well-worn embrace.

Her light whisper came to him like the sound wafted in the air. "I am something people celebrate or resist. I change people's thoughts and lives. I am obvious to some people, but to others, I am a mystery. What am I?" She'd mumbled it before he came upon her at the marina. Based on her emotions it troubled her. He'd promised not to pry, and the temptation was great, but he ignored his powers, giving her the promised privacy. He grinned as he took a draw from his beer. She pondered a riddle. Maybe allowing them to get to know each other naturally, without his powers, would be a riddle worth solving.

"What is it ye whisper Kat?"

She stared into her glass and shrugged. "Nothing really, a riddle I cannot solve." Even without his powers, he saw it in her eyes—the tightness in her jaw, the way her fingers fidgeted. It troubled her. The answer was easy, and with her sharp mind, she should be able to solve it. He huffed; a story might help, and the tale's message perfectly fit his Kat.

He reached out, grabbed the wine bottle, and filled her glass. "Sit back, Kat, and let me help ye with yer riddle. I'll tell ye a tale my ma told me as a youngling."

She obliged, settling into the crook of his arms like before while they lay back, watching the sunset over the Priory, her home. Evie was right. Tonight was a perfect opportunity for them to get to know each other better.

He started the familiar story like his ma, soft at first, with a plan to raise his voice and then lower it at the end. "Roran was a fifteen-year-old boy who lived with his uncle, Gannon, on a farm near the village of Crieff. His mother had died birthing him. While hunting, he heard a loud sound, like rocks falling. When he came upon the area, there was a large blue egg in the rubble. Roran knew a bit about birds, so he nested and cared for the egg, keeping it out of bad weather with a fire and blanket to keep it warm. Soon, a baby dragon hatched, and the two bonded. Roran named the dragon Eragon."

She blew out a breath, curiosity threading through her words. "Do dragons really come from eggs?"

Ceallach trailed his fingers on her arm. "Some, aye, but others, no. Depends on the type and their origins."

Kat pushed herself upright, twisting to face him with another question on her lips. "The one I saw in the Fae realm. He was greenish blue, and he flew. What kind was he?"

Ceallach drew her close again, his arms wrapping firm and certain around her. "A different kind." He waited while she sat for a moment, then sipped her wine as he took a pull from his beer. "Back to our story."

"In secret, he raised Eragon, starting as a youngling learning his way. Eragon and Roran become fast friends. Roran fed and cared for Eragon; in turn, the dragon taught Roran how to fight and ride him like a grand warrior. Each day, with his chores complete, Roran took one of the cows he'd raised and headed into the mountains to feed and spend time with his good friend. Roran grew into adulthood as time passed, but still maintained his care for his dragon friend, Eragon.

"Rumors in the small village of Crieff circulated about a massive beast roaming the countryside, creating fear throughout the village and drawing the King's interest and concern. He sent guards to Crieff to investigate. The King's guards learned from gossip in the pub that Roran had raised many cows but never sold any at auction, yet they disappeared.

"The following day, the guards cautiously followed Roran when he took one of his cows into the mountains. They hid and witnessed the huge dragon beast ravaging and devouring the cow. Fearing the great beast, the two guards attacked. Roran stepped between them, and one guard accidentally stabbed him.

"Eragon quickly scooped his friend into his arms, berating the guards. 'We have done ye no harm, yet ye come to kill me?'

The guards cowered as one replied. 'We come at the order of the King. The people of the village fear ye. Dragons are known to hunt and kill humans.'

"Eragon breathed healing breath onto his friend, then spoke softly. 'I will never harm the people of my best friend. I protect this glade from evil.'

"With Roran healed, he slid from Eragon's grasp. 'Go and tell the King of this. Leave us in peace as we have left ye in peace.' The guards left, informing the King, and many years passed. Roran fell in love, married, and had sons of his own who also befriended Eragon. Roran aged, but Eragon stayed the same. The day came when Roran died. Wishing his friend close to him, Eragon begged his family to bury him in the mountain where Roran had discovered and raised him. At the funeral, one of Roran's sons asked the dragon why he didn't age.

"Eragon bent his head close to the young man. 'I am immortal. I do not age like ye but grow wise with time.' He turned his tear-filled eyes to the youth. 'I will always protect this glen, but I will do so with a heavy heart. Each of ye will be born, grow to adulthood, and into old age, then die. As yer friend, I must see ye from birth to death as Roran ensured I had life.'

"Turning his gaze to his friend's grave, the dragon spoke. 'Value what time ye are given. Time is a fleeting thing, more precious than ye can ever know.'

"The boy turned to the dragon. 'In the end, it's not the years in your life that count. It's the life in your years, isn't it?'

Eragon nodded at the youth. 'Aye, boy, that it is.' "

Kat sat next to Ceallach while the last of the sun's rays skimmed the land, and the purple hues faded into deep blue, casting the boat in near darkness.

She sucked in a breath, and her voice laced with wonder in the question that followed. "Ye said ye ma told ye this story when ye were young. Ceallach, ye are immortal. Ye do not age."

He turned his head, eyes dropping to where she lay beside him, her presence pressing soft against his side. "I was born, and I've aged to adulthood. Age is just a number. Living life is the greatest gift that we could possibly ever have."

Her head tipped, curiosity flickering in her regard as she studied him. "My parents said the greatest gift is love. We should thank God for our best blessings, often the least appreciated. They consider their love their best blessing."

She blew out a sharp breath and adverted her gaze from his. "But what is love anyway? I've often

134

questioned the metaphysics of *what love is*."

Ceallach took her wine glass and set it aside with his beer. Taking her hand, he shared his thoughts on love and her explaining it so her scientific mind would understand. "Kat, love is the central metaphysical reality. Love is soul. Love is consciousness. Love is expressed through emotions and the mind but does not originate there." He brought their hands to his chest, opened hers, and placed her palms on his heart so she'd feel its beat. "Such a profound emotion's source is the deep self, the guiding energy behind the phantom play of the external world."

Chapter 10

Kat's hand on Ceallach's chest tingled with energy. His heart beat faster when he spoke words explaining what love was, and his voice reverberated in her soul. She inhaled and couldn't let it out. When his hand brushed her cheek, she finally released her breath. He'd said *love is expressed through emotions and the mind but does not originate there*. With her hand on his heart and hers beating a fast rhythm, she understood what he meant. Love came from within, and no logical reasoning of the emotion could make sense. She understood.

She blinked as she stared into his silver-blue eyes. "Love is something ye just have to feel."

He bent, brushing his lips over hers. "Aye, Kat." Her lips lifted, responding to the kiss, and her arms went around his neck, pulling him closer. She wanted to feel all there was with Ceallach: each emotion, each sensation, and each kiss.

As he delved deeper into the kiss, he pulled her closer till her chest became flush with his. The undulation of hard muscle brushed against her breasts, sending tingles through her. She responded to his kisses with urgency. He groaned as he pushed her back into their cozy nest, rubbing his body against hers, creating all sorts of little shocks to each area he touched. If this was what it was like with clothing on, what the hell would her body do if they were both naked?

Ceallach's head shot up, their gazes connecting. His first expression was one of shock, but soon, he grinned, and his eyes hooded. "Kat, ye do not know what ye think."

He bent, kissing her neck, and she took a shuttered breath. "I know perfectly well what I think." His tongue trailed to her ear, tracing the outer edge, bringing a shiver from her entire body. "Ye could stop reading my mind and make it a reality."

With a growl, Ceallach rose, lifting her into his arms as her legs straddled his body. "I'd shift us, but it would ruin the surprise. Evie and Aodhán's work would be for naught."

Kat lifted her head, and he turned, walking toward the hatch. "A surprise? I love surprises."

At the opening of the hatch, he lowered her, allowing her body to slide down his, each ripple of his muscles hitting her with tingles again. Her feet found the deck as she held on to his muscular arms. She loved his body and wanted to touch each part.

He shifted and waved before him towards the hatch opening. "Milady, yer surprise awaits." Knowing the layout beneath, she peered into the darkened area but didn't want to enter the blackness. Ceallach snapped, and the lanterns lit the space, teasing Kat to enter. She stepped on the ladder and held on to the railing since facing the front was harder, but she didn't want to miss the surprise by backing down. With each step, the table first appeared with a cooler set underneath. She stopped putting her hand to her chest when what was beyond was revealed. The bed had a similar setup to the cozy nest Ceallach had set up above, but this one had petals strewn all about. White petals as the scent of Camila filled the

137

air. She pushed off the last step and sighed at a picture-perfect love nest.

As Ceallach came behind her, his arms encircled her, and he bent, whispering in her ear. "Do ye like it?"

Kat rotated in his arms. "Like it? I love it." She tilted her head. "Does this mean ye want me?"

Ceallach's right hand brushed her cheek. "Kathryn. I have always wanted ye." The other came up, both cupping her face. "Since the first moment I saw ye, I knew ye were mine." He leaned in, inhaling near her ear with a quiet intensity—like a predator memorizing its mate's scent, then blew it out, humming as he kissed her softly.

She kissed his back, wanting this until reason and logic rushed into her mind. "Ceallach, yer are Fae, I am human. Evie says there is a law…"

He kissed her hard while he backed them around the table. He lifted her in his arms. "Kat, the laws be damned. Tonight, I want to share my soul with ye." As he lay her on the bed, the whisper of petals sounded, and the scent filled the room again.

He loomed over Kat with a grin, wicked and slow. "Wasn't there something ye wondered about earlier? Something about being naked?"

A grin broke free, and she dipped her head, heat creeping up her neck despite herself. "Aye."

With a wave of his hand, her and Ceallach's clothing faded. Too consumed with the sight before her, Kat didn't care that she lay naked on the bedding. Ceallach's body was perfect in every way. The chiseled muscles of his chest led into the angled curve of his hip.

His staff rose, her focus landing on it, and his chuckle filled the room. "Ye are pleasing as well, Kat."

Her gaze lifted to his, and he moved over her, covering her with the full heat of his body. Her hands met his chest, a jolt of energy sparking through her at the contact. As her palms smoothed over his broad shoulders, muscle shifted and flexed beneath her touch while he eased between her legs.

She'd had lovers before, but none of them held a candle to the man who now nestled against her center, confident and commanding. His length brushed through her curls, drawing a gasp from her lips and lifting her hips in an instinctive invitation.

She'd dreamed of this—of *him*—more nights than she could count. But nothing in her imagination came close to the raw, breathtaking reality of Ceallach—*flesh and fire, desire and devotion*—here with her now.

As he kissed her hard, his hand cupped her breast, fingers molding to her softness with a slow, deliberate squeeze. She kissed him back fiercely, gripping his shoulders like she needed to anchor herself—like letting go might send her spiraling.

He moved lower, mouth closing over her nipple, and the sharp pull sent flares racing across her skin. When he shifted to the other and sucked harder, she arched into him with a gasp, the pleasure striking deep and fast.

He sat back on his heels, gripping both breasts with reverent hands as he ground against her, his arousal pressing hot and insistent between them.

Slick with want, she met his rhythm, hips rising in silent, urgent response.

God, he consumed her—and they had only just begun.

Ceallach chuckled as he bent, kissed her, and released her breasts from his firm grip. "Ahh, Kat. Not too soon, *mo bruadarach*. I must worship ye first."

He began his descent with slow, reverent kisses—trailing from her mouth to her throat, lingering just long enough to leave her skin damp and tingling. The path he carved was warm, wet, then deliciously cool as the air hit it, and still he moved lower.

His lips found her belly, and she trembled. He shifted again, lifting his head, and blew gently against the curls between her thighs.

She squirmed, startled by the sensation—but not repelled. She liked it, more than she wanted to admit, even as a flicker of nerves sparked beneath the rising heat. No man had ever kissed her there before.

He blew again, slower this time, a tease she felt deep in her core—then one finger slipped between the curls, parting them softly, baring her to him with quiet reverence.

His breath flared through his nose before easing out in a slow, weighted sigh. "I will be the only one who kisses ye this way, Kat." He bent, kissing her with lips that were warm and soft, the sensation a teasing brush that felt like a tickle against her most sensitive skin.

His finger found her bud, circling gently—just enough to make her squirm, hips shifting beneath his touch.

Then he lowered again, his tongue replacing his finger in one slow, deliberate stroke. The heat of it against her—after the cool air kissed her bare skin—made her gasp, the sudden contrast pulling a whimper from deep in her throat.

His breath skimmed her skin, warm and close, as his whisper slipped past her ear. "Like lovely petals, folded in on one another till ye get to the prized center." He bent and covered her with his mouth, suckling with slow, intent devotion. The sensation hit her like a jolt—hot and electric—nearly lifting her off the bed.

Warmth, rhythm, the coaxing movement of his tongue, the pull of his mouth—it was too much, too good. Her body couldn't keep still beneath the waves crashing through her.

She tried to sit up, overwhelmed by the need to move, to do *something*—but his hand pressed gently against her chest, holding her in place. Not with force. With purpose.

That same hand slid lower, molding to every curve of her until it reached her center, and his finger joined his mouth—slipping inside with a sure, tender motion.

She cried out, hips arching, pleasure rising fast and fierce. Gods, he was unraveling her, and she didn't want him to stop.

Ceallach increased his pace, his mouth working her with deeper, more urgent pulls. The harder he suckled, the shorter her breaths became, the pleasure building in her like a storm with no end in sight.

She'd known pleasure before—once. Barely. A flicker compared to the fire Evie always spoke of. But this…this was something else entirely. Ceallach wasn't just touching her—he was *devouring* her, determined to wring every ounce of pleasure from her body like he had all the time in the world.

He hummed low against her, the sound rumbling through her, and the vibrations shattered her last bit of restraint. She arched back, heat flashing over her skin in a rush that left her breathless.

She reached for something—anything—gripping her legs to ground herself, but he pushed them open again with his body and free hand, growling low in his throat. Not asking. Demanding. He wasn't done.

Short, desperate gasps escaped her as the pressure inside her tightened, clenched, and finally—broke. Her body shattered in a blinding wave, and she screamed his name into the night, raw and wild.

His finger slipped free, but his mouth gentled, soft strokes pulling her back from the edge. She couldn't think—could only feel her heartbeat thundering in her ears, the ragged drag of her breath as her body tried to remember how to exist again.

For a moment, she floated—untethered, undone.

Then the soft whisper of his breath against her curls brought her back to earth. Back to him.

Her eyes dropped, and when she looked up again, his grin waited for her. "I hope ye enjoyed that."

She sat up, taking his face between her hands. "Good God, Ceallach, that was marvelous." She went to kiss him, and he pulled back, waving his hand. He came over her, kissing her, and his breath tasted minty.

She chuckled into their kiss. "Ye changed yer breath."

He spoke on her lips, "I tasted of ye."

She bit back a smile, savoring the friction of him sliding against her. "I wouldn't have minded."

His head lifted, gaze still fixed on her as if reluctant to break the moment. "I would have. I want everything about tonight to be perfect. Giving myself to ye is—it's something special for me."

She pressed closer, her palms exploring the breadth of his shoulders. "Is this yer first time?"

Ceallach moved until his hands cupped her face. "Sex, no. And I know this is not a first for ye either. But us together for the first time, it's…"

She stilled, her hands pausing against his skin as emotion surged through her—hot and unexpected. She'd been with others. She'd known pleasure before. But nothing like this. Not like *him*.

Her voice caught but didn't waver. "Magical. Something I've never had until you." Because this— *him*—was different. Ceallach didn't just touch her body; he reached the parts no one else ever had. The ones that ached to be seen, held, understood. With him, it wasn't about the act. It was about *everything*.

Ceallach kissed her softly as he slid into her, the slow stretch stealing her breath. He paused, drawing in a deep breath like he needed to ground himself. "I've waited my whole existence for you," he murmured.

He shifted, easing in the rest of the way, filling her fully—completely—with a soft, reverent sigh. The sheer intimacy of it, the way it was *him*, made her eyes sting.

He rested his forehead against hers and pushed again, and the sensation sent waves of energy rippling through her.

His hands found her breasts, steadying her, grounding them both as he began to move. Each thrust built the force inside her again—slow, steady, devastating in its intensity.

Ceallach kissed her hard, rising to shift her leg to his hip, and the new angle made her gasp as he sank even dccpcr.

He bent to kiss her again, slower this time, and the sensations poured through her—endless, consuming, wave after wave.

With each driving thrust, it felt like he reached deeper than her body—like he was claiming something sacred, something no one else had ever touched. Her soul.

Soon, the force of his rhythm overwhelmed her, sweeping her over the edge. Her body clenched around him as she cried out, the pleasure bursting through her in waves. She arched beneath him as he thrust harder, chasing his own release, the sound of their bodies mingling with the night air.

His grip tightened on her hips, anchoring her as he drove into her again and again, the rhythm relentless, consuming. Sensations surged through her—too much, too good—and she clung to his shoulders, desperate for something to hold on to, terrified she'd tumble right off the edge of the world.

Then he arched above her, head thrown back, and roared into the night. His body stilled—hard, shaking—before he pulsed deep inside her, heat flooding through her in a hot, startling rush. Her skin broke into a sheen of sweat, breath caught on a gasp, as he roared again, then collapsed over her, wrapping her in his arms.

He held her like she was precious. Like he'd never let her go.

Ceallach's breath came in ragged bursts, and he lowered his head, kissing her neck, her cheek—finally finding her lips and lingering there, as if she were the air he needed most.

He breathed into the kiss. "My soul. My mate." She came down from her high as he held her to him, still joined together. When she opened her eyes, his wings were out and curled around them, making a soft cocoon. "Ye are, okay? I wasn't, rough?"

She giggled, kissing the curve of his neck and tasting the salty-sweet sheen of his sweat. "No," she whispered, her lips brushing his skin, "I feel so satisfied." The words left her in a sigh, full and breathless.

He shivered as he slowly withdrew, arms never letting her go. His wings stayed curled around them, cocooning her in warmth, as if he couldn't bear to break the spell between them.

Kat nestled closer, heart still fluttering. She'd never felt so thoroughly unraveled…or so utterly seen.

His touch found her cheek, thumb stroking like he couldn't help himself. "Kat, ye are beautiful."

Her face warmed under his praise. "Ye are perfect."

Something in the gentle curve of his wings pulled her focus, soft and strong all at once. "Do they do that on their own?"

He brought them closer, touching her lightly, making the nest smaller. "At first, they popped out as a reflex. But now, they embrace."

Her eyes roamed, marveling at the uniqueness of him—especially his wings. Not just powerful, but beautiful—*like Loch Etive at dawn*. Deep blue where shadow lingered, rich green where the light touched the surface, and threaded through it all, a subtle iridescence that shimmered like morning mist catching the sun. His wings reminded her of that—the quiet majesty of water and sky meeting, something ancient and untamed, born not just of shadow and starlight, but of the wild, sacred magic of the land itself.

They stretched around her in a protective shell, warm and quiet, as if the world couldn't reach her here. "Yers are different than others." Ceallach nuzzled her neck, mumbling in agreement, his breath brushing her skin like a promise.

Kat melted into his embrace, every part of her fitting against him like they'd been carved for this moment. If she could, she'd stay wrapped in him forever—forget the dawn, the mission, the danger that waited beyond these wings. She wished the night would stretch on, endless and untouched.

"Must we go back?" She whispered.

His breath brushed her cheek. "Only when ye are ready, Kat. The boat is yers, after all."

A quick push upright sent her into the curve of his wings with a soft thud. "It is?" When he flinched, she laid back down. "Did that hurt?"

He held her tighter as if to keep her still. "Now that I have a grip on ye, aye, the boat is yers. A gift."

Every slight movement rubbed her against him, feeding the ache just beneath her skin. "I shall have to thank Evie."

His wings retracted and faded while he settled her in his arms. "Well, ye can thank her for the idea and the planning, but ye should thank me for the boat. This is my gift to ye."

She held him as she snuggled closer while memories of her and her brother sailing filled her mind. "Thank ye, Ceallach. I missed sailing."

He squeezed her once. "I know, Kat." Her boat, now the *Fairy's Wish,* that she had to clean and care for.

She started to rise, and he gripped her to him. "I already cleaned the deck. Take yer rest, Kat."

A sly wiggle earned her the squeeze she wanted, and a grin broke free when his arms held fast. "I wish I could stay here forever."

Ceallach held her without replying. She didn't need mind-reading abilities to know what crossed his mind—

the gathering and his duty. He'd explained it before, and she understood. She hadn't brought up him being a shield or his duty to the stones since his reactions were so intense.

Her voice barely stirred the air, words slipping out in a breathy whisper. "I just wanted ye to know how I felt."

He shifted toward her, catching her lips in a kiss before she could speak. "When this is all over Kat, I assure ye, I will be there with ye."

She returned his kiss but feared that fate would take over. They lived worlds apart, and reality loomed like a storm cloud on the edge of something beautiful. Still, Kat whispered the longing in her mind. *I wish fate bound us together.* Not just for tonight or in stolen moments, but truly—wholly—together.

Her ma's saying echoed as a tear welled in her eye: *If wishes were horses, beggars would ride.* It was the kind of truth that stung more than comforted. And yet, despite the odds, despite the thousands of reasons to let go, her heart held on to that fragile ember of hope, daring to believe.

Wrapped in Ceallach's arms, Kat fell into a deep slumber. A weightless sensation filled her head as her body began to float. She came to rest before the familiar passages of the maze—a choice again. Heady musk, the same scent she had smelled many times, floated around her, announcing the demon's arrival.

The man's voice rumbled in her ear. "Back again?" It moved to the other ear. "And after yer Fae lover?" She flinched at the sudden grip on her arm—strong, urgent— but when she spun around, no one was there. She yanked against the invisible hold, panic rising.

His voice hissed, "Fucked 'em good, I hope?" She pulled hard and stumbled when released. When she lifted her head, only two passages sat before her.

The sneer in his tone reverberated. "Come, Kitty, let's play."

"Don't call me that!" Last time, she'd gone right three times, so she started with left. She began with a brisk walk, left, and then left again. At the next fork, she chose right.

The man's voice came hard. "Have ye solved my riddle, sweet girl?"

She progressed on, keeping her step quick. "Yer childish riddle, Aye! I am something people celebrate or resist. I change people's thoughts and lives. I am obvious to some people, but to others, I am a mystery. What am I?" Coming to a dead end, she yelled the answer. "Age!"

Black smoke consumed her, and she bent, covering her head and holding her breath. When it faded, she lifted her head and faced another fork in the way. Right, she chose right and started the fast pace again as the man's taunting tone came to her. "Another riddle to solve so ye'll reunite with yer brother."

She skidded to a halt, her next breath flung out in a yell. "Liar! All ye give is one riddle after another, dangling a promise ye will not keep!" A force hit her body, thrusting it against the wall before she fell. She lay there, unable to draw in breath. The walls faded, and a path, clear to an opening, appeared before her.

"Lie? I do not lie." A rough breath flared from him, like a beast amused by its prey. "Solve the riddle, and yer brother ye shall see."

Finally able to draw in a breath, she breathed deeply once and then again, keeping her eyes trained on the opening.

His voice slithered through the air just as she pushed to her feet. "Here's a new one…I speak without a mouth and hear without ears. I'm invisible, but you can call for me. What am I?"

Knowing the answer, she took off running hard for the opening while she yelled. "Easy enough ye demon." She screamed the answer as it reverberated off the walls. "An echo."

His growl filled her head. "I shall kill Doug if ye don't bring me the stones." She reached the opening, the end of the maze, and jumped through, only to hit a barrier. She pulled back, and strong arms held her tightly.

They shook her a bit as Ceallach's voice spoke firmly. "Kat, wake up." His yell came hard in her ear. "Kathryn, ye must wake from this dream!"

A gasp tore from her as her body shot upright. Silver-blue eyes filled her vision, Ceallach's brows drawn tight, his hand already steadying her. His gaze searched her face, likely trying to read her mind, which she made blank. She pulled from him, and he gripped her harder, drawing their naked bodies together in an embrace as he settled them in the bed. Tucked into him like this, she could forget all her woes, yet the feelings from the dream lingered. Anger, frustration, and panic all wrapped together in a confusing ball she could not unravel.

Ceallach's fingers traced up and down her arm. "Kat, what was the dream?"

A small shrug rolled through her shoulders, the movement nudging her against his chest. "I don't know."

His fingers stopped. "Kat, I sense it. Yer emotions are in turmoil." A slow breath eased from him, the sound

149

brushing her skin, steady and close. "I don't wish to pry, but…"

She shifted to cut him off. "Then don't. And stop reading my mind."

Warmth swept over her when he shifted, drawing her in until the space between them disappeared. "I shall stop, but I know ye smelt the musk like before." A quick prod to his ribs earned her satisfaction, even if her exhale betrayed her irritation.

The gentle press of his hand urged her down, fitting her snug against his side. "I will keep my promise and stay out of yer mind."

Ceallach bent, kissing her head. "Ye will sleep deeply, Kat. And have only pleasant dreams." Her mind emptied, and her body drifted—weightless, untethered, like smoke carried on the wind as her lids grew heavy.

She drifted off as Ceallach whispered. "Have no fears, Kat."

She fell asleep, one deep and comforting. She dreamed of her and Doug, a fond memory she visited often. They were young teens again, sailing on Loch Etive. They'd learned to sail together and worked well as a team. He was always at the helm, and she was his first mate. They'd played pirates, and when Evie and Ewan were with them, Evie was always the princess needing rescue. The dream was a hazy memory that left her waking with tears in her eyes.

The sunlight shined across her face, and she rose to search for Ceallach but found herself in her bedroom at the Abbey. Kat sat up, glancing around her room, and her gaze caught something on the windowsill. A lone white flower sat winking at her in the early morning sunlight. She woke to a Camellia flower, but not Ceallach.

Rising from the bed, she crossed the chilled room to the sill, picking up the flower. "Ye may never be able to be my shield, but ye are my love."

Chapter 11

Stone crunched beneath her shoes as Kat stepped into the courtyard of Dunstaffnage Castle. A familiar giggle drifted to her, and she spotted Evie sitting beneath the low wall, Annie tucked close beside her. Behind them, the old stable ruins slouched in shadow, their crumbling walls still clinging to the shape of what had once stood proud. Once, that broken corner had been their kingdom—part fortress, part stage, part secret hideaway.

A soft ache of nostalgia stirred in her chest as she walked closer. How many afternoons had they spent here, pretending the world beyond the walls couldn't touch them? And now, watching Annie play in the same patch of shade and sun, it felt as if time had looped back on itself—the next generation's turn to make memories in the shadows of these stones.

Evie glanced up when she approached. "Hello, Kat. Glad I am to see ye."

Kat sat beside her friend, noting that her camera bag was there. "I texted before I came over. Did ye not get it?" Evie likely got lost taking pictures of the loch and chasing after Annie.

While she walked on wobbly legs, Evie held Annie's hands. "I'm sorry to miss your text. I tend to leave my cell in the bedroom when we are here." Evie smiled as she caught Annie. "Makes it feel like a vacation."

Kat leaned over, whispering to her dear friend. "I want to thank ye for the boat and sail trip."

With a glint in her eye, Evie grinned. "The sailing trip was yer promise to a Fae. The boat was all Ceallach's idea. He purchased it for ye."

Heat crept up her face. "He told me." The wind blew and she hummed as she spoke. "So, today is a lovely day to sit outside and play with Annie. Maybe take some pictures."

Her friend glanced around. "Aye, it is, but that's not why I'm here." Ceallach rounded the corner of the castle, followed by Aodhán, both dressed in their Fae clothing of suits made from incandescent fabric resembling organza. Each one's flowing long hair a complete contrast to the other, one near white and the other jet-black. Ceallach glanced back, saying something as his long hair parted and a pointed ear peeked out.

Evie waved towards them. "The men practice spells today." She leaned over, grumbling. "They argued last night after ye left from dinner about the other growing lazy in the human realm without practicing Fae powers." She giggled. "Over drinks, one thing led to another, and here we are to witness a duel. Of sorts."

Kat's gaze followed the men. Well, *Ceallach* was the one she couldn't seem to look away from. Even through dinner, she felt the weight of his attention—steady, unblinking—as if he'd decided she was the only thing in the room worth seeing.

His long, graceful stride reminded her of a lethal cat stalking its prey. When the picture hit her mind of Ceallach being a black panther, his eyes snapped to hers, wearing the same hooded expression he'd given her the other night when she imagined them naked together. The image of them making love flashed, and Ceallach tripped. He would have fallen had his cousin, Aodhán, not caught him. They exchanged a few remarks that ended with Ceallach punching Aodhán's arm.

Kat turned to Evie. "A duel? What type of duel?"

She shook her head. "Spells. They practice like Brigid and Morrigan taught Ewan and me as children." Both men shook hands and parted, taking a defensive stance while Evie nodded. "The same way the Fae train all their warriors. Using spells like in a Fae battle."

A charge stirred the air, prickling along Kat's skin like the sky before a storm—except the sun blazed, the sky an unbroken blue. Aodhán rolled his hands in a fast circle and threw one hand out. Ceallach tumbled to the side, and sparkles hit the air with a loud sound where he'd stood. As he came up, he threw his hand out, and flares of magic hit Aodhán's shoulder with a blast, knocking him back.

He righted, smirking when he yelled. "Come on, cousin. Certainly, ye can do better than that!"

Kat followed their every move in stunned fascination as she spoke aloud. "They aim to hit. They won't hurt each other, will they?"

Evie tucked Annie into her lap. "Naw, just a sting using enough power to stun only. The Fae use this exercise in fight training and power management. One must know how to cast and control the power they wield."

As the men circled, Evie turned to Kat. "So, yer evening with Ceallach on the Loch. Was it nice?"

Her cheeks burned as she dropped her gaze, but the images still pushed through—Ceallach's arms wrapped tight around her, the rough wood of the deck beneath her back, the press of his body claiming hers, slow and certain. "Shattering."

A boom sounded, and Ceallach called out. "Ouch, cousin. Stun only!"

Her focus went to the men as Ceallach circled Aodhán, each man similar yet so different. "Ceallach's powers differ from Aodhán. Why?"

Evie held Annie, kissing her head. "It would stand to reason. Aodhán's powers come from generations of Fae, passed down from a long line of kings. Ceallach, while from the same line, his more unique powers that come from his da." Ceallach threw a spell which went wide with a resounding report.

Kat turned to her friend. "His da? We didn't meet him when we went there for yer wedding?"

She shook her head. "No, he spends a lot of time away. A duty he must perform. Something about a promise made long ago."

An explosion sounded, and Ceallach yelled. "Son of a…Damn ye, Aodhán. Stun only!" Her gaze went to the men.

Ceallach stood holding his arm as Aodhán yelled. "Ha, focus ye nibit!"

He massaged his arm, and Kat spoke without looking at Evie. "Are ye sure they are okay to do this?"

Evie chuckled. "I am certain of it. The sparks show they practice. In real fighting, there are no flashes. Men playing like boys."

****

Ceallach rubbed his arm as he sent a mind message to Aodhán. *Stun only! Control yerself.*

The reply came with a spell. *Control?* The flares hit

Ceallach's hip, making him curse his cousin when it thundered.

Aodhán changed his circling to the other direction. *It is not I who cannot focus. Yer every thought and emotion are of the woman of yer affections who sits so close and consumes yer mind.*

He threw a spell, nicking the top of his cousin's head. *If they were discussing yer da and yer power's origin, ye'd listen in too.*

Aodhán stood upright with his arms down. *Kat doesn't know. Ye've made love, and she doesn't know?*

Ceallach flicked his wrist, and sparks hit Aodhán's knee, making him cry out and fall to the ground.

His reply came with a grimace. *She can't know. She won't accept me for who I am, what I am.*

Aodhán sat up, rubbing his knee. *An excellent fighter and good friend are what ye are, Ceallach. Yer powers are part of ye.* He rose, limping a bit. *But do not define ye.*

His cousin flung a spell as he limped, taking Ceallach by surprise. The ball hit him in the chest, knocking him off his feet. He flew back and landed on his ass. Sitting stunned, Ceallach stayed there staring at his smug cousin who spoke in his mind. *Every soul here can see she's yours*, Aodhán drawled, the words brushing against the edge of his thoughts. *Why can't you?*

Ceallach's jaw tightened. *Because the ritual doesn't bind her*, he shot back silently. *Because wanting her doesn't make it real.*

He swallowed, glancing across the yard to where Kat laughed, unaware of the war he waged with himself. *Gods help me*, he thought. *If claiming her were as simple as everyone believing she's mine…I'd have done it long ago.*

Power surged—someone gathered energy for a spell, but not from ahead where Aodhán stood. This pulsed from Ceallach's side where the air trembled with rising force. Someone else planned to enter the fight. With his senses on alert, everything went into slow motion. Aodhán stood relaxed, unaware of the threat approaching. From the corner of his vision, both women sat chatting, blissfully oblivious.

The air snapped as the ball came at Aodhán, traveling faster than a practice spell. Ceallach sent a counterspell, but the original spell was closer to Aodhán, who put up a block. When the hex hit the block, crackles flew out with a reverberating boom. Ceallach's counter hit the original spell, and the mass carried sideways towards the women. Aodhán yelled as Evie screamed, covering Annie with a raised hand, casting a shield over them. The sparks bounced off the bubble and flew into Kat's chest, lifting her from the ground and sending her backward over the stable wall, where she landed still on her back.

Ewan entered the courtyard. "Shit, I only meant to hit Aodhán!"

Ceallach's gaze focused on Kat, who lay unmoving. His heart lumped in his throat. Kat was injured. The thought struck his soul—deep, undeniable. Transporting to her, he knelt beside her. Ceallach reached his hand out, gently touching her chest. No breathing. He cried out, taking her hand in his and placing it on his chest, trying to send life-force energy to her. The others gathered around, and time caught up as Ceallach's heart beat a fast tempo.

He turned, yelling. "By the gods, Ewan. We were only practicing. Stun only!"

Ewan held his wife Lorelei's hand while she cupped her rounded belly. "I did. Kat will be all right, won't she?"

Ceallach bent, concentrating his energy between their held hands, the power connection between them. "She's not breathing!"

Aodhán folded his arms, concern knitting his brow. "Likely got the wind knocked from her. The spells were stun only, but I sensed more energy gather, like when my Ma is around."

Ceallach shifted his hand to her forehead, trying to search her mind. Blank. All wall like before, one foreign.

He barked, the sound raw, torn from his throat. "Now is a time I wish I had the full power of a dragon shifter, not part of one. The one that can heal near death for their soulmates." His hand moved over her heart again, fluttering but faint. "I beg the gods. I wish I had the same lifesaving power."

Aodhán unfolded his arms, putting one around Evie. "Ye do, in a way. Healing breath from yer da. But Kat's human. She's not yer soulmate, is she?"

Ceallach took a deep breath, held it while he heated the air like his da, making healing breath, and blew it on Kat's face. The white smoke encircled her face, shifted to grey, then dissipated in a slight stench. She inhaled hard, gasping when she took in precious air. Everyone seemed to sigh, but Ceallach gathered her in his arms, and his wings shot out. He held her tightly as he wrapped them around them both. He took another breath and held it, heating it again, mixing in his magic, then blew it on her face. White smoke covered her upper body, shifted to grey, and then faded again with the foul smell.

Her breathing evened, and she opened her eyes, staring at him. "I, what happened?"

Ceallach smiled as he blinked back tears. "Ye are fine, Kat." Relief flooded him so sharply his hands shook. He brushed a knuckle along her cheek, needing the contact to anchor himself. Gods, he'd nearly lost her. First the flame, now this.

His throat tightened. *How many more times can I watch ye slip away before I break?*

With slow, deliberate motion, Ceallach opened his wings, and Evie was the first to comment. "She's awake, thank God."

Aodhán hugged his wife. "Told ye, just had the wind knocked from her." He turned, punching Ewan. "Great way to return from yer honeymoon, nearly killing Kat."

Ewan flinched as his arms raised in defense. "I did not." Ceallach rose and helped Kat stand, but she wobbled a bit. His arm slipped around her waist before she could fall, holding her tight against his side.

"Easy," he murmured, his voice low and fierce. His hand splayed against her back, feeling the fine tremor in her spine. She weighed almost nothing pressed to him, each shallow rise of her ribs a reminder of how easily she could break—and the thought knotted his gut.

He dipped his head, searching her face for any hint of lingering pain. "Are ye certain ye can stand?" His thumb traced the curve of her hip, the contact grounding him as much as her.

She whispered lowly to him. "I went away to a place in the clouds. But ye called me back."

He held her to his side. *I will always call ye to me, Kat. Always.*

Energy rose in the yard, pulsing like thunder beneath still skies, putting Ceallach on edge. Ewan and Aodhán shifted their wives behind them, taking an active stance to cast a defensive spell—each shield before their maiden. A bright light and an explosion came from the Chapel, followed by silence. Ceallach sensed who'd come through the portal and sighed in relief. All the maidens and shields had arrived.

Laird Colin MacDougall rounded the side of the castle. "What the hell are ye kids up to? There has been nothing but large explosions at the level I haven't heard since Ewan sent his ship through the portal!" He came up short as the group of them stood staring at him. Each man posed before their woman, the shield in place for the fight to come. Ceallach stood at ease, holding Kat's hand as he watched the guardian of the Iona Stones. The people about to emerge from the Chapel in the Woods path would undoubtedly surprise him.

Colin searched each person's face till a movement from the path caught his attention. Three people strode out of the woods, each holding hands. If their garb of fur tied to make capes and tunics over long pants with lace-up boots gave them away, the shield and weapons strapped to them spoke of where and when they'd traveled from. Colin stood frozen, eyes shining with tears, his mouth slack. All three approached him, oblivious of the others in the yard. A tall man, a young boy, and a very tall black-haired woman who resembled Colin stopped before him.

The woman stepped forward, taking a speechless Colin into an enormous hug, "Hello, *deartháir, my brother.*"

Colin rasped, returning the embrace. "*Mo deirfiúr,*

my sister." They stood staring at each other as they still held each other. "Ainslie. It is…" He choked with a sob. "So, good to see ye."

Bree rounded the castle corner, calling out. "Colin, did ye find out what the kids are doing?"

She froze, then ran forward, crushing Ainslie into an embrace as she pulled her from Colin's arms. "I knew it! The booms are always the portal!"

Bree stood back with tears in her eyes. "Sister, it is so good to see you!"

Ainslie patted Bree's shoulder. "It is good to see ye in such good health."

The man strode forward, taking Colin's offered hand, and they clasped each other at the elbows, patting each other's shoulders. "Laird MacDougall, Colin. It is good to see ye again." His English carried a heavy accent, but considering it wasn't his first language, Ceallach smiled.

Colin slapped him on the back. "Rannick MacRaghnaill, I see ye have treated my sister well." He stooped to the youth between the two adults dressed like Viking warriors. "And is this, Ronald?"

The youth stood tall, glaring back. "I am Ron, the fiercest fighter in the land. My ma says ye are my uncle from the future."

Bree gasped. "Colin, you refused to read about Ainslie in the past, but you know her son's name."

Colin stood brushing the youth's hair. "Aye. I read them when ye left the scrolls out and weren't around."

Ron's gaze took in the yard and castle. "The castle is huge, Mother." He turned to Ainslie. "I doubt the Lord of Lorne knows what he has up against him, building a fortress this large."

161

Ainslie patted her son's head. "It's his son, Ewan, that has that task." She turned to the others in the yard, her assessing eyes traveling over each couple.

It was Ewan who stepped forward first. "Auntie?"

Ainslie's grin went wide. "Ewan, ye do look like yer da." He strode forward, taking his aunt in a hug.

He nearly dragged her toward his wife. "I want ye to meet my wife, Lorelei. We've just returned from our honeymoon."

Ainslie stumbled along and took Ewan's wife's offered hand as Lorelei gave her formal Tilinkis address. "I am happy to make known Ainslie, Ewan's aunt. Rannick, his uncle, and Ron, his nephew." She bowed over Ainslie's hand.

When she rose, Ainslie gave Ewan a raised eyebrow, making him chuckle. "She's Fae auntie from the merfolk. Long story." He moved, taking Lorelei in his arms and rubbing her rounded belly. "She's expecting our first. A boy. I feel it."

Evie moved forward, and Ainslie turned to her. "You must be Evie." She touched Annie's head, who wiggled in her ma's arms. "And who is this bright sprite?"

Aodhán shifted behind his wife, putting his arm around her. "Sprite is the right nickname. I am Aodhán, son of Brigid and grandson of Dagda, King of the Tuatha Dé Danann. Evie is my wife, and the sprite is Annie, our daughter."

Ainslie's gaze traveled to him, and Kat pushed forward. "Dash, I have heard so many stories about ye! A woman Viking warrior." Keeping close, Ceallach shadowed Kat in case she faltered. When she reached for Ainslie's hand to shake it, her movements looked steady, sure. Relief loosened the knot in his chest—she'd regained her strength faster than he dared hope.

Ainslie glanced from one to the other. "I am sorry, I don't recall Colin and Bree having another." She tilted her head. "Ye do resemble Marie Murray, though. I mean MacArthur."

Kat tossed her head back, laughing. "I should. I am her daughter."

Ainslie's gaze landed on Ceallach, and she tilted her head. "Ye look a lot like Morrigan, the Fae."

Ceallach bowed in formal address. "I am her son, Ceallach. Cousin to Aodhán and grandson to Dagda." Her eyes went between him and Kat. As her mind made the connection, a wide grin filled her face.

Ainslie nodded while her gaze roamed the yard. "Nice to meet ye." She shifted her weight, and her gaze came back to Colin. "Doug, where is Doug?" Everyone glanced down, moving a bit.

Bree stepped forward, taking Ainslie's hand in her arm. "Why don't ye all come in for refreshments, and I can tell you about Douglas MacArthur. Doug's story is so romantic! Similar to yers!" Bree led Ainslie towards the castle. "He fell in love with Abigail, a woman from the Caribbean in the seventeenth century. He stayed and led an era from slavery into a prosperous business."

Rannick and Ron followed Ainslie while Colin strode beside them. "Took ye long enough. We've waited."

Rannick nodded as he walked beside his brother-in-law. "We had trouble with the portal. No one's used the doorway since ye traveled it."

Ewan and Lorelei followed Colin, and he huffed, "All is well with the Lord of Lorne?"

Rannick chuckled. "Dougal is angry that he cannot come himself. Dagda's summons were very specific. Ainslie, myself, and her arguing got young Ron along."

Aodhán, who fell in step beside his wife who carried Annie, followed, leaving Ceallach and Kat to bring up the rear. Kat stepped back, and he waved to her to precede him. She moved past him, and a waft of her scent teased his senses. Camellia flowers, smelling exactly like the bed they'd made love in.

Rannick's tone grew firm when he spoke to Colin. "We face a battle?"

Colin glanced back, eyeing Ceallach as he replied. "Aye, but it would be best to wait. I'm sure we'll have a meeting soon. Save yer questions for then." Ceallach nodded to Colin, who nodded back before focusing on the path before him.

Aodhán turned a bit while the group proceeded towards the castle. *Will ye tell them?*

A muscle ticked in Ceallach's jaw as his gaze shifted aside. *Tell them what?*

His cousin huffed. *About the unknown source overpowering the block. It carried the faint scent of musk.*

Ceallach's gaze returned to his cousin. *Ye and I cannot tell the exact source, and until I can, I won't alarm them. They have enough to face as it is.*

Aodhán faced forward, shaking his head. *Cousin, they face so much. The battle of good vs evil is upon us. Are they ready?*

He eyed the group before him, praying to the gods that this was enough. *They have to be. The fate of the realms is in their hands.*

Chapter 12

By morning, the Great Hall buzzed with murmurs and the shuffle of shoes on stone. Kat stood near the edge, fingers twisting together, the restless motion as constant as her thoughts. Around her, everyone took their place, all eyes eventually drawn to where Ceallach would soon appear to discuss the gathering. Colin, Laird Mac, stood with Bree at the back of the couch while they mumbled back and forth. Her parents, Marie and John, sat on the left end of the sofa. Her da's arm was over the back of the couch, but close to her Ma. A familiar image Kat had seen a million times.

Ainslie stood beside her brother Colin. The two were inseparable since she returned to the future. Her rather intense, large warrior of a husband stood beside her, his gaze scanning the room, ready to go to battle at any moment. He pulled and shifted his jeans again, reminding Kat of his comments about wearing modern clothing to *fit in*. He'd called it confining even if his wife Ainslie had explained the fabrics were all spandex and flexed with his body. Ewan kneeled behind Lorelei, who sat in the large chair perpendicular to the couch, rubbing her rounded belly.

Moira and Dom sat on the right side of the couch. Their heads bent while they cuddled. It seemed their newly wedded bliss continued into their fourth year of marriage. Evie, her BFF, was beside her with her husband, Aodhán, as they stood before the fireplace. No fire burned today, but a chill permeated the room, or maybe the cold was Kat's dread.

Ron, Ainslie's son, Annie, Evie's daughter, along with Olivia, Moira's daughter, had been tucked away in the playroom upstairs with Mrs. A. The ones that were not a maiden of a stone or a shield were not there, except Kat.

She fidgeted with the longer top over her jeans as Evie bent over, snorting. "Stop being nervous."

Kat grumbled at her friend. "I can't help it. Ceallach thinks I should not be here and will be angry that I am."

Aodhán leaned across his wife. "Nonsense. Ye are part of the family. Just because ye don't have a stone doesn't mean ye can't know." He stood huffing. "Seems insulting to leave ye with Mrs. A like a child." He pointed at her. "Yer mind is the sharpest in the room."

As Ceallach swung into the room, he came up short when his gaze connected with hers across the vast space. He wore his Fae suit, the organza type fabric that almost glittered in the sunlight. When his expression shifted into a frown, his hair fell away, exposing his pointed ear.

With a scoff under his breath, Aodhán spoke aloud. "Well, now we can begin." Tension crackled between them, Ceallach's eyes flashing as he locked his glare with his cousin's. Neither moved, the pause marking mind speak between them.

Colin shoved between them. "Stop yer mind talk. Speak aloud."

Evie cleared her throat. "Da, I don't think ye want to know what they argue over."

As he spoke, Ceallach crossed the room. "I asked all the maidens and shields to attend." When he arrived before her, he stopped and turned, facing the room, blocking her view with his broad back as he spoke. "Kathryn Marie McAuthur is neither. She should not be here."

She elbowed around his large frame, surprised he didn't try to stop her. "I want to help. I'm sure there is something I can do."

A low, rough sound rumbled behind her, the warning clear in Ceallach's voice. "Staying away is how ye can help."

Her ma rose, crossing, taking her hands in hers. "Kat, dear, I am certain ye mean well. But maybe Ceallach is right." Her ma's *Dear* used again. She brushed her hair, despite it not being in her eyes. "Someplace ye can be safe."

Kat huffed, yanking her hands from her ma's as she stepped back. "I am not a child."

Marie moved towards her, but Evie stepped between them. "I am sure having Kat in the meeting will do no harm." Her stare met Ceallach's. "As long as she is not part of the actual gathering." The two stood there, maybe making mind speak? Kat didn't know and grew tired of all the arguing over her.

Her da rose, putting his arm around her ma. "She should stay. Who knows, maybe her knowledge of physics may help."

Whatever argument Evie and Ceallach had, it seemed Evie had won since Ceallach sighed. "Fine." He pointed at her. "Ye will stay out of the actual gathering." Lowering his hand, he crossed to the other side of the room, took a deep breath, and turned, facing all. Each person's expectant gaze fixed on him. Kat shivered, wondering how he held all the weight of his

167

responsibility so well.

Ceallach's voice rang over the room. "The gathering is upon us, and we all must be ready."

Colin folded his arms, bracing his feet apart. "How will we know when it is to start? What will ye require of us?"

Ceallach nodded. "That is what today's meeting is about." He unfolded his arms and gestured broadly, motioning to each of the women scattered around the room. "All the women, the maidens, must gather and call the stones."

Moira sat forward. "Call them? How?"

Aodhán nudged in front of Ceallach, facing the rest of the room. "Let's keep the questions at bay until Ceallach can finish. I suspect he will give us all we need if we allow him time to explain."

He returned to his wife's side as Ceallach nodded to his cousin. "Thank ye, cousin. If I can describe everything first, maybe it will all make more sense."

A rough rumble scraped from Colin's throat, sharp enough to catch Ceallach's ear. "Nothing from the Fae makes sense." Bree tapped his shoulder, but he only grunted in reply, eyes fixed ahead without turning.

Ceallach waved to the women again. "The maidens must gather to call the stones. If ye can all stand?" With a ripple of magic stirring the air, he waved his hand. In an instant, the couch, chair, and coffee table before the fireplace shimmered, then blinked out of sight—leaving the space bare and waiting.

Bree huffed. "Well, I hope you will return my furniture when you finish. Some are precious antiques."

Ceallach nodded. "Aye, of course. Bree ye will stand closest to the fireplace, on the right. Next to her is

Moira and then Lorelei." He proceeded to each place, indicating where each woman should stand, then strode to the opposite side, opposite the fireplace, eyeing her.

Kat stepped back under his glare, and Evie took her hand in hers, sending a mind message. *He isn't mad, Kat. He's worried.* Evie's focus met hers. *He doesn't want ye hurt.*

Ceallach waved to the place before him. "Marie, yer place is here opposite Bree." He moved aside as her ma took her place.

"Next to Marie is Evie, and last is Ainslie." Evie released Kat's hand, taking her place.

He turned, pointing next to Bree. "Beside Bree is Moira, and then Lorelei is at the end."

As each woman shifted to her place, Kat had to move to the other end of both lines. When she arrived next to Ceallach, he strode through the middle.

At the fireplace, he turned, facing the room. "And each man, as the shield, must protect them."

The men relocated, positioning themselves behind each of their women. Arriving behind Bree, Colin bent, kissing his wife on the cheek.

As John nudged behind Marie, he chuckled. "Nothing to *quarry* about. You'll do great at this!" Marie twitched, giggling.

When Uncle Dom moved behind Moira, he touched her shoulders. "Always have hope." As Ewan went behind Lorelei, he placed his hands around her, rubbing her round belly and letting them fall to his sides when she wiggled. When Aodhán stepped behind Evie, his eyes moved between her and his cousin.

Ceallach stood before her, the people who meant everything to her between them. The weight of fate pressed down upon them all, yet she remained an outsider—watching, powerless, aching to be part of the most crucial endeavor of their lives.

Her heart thundered in her chest, and she looked at him, pleading without words. She wanted nothing more than for him to cross the room, scoop her in his arms, and carry her away. Them—together. She longed for the reckless certainty of his embrace, the fire that had once burned between them.

His gaze locked with hers for a breathless moment, and hope flared in her chest. Then he blinked, his lashes shuttering his intense gaze. His breath hitched, and when his eyes lifted again, he looked past her—deliberate, distant, like she no longer mattered.

Her stomach twisted. Ceallach's avoidance was what he didn't say aloud. *This isn't our time.*

Not their time. Not their story.

A sharp pain lanced through her, but she refused to break. He had warned her and told her she didn't belong there, in their mission. But God help her—she *was* a part of this. Of him.

Tears burned, but she refused to let them fall. If he wouldn't choose her, she would have to find a way to make him. No matter what it took.

****

When Kat stood before him, her gaze pleading, he nearly strode forward to offer his hand. When her thoughts flashed into his mind *Her wanting nothing more than for him to cross the room, scoop her in his arms, and carry her away. Them—together.* He had to break eye contact and blinked back tears. He should never have spent time with her. Focusing on his duty, the gathering was what he needed now.

Ceallach avoided her regard as he spoke. "Each shield must align with each stone. The shield uses his emotions to protect the maiden of each stone. The woman calls the stone filled with his, well, their emotions. The maiden comes forth, offering the stone for the gathering. The shield's powers protect the maiden." He took a breath and waved his hand for emphasis. "Each shield cannot fail. If the shield fails, the stones become vulnerable to the evil Fae."

John placed his hands on Marie's shoulders, stepping closer to her. "Each maiden holds each stone. Ye mean the women and the stones become vulnerable to the evil Fae."

Aodhán did the same to Evie, his hands on her. "And now ye understand yer duty as a shield."

Ewan shifted closer to Lorelei, wrapping his arm around her and placing it on her rounded belly. "I am not so certain about this. Lorelei is expecting." Ceallach sensed the babe shift at his da's touch. The young one was strong and would endure well.

With measured control, Ceallach folded his hands behind his back. "All will be well. Ye have powers, Ewan. Ye will use them as her shield."

Colin stepped before Bree, a shield before her, without even thinking. "But John, Domonic, and I do not possess Fae powers. How will we be able to protect them?" Colin's instincts would serve them all well. The good Fae counted on Colin's strong emotions, even if he sometimes lost control.

Ceallach eyed each man in the room. "Ye are connected to yer maiden's stone. Yer emotions, yer love for yer maiden will be yer power."

Bree pushed around Colin into the center of the

group. "Wait, we've aligned in the same order as the Chapel windows." She gestured to the left side. "Love, Hope, Faith." Turning, she waved to the right, where Marie, Evie, and Ainslie stood. "Fear, Doubt, Lust." She rotated facing Ceallach. "The gathering is in the Chapel in the Woods."

Ceallach stood immobile. "Ye state it, not ask."

Marie pointed to Bree. "When they built the chapel, they positioned the center of the cross precisely in the center of the chapel, pointing east and west."

She folded her arms, chewing her thumbnail. "Emily believed the circular stained glass above the altar and door held magical properties, believing that light from the west window at dusk hit the center of the chapel. The stained-glass pattern Bree saw in the past now matches the flooring. The cross. She always thought the chapel held mystical power when the shadow crossed the pattern on the floor."

Bree turned a full circle. "Yes, each time magical events happen in the chapel, it's always the center, over the cross." She stood in the center as she whispered. "The Stone of Destiny, it's in the chapel."

Ceallach nodded. "Ye are exactly where ye will be when the stones come together, Bree. Love is the strongest power of all. It is through the Stone of Love the stones must travel."

Colin folded his arms, glaring at Ceallach. "What of the maiden's sacrifice? If Bree is to gather the stones, the evil Fae will target her above all the others." Bree's breath hitched. She *was* truly afraid of the prophecy, as she should be.

Ceallach glanced down. "It has been her they've targeted all along, Colin." He stood taller, staring straight ahead while he told them his life's purpose. "Now ye know my duty. I am the shield of the stones. I will protect ye all." They all gaped at him, wearing the same expressions—eyes wide, mouths parted, struggling to grasp what they'd just heard. But beneath that shock lay something heavier, more complex. Doubt.

It wasn't just disbelief in his words but a quiet storm of fear and uncertainty in each of them. Doubt that he was strong enough. Uncertainty that any one person could stand between them and the dark tide bearing down on their realm. It pressed against his mind like a cold wind—sharp, biting, relentless. Some doubted because they had seen too much failure. Others because they had lost too much hope. And a few, perhaps, because trusting him now meant letting go of their fear—which was the hardest.

But buried in the silence, there was something else too. Subtle. Heated. Arousing in a way they hadn't expected. For some, doubt tangled with desire—a primal reaction to strength, to the raw certainty in his stance, to the fierce promise in his voice. The fire in his eyes stirred something deeper, something reckless. The hunger for success whispered alongside their fear, a flicker in the dark, undeniable and dangerous.

"I've trained my entire life for this," he said, voice steady though his chest tightened under the weight of their unspoken fears. "I will protect ye all or die in my duty."

Ceallach wasn't asking for blind faith, not needing them to cast aside their doubts entirely—only to let him carry them for a while. He had to have their trust, even if it flickered, and fragile as candlelight. He would stand using their hope for guidance, their faith for courage, and

173

their love for strength.

And perhaps, in the lingering heat of their gaze, in the breathless pause between heartbeats, he would draw from their longing too. Let the pulse of desire lend him another edge. Because if he faltered now, they would fall with him.

His cousin folded his arms and sent a mind message only to Ceallach. *Ye aren't going to tell them?*

I've told them all I'm required to. They have all they need. Ceallach's mind snapped back.

Aodhán pushed past Evie, towards him. *The new guardian, the fact their guardianship is over. And who is the new guardian?*

Ceallach remained silent, and Bree went to Colin, going into his arms as she whimpered. "The maiden's sacrifice you cheated before still haunts us." Each shield took each maiden in their arms. Tension pressed against the walls, thick with unspoken fears, flickers of hope, and the sharp sting of doubt. Every breath carried the weight of what no one dared to say. Bree's fear and worry. The sense of each man wanting to lay down his life for the woman he held. Combined like this, they almost overwhelmed Ceallach, but one person's emotions rose above the others, sharp, vivid, and unmistakably hers. Kat.

Her feelings surged through him like wildfire, hot, aching, furious. Not at him, not entirely, but at the circumstances that kept her outside. Her frustration burned brightly, edged with the sting of betrayal. Being left out was what she hated. Those she loved saw her as fragile, when she knew damn well, she could hold her own. Longing laced through her anger, not just to fight, but to stand beside them, to matter in the way that counted most. She didn't want to be protected. She wanted to be trusted.

Ceallach's heart went out to her. That kind of fury came from love, from the ache of being sidelined by someone she would die for. And she would die for him. Her emotions clung to his like a second skin, raw, pulsing, impossible to escape. But he dared not look at her. If he met her gaze, he would cave. He would cross the space between them, take her in his arms, and surrender everything he had—his duty, his vow, his restraint. He would give her everything she wanted and then some, not because she demanded it but because a part of him needed her just as fiercely.

No. Ceallach had to stay the course. This moment wasn't about desire or love or even fairness. This was about survival. And if he let himself fall into her now, the rest of them would fall, too.

Still, her emotions haunted him, clinging like a phantom touch. Her pulse thundered in his blood; her fury burned through his bones. And the gods help him. Part of him *wanted* to fall.

Kat shoved into the group. "I want to help." She glanced around her. Her love for all the people in the room radiated from her. "My emotions can help power the stones."

Marie strode to her. "Dearie, ye are safe staying away."

Her ma's regard shifted as John stepped to them. "Aye, Kat."

Both parents took her in their arms, trying to comfort her, but he sensed she wasn't having their coddling care. She wanted to help and to be included, but he needed her to stay away. He wanted her safe and away from the stones.

She glared at Ceallach when he spoke. "Evil is where ye least expect it. Ye all must be on guard."

Kat yanked herself from her parents' arms. "None of ye care." She spun on her heel, footsteps sharp against stone as she rushed out, the sway of her hair the last thing he saw before the door swallowed her whole.

Marie started to go after her as John took her in his arms. "Marie, let her have her cry. She'll come to terms with her feelings." The front door opened and slammed shut. No small feat. The entry was solid oak, and Kat was a petite woman. Her strong emotions echoed through the room, hitting Ceallach multiple times, each one hurting more.

Colin stirred next to Ceallach. "How will we know when the gathering is to start?"

Ceallach gave the only answer he could. "Ye will know, ye will feel it."

With a flick of his hand, the empty space stirred—wood scraped faintly against stone as the couch and chairs slid back into position, the room settling as if it had never changed. "I suggest ye all take a respite." Not wanting to face more questions than he had answers to, as well as ones he could not share, Ceallach twisted his shoulders to transport from the room. But it wasn't his bedroom where he sought solace. He arrived at the stable ruin. The place where Kat sat on the other side, as sounds of her sniffles filled the air.

****

Kat drew her knees tight to her chest, arms wrapped around them, her chin resting on the ridge of bone. The hollow ache inside didn't ease, but she held herself anyway, as if the pressure alone might keep her from

176

coming apart.

Lifting her head, she wiped the tears from her cheeks and scolded herself like Evie had time and time again. "Come on, Kat, get yerself together." She wiped her runny nose, smearing the moisture on her jeans. She spoke, mimicking her bother Doug, almost feeling his punch to her arm. "Kat. Chin up." Kat sighed as she rested her chin on her knees. "They all have their place. And me? I'm just the one no one trusts to do anything."

Ceallach's voice came softly. "That's not true."

Kat jolted, falling sideways. Ceallach was beside her before she recovered, taking her in his arms. At first, she wiggled in protest. Emotionally waned and worn, she eventually gave into the comforting feeling of his arms around her.

Care washed over her, easing her headache and drying her eyes. "Ye do that every time we are together. Weave yer magic, making everything all better."

He shifted till he sat cradling her in his lap as he brushed her hair from her face. "I do?"

She huffed. "Don't play the innocent. Ye use powers all the time."

Fingers grazed her cheek. "Is it a crime to want to make ye feel better, to make ye happy?"

Kat tucked into his embrace, finding a familiar comfort there. "Not a crime. I worry I'll grow dependent and will miss ye when ye leave." She sighed. "Why can't I be part of the gathering?"

Ceallach squeezed her to him, and she laid her head on his chest as his voice vibrated when he spoke. "Kat, ye will only get in the way. Ye are not a maiden." His deep breath shifted her head, and the air shuddered with the weight of his statement as he exhaled. "I would have more to worry over since Colin must protect the Stone of Love, and Bree is the maiden of all the stones. The maiden's, the shields, I must protect all of them." Evie's comment from earlier rang in her mind. *He isn't mad, Kat. He's worried. He doesn't want ye hurt.*

A thumb on her chin lifted her face until she looked at him. "Evie is right. I don't want ye hurt, Kat." He read her mind again, and she was too wrapped up to get angry with him.

New tears filled her eyes. "But I want to be a part. Doug is a part, even if he isn't here. Everyone has a duty to help. Why not me?" As she looked at the chapel trail before her, she wondered about Doug. What was he dealing with, and did he have anything to do for the stones?

Ceallach's fingers wiped her tears away while he whispered. "Close yer eyes, Kat. Let yer mind free yerself of all these worries." As his fingers brushed gently over her lids again, a lightness unfurled inside her. Ease washed through her, soft and steady.

His murmur came again. "Worry not for yer brother." A bright light flashed, and her mind's eye opened to a scene, like a dream—an unobserved bystander to the world around her. Rows of chairs stretched in neat lines, and were filled with shadows shaped like people. Their whispers curled together like smoke, too soft to catch, but heavy with expectation. Kat hovered at the edge, a stranger unseen, watching the hush ripple as if the air itself waited. A wedding. She knew it without seeing the bride—just the way the air thickened with hope and the weight of promises about to be made. Everyone turned to the back, and a beautiful, auburn-haired, short woman proceeded down the aisle in a white linen dress. The love and happiness surrounded Kat, washing over her like waves. The woman's smile went wide when she arrived at her groom, and when he moved forward to take her hand, the groom was Doug. Kat's breath whooshed. She witnessed her brother's wedding!

The picture flickered like a movie, and she floated over a bedroom—as if she sat on a rafter peering inside. A baby cried from the crib, and a man crossed the room cooing. He took up the infant, and when he turned, Doug held the baby. The same woman, his wife, crossed and stood together, and the babe quieted. Doug glanced at his wife, his expression soft as his love and care came to Kat. He was so happy.

The picture shifted again. Doug stood steering a ship, But not any vessel. Kat knew this one. He sailed *The Faithful*, Ewan's Galleon he'd left with Doug in the past. Doug sailed into the sunset with a smile as his contentment came to her. The scene wavered, and the view of the chapel's trail came back into her sight. She hiccupped and held on to Ceallach. He sat holding her as the scenes played out in her mind. Doug, in the past, was joyful and content, making her happy and sad at once.

Ceallach kissed her forehead. "Aw, Kat, I showed ye those things to make ye glad, not sad."

Her gaze rose. "I just want to go away, where all these troubles don't exist. I want to be free."

Ceallach rested his forehead on hers. "Ye truly wish it. An escape?" His lips lowered to hers and flitted across them in a brief kiss. When he lifted his head, Kat nodded.

He kissed her lips as he whispered. "Meet me in yer dreams, Kat."

Her body jerked before she forced herself still, pulse drumming too loud. She shoved the memory back, sealing the images behind the thrum of her heartbeat. She wouldn't let him see—wouldn't let him know.

The words shot from her mouth, rough and louder than she meant. "Not my dreams. When I'm awake." Ceallach stared at her, blinking. Had he read her mind?

Focusing on the trail, she thought of being free, and he tucked her into his arms. "As ye wish. Tonight, at dusk, ye will meet me by the loch where we picnicked, and ye shall have yer escape."

Kat blinked. "I will? Like a date?"

Ceallach held her in his arms. "Aye, a date, sweet Kat. But for now, I only wish to hold ye."

Chapter 13

The brush glided through her hair in slow, thoughtful strokes. Kat sat before the vanity, the fading light catching the copper strands like flame. Tonight wasn't just a date—it was an escape. That's what he'd promised.

Her fingers paused at the final stroke. She set the brush down gently, as if breaking a spell, and swept a touch of powder across her cheeks. The cool silk of the makeup calmed her skin, a small ritual of renewal. She'd woken late in the afternoon, curled in the hush of her bed chamber, the aftertaste of tears still on her lips.

Warmth lingered on her skin, a ghost of Ceallach's arms wrapped tight, as if he'd never let her slip free. Doug's presence lingered too—softer now, not aching but warm, like sunlight on stone.

But Ceallach's voice was what she kept hearing. His final words before she'd drifted to sleep echoed in her mind, low and certain, like a vow whispered in the dark.

He'd flashed them into her room, laying her on the bed and kissing her forehead. "Till tonight, Kat." Her hand froze, the brush suspended as she recalled the light caress of his lips on hers when he kissed her before leaving. After she'd drifted into a deep sleep, the dreams that had plagued her lately interrupted her rest. Throwing the makeup brush down, she stood, wanting to dress for the night. She picked up her short skirt, tossed the garment down and opted for a dress. She removed her shirt and pants, slipped her dress over her head, and wondered what Ceallach would consider an escape. The sunlight shifted, casting the room into golden hues. Was it dusk already?

Kat edged to the window, the sun brushing gold across the hills. She leaned out, drawing in a deep breath—warm air kissed with the tang of salt and the sharp bite of loch wind.

A freezing chill washed over her body as her vision dimmed. That voice rang in her mind, the demon from her dreams. "Hello Kitty, how has it been since we last met?"

Her fingers curled tight on the windowsill as the man took over her mind. She knew she was awake but couldn't maintain control. Opening her mouth to scream, she pressed hard, yet nothing came out. She tried to breathe, and her body froze. Her mind rebelled. *Don't call me that!*

His low chuckle filled her head. "I shall say and do what I wish. Tell me, dear, have ye found my stones yet?"

Kat gripped the windowsill harder, finding the frame the only solid piece of reality at the moment, grounding her. "I don't know where they are." She yelled the last. "And I wouldn't give them to ye if I did!"

Her body lifted, weightless and wrong. She dangled from the windowsill, fingers arching around the wood— the only thing between her and the two-story drop below.

The demon's deep voice tickled her mind. "My stones, ye will get me my stones." Shaking her head, she faltered and had to shift to grip the sill better.

A sigh echoed in her head. "I would hate for

anything to happen to the brother ye care so much about."

Her fingers began to slip. She shifted, readjusting each hand to find a better grip. "No, Doug is fine! I've seen it." Her body lifted and slammed against the Abbey's rough bricks, but her hands held firm. She hung there for a moment, her breaths raging as her strength waned.

His voice teased her, and he whispered. "Tell me, Kitty, what ancient invention allows people to see through walls?"

Her grip tightened, fingers burning as she shouted. "Another riddle? I think not!"

Her body hit the wall again, but her hands held firm, and his voice yelled. "Tell me the answer to the riddle, and I shall free ye." The last came as a moan, teasing her. "Give ye that escape ye so wish."

Running the riddle through her mind while her fingers began to slip again. *An invention to see through walls.* She had to have the answer. The two-story fall would certainly hurt if not kill her. *See through walls?* She glanced up at her fingers on the window's edge, and the answer came to her.

A ragged cry ripped from her chest, "Window."

She slammed onto something solid, the shock snapping her upright. Breath ragged, she glanced around—her bedroom floor. She rubbed her arms, certain the pain that radiated up them was no dream but reality as she asked her mind if this was real or a dream. The demon chased her in her waking hours as well as her dreams.

Wiping her hands on her face, she moaned. "Is there no escape at all?"

Kat stood, brushing her hands down her dress, finding everything in place. No evidence of her ordeal showed. Shaking herself, she slipped on her sandals, turned from the window, and left her bedroom with the feeling she'd left the demon behind.

With a clearer head, she proceeded through the Abbey, her parents nowhere in sight, and went out the doorway to the garden to meet Ceallach in the same spot they'd picnicked at days before.

Arriving at the place, she faced Loch Etive and the setting sun. Its warm hues of orange and red dazzled as the sky slowly shifted into blue and purple. Sunsets were the prettiest in the summer in Scotland. A breath blew on her ear, making her jump and scream.

Strong arms encircled her, stilling her. "Kat, it's only me."

She turned and found Ceallach holding her as she took a deep breath. "Sorry, ye startled me."

His hand brushed her cheek, and a soothing sensation washed over her as he grinned. "I am sorry, *mo bruadarach*. I didn't mean to."

He bent, kissing her, and the world tilted; she grew dizzy, and she floated as he held her.

Her feet touched something solid while Ceallach blew on her cheek. The dizziness faded, and she opened her eyes to see silver-blue lighting Ceallach's face. "Where are we?"

He took her by the shoulders, turning her as he remained at her back, his body's warmth a constant reassurance of his protection. "Yer escape, *mo bruadarach*."

The land shimmered in a silver-blue hue, touched by moonlight that seemed to have lingered there for a thousand years. A grand gate stood at the entrance—tall, ornate, forged of white stone veined with shimmering threads of starlight. Intricate vines wove through its delicate frame, curling around an empty circle in the center, waiting for a symbol, a name, or a soul to complete it.

Beyond the gate, the tranquil land stretched out like something from a dream, or a half-forgotten memory. Though the lake anchored her view with its cascading waterfall, the rest slowly unfolded, revealing itself only to those granted the right to see. The sky above shifted darker, the twilight deepening into velvet indigo just as the gate opened with a soft sigh. The lake caught the change in light and transformed into a mirror of silver, rippling under the moon's touch. The waterfall glowed like liquid crystal. The fall of water soft and rhythmic, like the breath of the realm itself.

Clusters of flowers bloomed along the water's edge, lunar blossoms with petals that glowed faintly, casting a pale light over the cobblestone paths. Some swayed though there was no wind, humming with quiet magic. Silver-leaved trees arched over the garden paths, their trunks smooth and warm to the touch, their branches hung with starfruit that pulsed like tiny lanterns in the night.

The air smelled of something sweet and otherworldly, like jasmine and wild mint and something softer, unnamable, that tugged at the edges of memory. This place wasn't just beautiful. It was sacred. Timeless.

Ceallach took her hand, leading her into the area as the white whole moon rose above them. "This is the Moon Garden. A scared place in the Fae realm."

White flowers and silvery foliage surrounded the

waterfall, glowing in the moonlight. A smile tugged at her lips, light and untouchable. Everything felt thinner here—like a dream. The peaceful sounds of their feet rustled in the grass as a cool evening breeze blew through, creating a shiver.

Ceallach pulled on her hand, drawing her into his embrace. "Yer escape I promised, *mo bruadarach.*"

He turned her till she faced the waterfall again, his body flush against her back as he trailed kisses down her neck, and his hands roamed her hips. "Ye are beautiful." Kat tried to turn, but he held her firmly. "No, enjoy yer escape."

She tilted her head as he drew up her dress, and his kisses progressed along her neck to her shoulder. When his hands brushed her bare thighs, she had to grip him for stability. His teeth nipped her neck while one hand slid under her skirt and the other rose, pulling her dress top down and exposing a breast. As his fingers dipped into her underwear, his tongue tickled her neck. When he tugged the panties down, she wiggled, stepping free of them.

Ceallach's chuckle tickled her ear. "So eager." His fingers tickled her private area, and he lightly sucked her earlobe, sending shivers over her body. A sigh brushed her ear, followed by his hand, slow and sure, cupping her breast. When he parted her, rubbing her little nub, she arched into the caresses. Each stroke of his fingers through her wetness sent her legs trembling, barely keeping her upright. He stood firm, allowing her body to flex against his while his hands worked magic on her. One at her breast, the other teasing her into a wicked journey. Teeth nipped her neck, a tease of pain before his finger pressed deep, coaxing a gasp from her.

She whimpered, wanting more, and his chuckle came to her. "My sweet siren, ye are a delicate treat." Kat turned in his arms, not wanting to delay more, forcing him to withdraw his hands.

As she dipped her head, she pulled the other arm free from her dress. "I am? Yer sweet treat?" She lowered both arms of her dress, then released it, allowing the fabric to billow and fall to her feet. As she moved free of the garment, she drew her fingers up, and his arms tilted, till hers encircled his neck. Her body came against his hard one, fully clothed.

She kissed him once, then pulled back. "Where is my treat?" Her mind's eye flashed an image of his naked body. He growled as he pulled back from her embrace.

His arms twirled overhead, and then his clothing vanished. "Yer escape, yer treat is here." His hands rested by his sides, palms open in submission.

Kat moved toward him, lifting her finger to his lips, and he kissed the tip. She drew her nail down his chin, throat, and chest, wondering how far he'd allow this game to go and how far she wanted to take it.

He took a deep breath as she trailed her finger lower. "My treat? Is he mine to command?" Ceallach reached for her, and she shifted back. "Not yet." She gave him a wicked grin. "My treat, my command."

He clenched his fists, and his voice rumbled. "Yers."

Kat shifted closer, kissing his collarbone. His hands came up, gripping her arms. She stepped back. "No touching."

Ceallach gripped her harder as he bent to kiss her, and she moved aside. "Mine to command." He froze, his swallow audible.

She shifted and kissed his ear as she whispered. "No

touching without my command." He released her so fast she had to catch herself.

A growl curled from his chest, rough-edged like a tiger stalking its prey. "Yers."

Kat stared into his eyes, which sparkled like fireworks. Ceallach's arms flexed again, and she ran her hands over his shoulders and then his chest, marveling as he jumped under her touch. She bent, kissing his chest, then licking her tongue through the springy hairs down the middle. Her hands rounded to his backside, causing him to flex. Her fingers tightened in answer, her tongue trailing lower with greedy intent. She knelt before him, her mouth at his belly button, her hand gripping his ass.

Hard and waiting, he jutted toward her, the heat of him daring her closer. Kat had never been this close to one before, and she studied him there for a moment, noting the veins pulsing. He twitched, jumping, making her smile. Did she affect this man, this mysterious Fae?

Everything about him was rock-hard. Kat dared a glance at his face, and the firm set of his clenched jaw told her she had affected him as she desired.

As she kissed his navel, her whisper teased while she watched his expression. "I've always wondered." She licked again, allowing her tongue to trail lower. "What a Fae tasted like." Laving the tip of his desire she reveled when his hands gripped her arms. She pulled free. "My command, no touching."

IIis hands dropped to his thighs, a low rumble vibrating in his chest.

Kat gripped him firmly at the base, feeling the twitch of response as his hips jolted beneath her touch. Her other hand slid around to grab his ass, drawing him closer as she lowered her mouth over the tip. She kissed him there, slow and deliberate, before letting her lips part and pulling him in. He pulsed against her tongue.

His sigh—rough, raw—brushed her ears like wind in a storm. She eased back, licking her lips, then took him again, deeper this time, savoring the stretch and heat of him. When he throbbed in her mouth, she started a slow rhythm, bobbing forward and back, remembering the way girls in college had whispered how the act drove men wild. But he wasn't just a man—he was Fae. And she wanted to know what *this* would do to him.

His hips began to match her movements, every flex of his body meeting hers. His panting grew heavier, louder, wrapping around her like heat. She quickened her pace.

A growl tore from his throat as his hands dove into her hair. He tried to guide her, but she swatted him away without missing a beat, taking control with every steady stroke.

Arms gripped under her arm as he pulled her up and captured her mouth with his. The kiss stole the breath from her lungs. His growl didn't fade—it melted into the kiss, into the way his mouth claimed hers like he couldn't get close enough.

They moved as one, spinning, lifting. His body molded to hers, hands everywhere, mouth devouring, need crashing between them like waves breaking over rock.

They lifted into the sky, pausing, and his kiss slowed, his breath on her lips when he spoke. "Kat, ye wicked siren, ye tempt me beyond reason." He kissed her again as they floated down, landing next to one another, wrapped in each other's arms.

He held her as his breathing subsided, and her hand

caressed his chest. "We flew without yer wings."

A little out of breath, he replied. "Floated. Wings—are only needed—for flying." He rolled on top of her, sliding himself against her heat. "Kat, ye almost had me…" He kissed her, rubbing against her. "Lose myself."

Gripping his ass again, she loved the way the mounds of flesh flexed. "Mine to command."

He rocked against her again, hitting that spot. "What does my temptress command?"

She arched into his caresses. "Make love to me." With the next thrust, he drove into her in one smooth, urgent motion, pulling a cry from her lips.

He thrust again. "Command me."

She surged up, capturing his mouth in a fierce kiss. "Loose yerself in me."

Voice rough with restraint, he paused. "Kat, if I let my lust loose, I…"

Kissing him again, she tugged him closer by the hips. "Ye will not hurt me—unless ye do not take me now!"

His growl rumbled low and dangerous as he pressed into her, slow and deep. She sighed, her breath catching as he buried himself completely.

When he pulled back, she whimpered. "Please, Ceallach. I want all of ye."

On the next push, her plea came on a breathless whisper. "Please."

He slammed into her, the force shifting her across the soft ground. She wrapped her legs around him, urging him on with the grip of her thighs and the pull of her hands on his ass.

As he drove in again, another growl curled hot

against her ear.

The next thrust had her arching. The one after left her gasping. He rose above her, powerful and relentless, one hand gripping her shoulder for leverage as he pounded into her.

The stretch, the pressure, the consuming fullness—each motion sent fire racing through her limbs. She ached for his possession, for everything he gave and withheld.

Another hard thrust, another deep growl in her ear.

Their bodies moved as one—his pace matching her frantic pants. Then he bent low, teeth grazing her neck before he bit, hard, claiming her as he drove into her again and again.

Each brutal thrust struck her center, her most sensitive place. She writhed beneath him, breathless, unraveling. The tension coiled, stretched tight, and with one final, devastating push, she cried out—stars bursting behind her closed lids.

In one fluid motion, he swept her into his arms as he dropped to his knees, hands gripping her hips with possessive strength. She locked her legs around him, anchoring herself as he drove into her, thrusting deep while pushing her down onto the full length of his hardness.

Again and again, he moved, relentless, their faces so close she could taste the breath between them. When he thrust deep and held, his eyes flared silver—wild, unguarded. His body arched, and he roared to the sky, pulsing hard inside her in a fierce, rhythmic wave that echoed through her center.

He drew back only to plunge into her again, bellowing as release overtook him.

A shudder rolled through him, and his arms instinctively rose to steady her—but she clung first, holding tight, her grip fierce and trembling, gripping him like a lifeline.

They rolled to their sides, each holding the other as they caught their breath. Ceallach slowly pulled himself from her. At first, her body didn't seem to want to let go, but they separated with a long sigh at the same time. Their breathing subsided, and stars still danced behind her lids each time she closed them. Her head spun a little, and when her breathing came under control, she found herself in the same place, in Ceallach's arms.

Ceallach held her close, and the breeze blew over their heated naked bodies. He hummed as his heart beat hard. "Yers, my temptress." He chuckled. "Did ye enjoy yer treat?"

Kat snuggled into his embrace. "Aye."

She lay there for a moment, her ear on his chest while his breathing slowed and his heart calmed. She drew circles in his chest hairs, delighting in being with him, no matter the realm. She wished this didn't have to end. Time seemed to fly when she was with him, but she relished each moment, knowing he would soon leave her life.

Ceallach grunted. "I will not leave ye." He gripped her hand, raising her knuckles to his mouth, and kissing each fingertip. "I can come and go as I please. The rules of time limits between realms do not apply to me."

Kat yanked her hand from his. "It would be nice to be with ye for once without ye knowing my every thought."

He grabbed her hand again. "Such pretty thoughts they are that match such a beautiful woman." He placed her hand back on his chest. "Part of yer escape is a restful sleep." She sat up, and he pulled her back into his embrace. "Take yer ease, Kat. I know ye have had troubled sleep." As she settled back into his arms, he took a deep breath and exhaled. "Come, let me tell ye a tale."

Kat sighed, already tired from their activities. "A story would be nice. Ye tell them well."

He shifted, and his chest shook with a chuckle. "Aye, well, ye are a good listener. Once upon a time, there was an island where all the feelings lived: Happiness, Sadness, Knowledge, and all others, including Love. One day, the gods announced that the island would sink, so all constructed boats and left. Except for Love."

Kat yawned, and Ceallach bent till she glanced up at him as he spoke. "Ye aren't already asleep? I've only begun." She shook her head while she relaxed, fully anticipating his calming voice.

"Love was the only one who stayed. Love wanted to hold out until the last possible moment. When the island had almost sunk, Love asked for help.

"Richness passed by Love in a grand boat. Love said, 'Richness, can you take me with you?' Richness answered, 'No, I can't. There is a lot of gold and silver in my boat. There is no place here for you.'

"Love decided to ask Vanity, who also passed by in a beautiful vessel. 'Vanity, please help me!'

"Vanity answered, 'I can't help you, Love. You are all wet and might damage my boat.'

"Sadness was close by, so Love asked, 'Sadness, let me go with you.'

"Sadness sighed, 'Oh… Love, I am so sad that I

need to be by myself!' " Kat hummed; sadness was something she understood all too well. Being alone, though, wasn't always the answer.

Ceallach squeezed her once as he continued. "Happiness passed by Love, too, but she was so happy that she did not even hear when Love called her.

"A reassuring voice sounded over them all. 'Come, Love, I will take you.' The speaker was an elder from the traveling group of seniors. Feeling so blessed and overjoyed, Love forgot to ask the elders where they headed. When they arrived at dry land, the elder went his own way." Her brows pinched, mouth tightening with her thoughts. Love going on full trust, not knowing where. That was, at times, how she felt.

Ceallach brushed a kiss on her head. "Realizing how much he owed the elder, Love asked Knowledge, another elder, 'Who helped me?'

" 'That was Time.' Knowledge answered.

" 'Time?' asked Love. 'But why did Time help me?'

"Knowledge smiled with deep wisdom and answered, 'Because only Time can understand how valuable Love is.' "

Kat glanced up at Ceallach. "Love?"

He grinned at her, almost teasing her, and she folded her arms. "Ye know, the old masters, such as Michelangelo, placed the symbol of love in David's eyes. It's not just the shape of a heart, but a Möbius strip of energy that creates matter through this eternity knot with the indifferent empty space. This renders information, in essence, love, eternal for as long as time endures."

Ceallach kissed her while she finished the last word, whispering into the kiss. "Time endures all, Kat. Time is everlasting."

She hummed into the kiss. "Love, Ceallach?" He kissed her deeply, his tongue tangling with hers, coaxing a moan from her throat.

When he finally pulled away, his voice came with a whisper of softness. "Aye, I love ye, Kat."

Her eyes snapped open. "But the gathering…"

He claimed her mouth with heat and hunger, then pulled back just enough to speak, his breath still mingling with hers. "Time will figure this one out, Kat."

She pushed against him. "But what about after, what will happen… to ye, to us?"

He turned, taking both her hands in his. "I vow at this most sacred place I bind myself to ye Kathryn Marie MacArthur. With my body and my vow, we shall love one another in all the realms. I promise, Kat, in the end, I *will* find a way for us to be together." Ceallach kissed her, and she nodded, responding to the kiss and his vow.

Her vision blurred, the sting of tears rising fast, and his head lifted as if he felt every drop. "No tears, Kat."

She licked her lips. "But I love ye too. I vow to ye as well. Us together."

A quake of heat passed through him before he calmed, his lips finding hers once more before he gathered her close. "No more tears, Kat. Sleep, ye need yer rest." She lay in his arms, content, spending the rest of her days there. As her lids grew heavy and her body grew languid, Ceallach whispered. "Sleep, my Kat. In the Fae realm, no one shall disturb ye."

Chapter 14

Ceallach lay with Kat in his arms while she peacefully slept. His fingers caressed her face again as he sensed her mind at ease, the deep sleep he sent her working. With the coming gathering, sleepless nights had plagued her. She shouldn't fret, but she did. The human mind was a complex and vast maze of thoughts and energy. Some powers the humans had barely even tapped into their full potential. He kissed her forehead again, relishing holding her as he'd always dreamed. Naked in the Moon Garden in the Fae realm.

The energy shifted—familiar, expectant, threaded with an undercurrent that always managed to stir something deep in him. Not power that threatened, but one that demanded awareness, like the echo of a voice he'd known since his first breath. Ceallach didn't need to turn to know who approached. With a flick of his hand, their clothing shimmered into place, the spell effortless, instinctual. Still, he kept Kat in his arms, unwilling to let go—*refusing* to let the moment slip away just because someone had crossed into their sanctuary.

Morrigan, his ma, stepped near his feet, blocking his view of the waterfall and valley beyond.

Air shot through his nose, edged with frustration. "Mother, ye interrupt my evening and block my perfect view."

A similar action escaped her, sharp and stubborn.

"Perfect view, my ass." She pointed at the woman blissfully sleeping in his arms. "Perfect? This is nothing but trouble."

Ceallach shifted. "Shh, she needs her sleep."

A short breath puffed from his ma, sharp as a scold. "Shh, what crap. Ye sent her to a deep sleep." She folded her arms. "Mating with a human is against the law."

Ceallach stared at Kat in his arms. "An old law." His eyes rose, challenging his mother. "One many have broken for love." Sitting up, he glanced around and replied sarcastically. "Where is the Fae Council? Not here? Because the leader married a human last year." He settled back next to his sweetheart. "Kat is my love, my soul mate."

Morrigan stared at him a moment, her stare not discomforting. "The game ye play, chasing a human doesn't help matters. Ye must focus, Ceallach. I sense evil all around the MacDougalls now that the gathering is upon us." She sat on a rock beside them. "Ye must take care. The gathering is important."

His breath slipped out slowly as he drew Kat tighter against him. "I know. Not only have I sensed the evil, but Aodhán has as well." Changing the subject, Ceallach sighed. "Has da been back yet?"

Redness bloomed across her cheeks, a flush she couldn't hide. "Eragon is protecting the gale again."

Ceallach noted his mother's blush, then her woeful smile. "It's been almost a thousand years in the human realm. Must he protect them still?"

Morrigan fluffed her skirt out, avoiding his glare. "He made a promise when the young lad saved him." Her gaze rose as she waved her hands out. "He is what he is. Ye should know this, being his son." She looked to the valley before her—her eyes seemingly not focused on anything. "But he visits often." She turned to him, her focus moving to Kat in his arms and then back to his. "As soul mates in the Fae realm, we shall have eternity together." Morrigan nodded. "As it is with all soul mates."

Ceallach glanced down at Kat's relaxed face. "Soul mates."

Morrigan stood shaking her dress. "Aye, well. Enough play time, my son. Ye have yer duty. Now is the time to focus on the stones and Bree." Her gaze traveled over Kat again. "Love must wait for another day." Tilting her head, she grinned. "I admit, Kathryn is a lovely girl for a human."

She sauntered away, calling over her shoulder. "Do not dawdle, son. Mary and Roderick MacDougall approach. Yer time in the Moon Garden is almost up."

****

Kat strode into the kitchen of her home after sleeping blissfully late this morning. She'd expected to wake in Ceallach's arms in the Moon Garden in the Fae realm, but comfort settled over her—familiar walls, familiar scents, wrapping around her like a well-worn blanket. The white flower left on her windowsill sat in their special box, a reminder from Ceallach of his care.

Her ma greeted her with her usual cup of tea. "Good morning, sleepy head."

She took the cup, replying. "Aye, I did sleep late." She took a sip and then turned to join her father at the breakfast table. "I feel refreshed."

As she sat, her da, John chuckled as he spoke. "I slept like a rock last night."

She stared at the back of his newspaper while his

voice came from behind. "I just laid still. All night." Her ma barked a laugh.

Kat tilted her head, not missing a beat. "Dash da, when were rock puns the funniest?"

Her da flipped his paper aside, smiling at her. "During the Stone Age."

Who reads an actual paper anymore? Her da.

Fingertips drummed lightly on the table, her ma's silent nudge for attention. "Ye know, Ceallach is such a wise man."

Evie grabbed a toast from the toast holder and spread butter over the top. "He's Fae, *mother*." Mother, she emphasized, hinting her ma was being simple.

Kat bit into the slice as her da spoke from behind his paper. "Yer ma and I," he folded the paper, smiling at her. "We've had a change of heart towards Ceallach."

Her ma took her hand. "If Evie and Aodhán can make a relationship work, then maybe there's something for ye and Ceallach."

As he flipped the paper back in place, her da spoke—his grin clear in the lift of his voice. "Plus, it would be nice to have Dagda as a relative. A Fae king as yer father-in-law."

Kat finished off the rest of her toast and brushed off her hands as she rose. The thought of Ceallach as her husband made her breathless, nearly weakening her knees. She put her cup in the sink and stared out the window at Loch Etive. The old saying crossed her mind: if *ifs* and *ands* were pots and pans… She mumbled. "I'd be a fly on the wall if the right man came along."

Her ma set her cup in the sink. "What was that, dear?"

Kat shook her head. "Nothing, ma. I'm headed out."

She spent the day on her boat, cleaning and setting everything to order as she liked. When she first walked up to the vessel, she grinned. Hamish had already painted her new name, *Fairy's Wish*, in swirly cursive on the side. When the sunlight hit the name, the words glittered, making Kat smile.

She didn't sail. The vessel needed at least two to sail, and with everyone preparing for the gathering, she didn't want to intrude. She didn't see or hear from Ceallach either but figured he was the busiest of all, overseeing this battle between good and evil. The one thing that kept her going was Ceallach's promise. *I promise Kat, in the end, I will find a way for us to be together.*

In the end. So, for now, she'd wait, content with his vow of love.

****

Two days had passed since her night with Ceallach, and there was still no word from him or Evie. Kat dug the hand spade into the soft earth while she helped her ma weed the garden around the private house area of the Abbey. The job was a yearly routine that, as children, she and Doug had reveled in since they got to get dirty making mud pies, but as they got older, their ma had required actual work from them. Kat pulled a weed and threw the offending plant in the bag with the giant pile while memories of her brother flooded her mind. She welcomed them. Last night's dream flashed again, coming all too clearly into her mind. The twists and turns in the maze were more familiar to her now. She ran through without any dead ends. That is, until black smoke stopped her, and the evil voice offered a riddle— solve it, and she'd find the end...and her brother. Last night, she'd been unable to, and the moment tickled her mind now.

It can't be touched and can't be felt. It can't be seen, heard, or smelled. It lies behind stars and under hills, and any empty holes it fills. It comes early and follows, ends life, and kills laughter. What is it?

Her ma leaned over from the bed of soil beside her. "What was that, Kat?"

Kat shook her head. "Nothing, ma." And dug into another weed, harder this time.

A guttural roar split the distant sky—deep, primal, and thunderous, like mountains grinding against one another. The sound echoed through the valley, shaking the very air with its fury. Kat and her ma froze mid-glare, eyes snapping to the horizon. Then came another cry, higher in pitch but no less terrifying, piercing, shrill, almost metallic, like rage made a sound. The shriek soared above the first, a hunting call laced with triumph or warning. The silence that followed was tighter than a drawn bowstring.

John, her da, came around the corner. "Ye girls, okay?"

Marie stood, wiping her hands on her apron, "Aye, it came from a distance."

A second cry rang out, then a deeper roar thundered in reply—shaking the air with power. Kat shook her head. The second roar—*a clear rage-filled challenge*. She glanced around, noting that the guests on the other side of the abbey yard did not react. Could it be she and her parents were the only ones who heard?

The air thrummed with a soft, silvery chime, each note prickling along her skin as if something unseen stirred close. As Kat stood brushing her hands free, a man materialized before her. She pulled back, putting her hands up, until the form took full shape as Ceallach.

His eyes rested on her, brows creased as he spoke firmly. "John, Marie, yer time is upon ye. Ye must come with me now." He held his hand to the side, not out to Kat. She stepped back, glancing down, unable to meet his tense glare as she sensed her parents move toward him.

Her ma's voice carried. "Kat, ye stay here, dear. Go inside till this is all over." Kat turned on her heel, each step hard and fast. She couldn't watch them go—her him. Off to a battle that split the world between light and shadow, and she was left behind to count the silence.

Ceallach's voice whispered near her ear. "Remember my vow, my promise, Kat." Tears gathered as she turned. From a few feet away, Ceallach held each of her parents' hands. With a twist of his shoulders, all three began to diminish.

She called out. "Ma, Da!" As they wavered, the last image implanted in her mind was her parents' smiles and Ceallach's firm frown, and then all three diminished from view.

Kat stood immobile, feeling like they'd left her in the darkness in full daylight. The sun still burned overhead, but the warm rays touched nothing inside her. She had never known silence could feel so loud, pressing against her ribs, echoing with the footsteps that walked away from her. Not out of cruelty—but out of duty. Out of belief that she wasn't meant for this part of the war. That she couldn't help. That she wasn't chosen. And that cut deeper than any blade. She wasn't afraid of the danger they faced—she was afraid of being forgotten while they faced the battle.

More animalistic roars came, piercing the sky. The people around her went on, oblivious to the battle at hand. She pictured the Chapel in the Woods, all the people she loved in the world lined up as they had in the Great Room, preparing for this day. Would they all survive? She huffed; would any survive?

Kat packed the gardening supplies, trying to take her mind off the monumental event not far from her home. She piled all the tools into the wheelbarrow and hauled the load to the shed as another rumble hit the skies, the strain not distracting her thoughts.

A deeper roar answered, followed by a boom louder than she'd heard before. The resonating explosion reminded Kat of the Fae fight in the yard. Larger and louder. These must be Fae spells cast for battle. She dropped the handles and shut the shed door with a bang, hoping the hard act would elevate her frustration. But her emotions stayed on high. Another explosion and one more echoed across the valley.

Kat walked fast toward her home, boots crunching the gravel path in an urgent rhythm. The wind had picked up, carrying the brittle scent of pine and something older, wilder. Then came a long, lone howl that sliced through the quiet. A call that rose from the distant hills, high and mournful, stretching on like a sorrow that refused to end. Cold and aching, the sound curled around her spine, full of longing and loss. The sound wasn't just the cry of a creature; this was a raw and ancient lament echoing across the land like a ghost remembering a name.

She froze, breath catching, heart thudding against her ribs. The world seemed to hold still, listening. Then the sound faded, swallowed by the trees, leaving only silence behind. But the feeling lingered, lonely, sad, and somehow called her.

Kat turned, running to her car, unable to resist. Her friends and her family were in danger. Her love defended them all. She had to be there, had to try to help. Tires crunched as she slid into the seat, snatched the hidden key, and fired the engine to life. She had to know if those she loved survived.

After driving across Dunbeg like a maniac, Kat skidded to a halt near the stable ruin wall at Dunstaffnage Castle. She'd driven across the lawn, but she didn't care. All she cared about were her family and her friends. Kat tumbled from the car and righted herself, running up the path towards the Chapel in the Woods. Booms and roars filled the sky, so loud her ears numbed with vibrations. Not heeding the fear in her heart, she ran into the chapel clearing, and the doorway to the nave stood open. She ran towards the chapel, and another bellow pierced the sky. Before crossing the threshold, she glanced up and a dragon, black as night, flew overhead, a tail clipping the roof and sending debris everywhere.

She screamed and ran into the safety of the religious building to come skidding to a halt. Everyone stood in their places like they had the day of the meeting. Bree, in her typical khakis, and a tee held by Colin in his jeans, was before the window for love on her right, and her ma and da in their work clothing to her left, before the window for fear. As her eyes followed, all the others lined up till she came to the altar where Ceallach stood, his wings out, arms raised.

When she gasped, he lowered his arms, and his glare met hers across the nave. "No, Kat!" He flung his hand out, and something hit her. She fell as darkness consumed her.

****

Ceallach flung his hand out, sending a spell toward Kat. When the force hit, she jolted and crumpled. Her body disappeared, and he sighed in relief. Knowing she couldn't resist staying away from the gathering, he feared it'd come to this. However much his act pained him, he'd prepared for her arrival. There was only one place he could send her where she'd be safe and occupied for a while. He only hoped he bought enough time till the battle ended.

Marie's scream tore through the air, sharp enough to make Ceallach's spine bristle. "Kathryn!"

Then her da's roar followed, thick with fury. "Damnit, where did she go?" Another dragon screeched in the air as an explosion hit the roof.

Bree's voice cut through, strained and urgent. "Colin, do something. They tear apart my Chapel!" Colin held her firm in his arms while she tried to wiggle free.

Another deep roar and crash came as debris fell from the ceiling, which Ceallach's minor protectant spell had blocked and needed little energy to manage. Everyone covered their heads, but Ceallach kept an eye on the roof. The frame was about to give way soon. He needed to see which dragon was which, to know who to focus on. He needed to help her transition of the Iona Stones.

Aodhán called out over the commotion. "Where did ye send Kat?" Another crash and more rubble fell, opening the rooftop, his shield protecting all within.

Ceallach yelled back, adding magic, so all heard over the dragons. "To the Fae realm, the labyrinth." As more debris dropped, another boom hit the roof, and a black dragon flew by. So, the evil one appeared, and he's exactly who Ceallach suspected he would be.

Evie's cry cracked, like glass splintering in his ear. "Manix, he's here!"

John's shout punched through the noise. "A maze in the Fae realm?" Marie held on to her husband, and her fear for their daughter flooded Ceallach's mind.

Aodhán held his wife tightly as he called out. "A large maze that's difficult to solve. Don't worry. She is safe."

In his jeans and loose shirt, Ewan held a shaking Lorelei while her white dress floated around her. "The badman, he's here."

Ewan whispered something in her ear as his words came to Ceallach. *I've beat Manix before, love, and we are all here now. We will win.*

Manix flew, hovering over the group, his focus turning to Evie. He held his claw out, sending a spell, and Ewan threw up a blocking power, hitting Manix and forcing him to tumble back, falling from the sky. A loud splash of water and a resounding blast came as the ground shook beneath them, signaling Manix had fallen into the shallows of Loch Etive.

A white dragon flew by, landing on the edge of the chapel wall. Her pure white wings glittered as she folded them in. Ceallach had not expected such, but she was there before him. An *aingeal* in every sense, clothed in the mighty form of a dragon. Light spilled across her incandescent scales, each one catching the sun like fire caught in crystal. Her radiance didn't burn—it *blessed*, and in that moment, he could only stare.

She hovered for a breath, her luminous eyes sweeping the gathered souls below. Then came a single, aching wail—low, mournful, and impossibly tender.

The dragon inside Ceallach went still. He felt her

sorrow as if her emotion were his own, her heart laid bare. No malice touched her intent. Only grief. An unbearable weight of caring too deeply. She honestly did not wish any of them harm.

A sharp breath hitched from Evie, catching like a snag in cloth. "Her sorrow, I sense her feelings. Why is she so sad!" Even from the nave, the white dragon's mournful note rippled through the half-blood Fae, brushing Ceallach's senses like a sorrowful wind.

Dominic held his wife Moira both in shirts and pants as he yelled. "I don't give a shit what they feel." He turned to Ceallach. "Let's get this thing going before they tear us all apart!"

Energy built—thick and volatile, crackling through the air like a storm breaking a leash. The ground hummed with power, the sky seeming to hold a breath. Then, with a sudden, violent snap, a force tore through the clearing and slammed into the white dragon.

She screamed—an agonized cry that echoed off the stones—as her wings flared wide and lifted her into the air, pain driving her ascent. Manix followed close behind, his dark form streaking through the sky in ruthless pursuit.

Ceallach needed to initiate the gathering. He wasn't sure how much longer the white dragon could hold out, and he could only hold the master protecting spell for so long to kept the maidens safe. He raised his hands to the sky as his wings flexed farther out. He summoned the elements—*all* of them. Earth groaned beneath his feet, ancient and awakening. Wind howled in response, circling him like a living force. Fire sparked at his fingertips, eager, volatile. And air—the very breath between worlds—thickened, drawing tight like a bowstring.

Ceallach opened himself to their power, feeling each one answer his call with primal urgency. Magic surged through him, raw and unfiltered, as if the land itself knew what approached.

This was no simple spell. This was a reckoning. The storm would break—and he would be ready.

Aodhán sent him a mind speak. *I hope the labyrinth will be long enough for Kat. She's safe until she figures out the maze. Yet, she's smart. Ye may not have enough time.*

Ceallach replied, the message mixed with a prayer. *Time is what I pray for.*

Chapter 15

Kat rolled over, dizzy and nauseous as she dry heaved. The world still spun, and she tried to grip the ground but could not hold anything. Holding her palms flat, she pushed up to a familiar view. The sandstone wall from her dreams. Was she in a dream? Pushing against the wall, she stood on shaky legs as she turned. The only way out was to her right.

She called out, "Hello, anybody there?" Her voice echoed into the emptiness as though the space itself had no end. She took a deep breath and another while she gained her bearings. Taking small steps, she proceeded forward, uncertain if she was in a dream or real life.

She yelled again into the empty space, "Hey!" Her voice echoed as before. Her steps quickened, breath tight as the path split ahead. She stopped, and her memory flashed. *Men go left because women are always right.*

She was in the maze, the one from her dreams. Slowly turning a full circle, she searched for something hidden within or without. Right, she needed to go right. When she turned that way, flashes of memory came from her dreams. Up ahead was another turn. Right would be the black smoke; left, who knew? She jogged to the fork and took the left. More memories came to her—another left, then the two rights. As her confidence rose, she picked up speed—the end, she had to get to the end.

Something nagged her mind. Someone followed.

When she turned to look back, she hit something solid and fell on her back. Black smoke circled her like in her dream. The familiar heady musk scent accompanied the fog as the fog swirled around her. She scooted backward, trying to escape the black mist, but the cloud followed.

A low rumble crawled through the air, heavy and dark, curling around her like a voice that knew her name too well. "And where is my lovely pet going now?"

Backed against a wall, Kat used the surface to leverage herself to stand. "Out of here!"

Laughter slid from him, low and rough, like a secret meant just for her. "I think not, Kitty. Come, let's play a game."

Her shout snapped through the air, cutting just as hard. "No! I won't play your games anymore!"

He bellowed, forcing a gust on her face. "Ye will if ye want to see yer brother alive." The wind blew the smoke away, giving her the view of her path forward. She took off at a run with the intent of finding the end.

The evil chased her, his breath in her ear as he spoke. "That's not the way we play, Kitty." At the fork, she took the left without question. She had to survive to the end.

Her steps faltered at the dead end, chest heaving, each breath pounding like a drum inside her head. She turned a full circle, but the way back was a whole wall again. He'd truly trapped her now.

Black smoke coiled back in, the voice slithering through the fog like a shadow come to speak. "Come, Kitty. Ye haven't solved my last riddle."

Kat screamed as loud as she could, enhancing the thought with as much mental force she had. "No, ye are not real!"

The smoke curled in on itself, rising higher—taller

than she was, though that wasn't saying much. Shadows shimmered within the haze, coalescing into something more.

The shape drifted forward, silent, unbound by gravity, as if the very air bent to his will.

Her breath caught. The swirling mist peeled away in wisps, revealing the figure of a man where there had been none before—as if he'd stepped from another realm entirely, summoned by magic and smoke. He was older, yet handsome with dark hair deeper than Ceallach's, if that was possible. Trimmed sharp along his jaw, his beard angled clean in a way she'd never seen before. The heady smoke wafted stronger now, almost dizzying. When he floated toward her, the air itself seemed to still. His smile curved with eerie grace—beautiful and wrong all at once—and his expression chilled her to the bone. She wanted to look away, to run, but something in his presence rooted her in place, ancient and unknowable. Curiosity surged, reckless and defiant, rising above the warning drumbeat of her instincts.

Her voice slipped out, barely a breath. "Who are ye?"

His mouth didn't move, but his voice came to her. *I am Balor, King of the Fomoire, the evil Fae. Kitty, ye must answer my riddle if ye want to see yer loved ones again.* Taking her chin in his firm grip, he kissed her full on the mouth.

Lifting his head with a grin, he gripped her hard. *It can't be touched and can't be felt. It can't be seen, heard, or smelled. It lies behind stars and under hills, and any empty hole it fills. It comes early and follows after, ends life, and kills laughter. What is it?*

****

211

Another explosion cracked the air, spewing rocks in every direction. The white dragon veered hard, her wings clawing for balance, but Ceallach caught the tremor in her flight. She didn't flee. Could've soared off to the safety of the skies, but she circled back—closer to the chapel. Her gaze cut to the walls, to the mortals sheltered inside, and her tail lashed, a flick of frustration. She knew Manix aimed for more than her. She stayed for her duty, despite knowing each blast chipped at her strength. Ceallach had to start the end, or Manix would wear them all down, gaining all the stones for the evil Fae and tossing the realms into dark times.

He shouted, his voice laced with raw magic, tearing through the chaos like a blade of wind. The clang of steel and cries of battle fell away as his words echoed, impossible to ignore—commanding, unyielding, and heard by all. "Each maiden must go to the box under their window and call their stone."

As each woman proceeded, Bree hesitated. "My chapel."

Colin embraced her as they shuffled toward the window for love. "Shh, Bree. Ye rebuilt the building before and shall again." He kissed her, and his whisper came to Ceallach's mind. *This is only a building. Ye, my love, are more important than anything.*

She is more important than anything, echoed in Ceallach's heart. He shook his head. He needed to focus. Kat was safe.

Ceallach raised his arms, bracing for the surge as his shield spell shifted, his voice cutting through the storm as he called out. "The shield must position himself behind the maiden so she may call the stone." Each couple obeyed, moving into position while Ceallach anchored the master shield, the magic flaring to cover every soul beneath. "Now, using yer love for one another, call yer stone. Focus on each emotion and fold them over with yer love for your mate."

Colin held Bree, their love a visible current between them, and the Stone of Love rose from the box beneath the window, drawn to Bree's open hands. The red, heart-shaped gem pulsed with a radiant glow as the stone settled into the maiden's grasp—just as Manix's roar tore through the air. Ceallach braced, channeling more power into the shield, locking the barrier tighter around them.

Across the nave, Marie clasped the Stone of Faith. The gem ignited in a steady violet light as she and John met each other's gaze—one look, full of unshaken belief—before they turned their attention fully to the stone.

Moira's hands glowed green as Dominic held her. "I'll be damned, this works!"

Evie and Aodhán's bond burned bright, unquestioning—and the Stone of Doubt rose effortlessly into her hands. The yellow gem shimmered as the absence of hesitation between them surged, transforming uncertainty into power.

Lorelei reached for the Stone of Faith, the sacred gem her people had venerated for generations. The moment her fingers touched the rock, she cried out and doubled over, as if the weight of that legacy struck her all at once.

Ewan yelled over the dragon's roars. "Ceallach, now would be a great time to finish this. I think Lorelei may be in labor."

His wife spoke between clenched teeth. "Love, I believe your son wants to meet you now."

Ceallach risked drawing power from the shield, exhaling a healing breath toward where Ewan held Lorelei. The white mist swept over her—then dulled to grey, the telltale shimmer of energy spent and healing complete.

Lorelei took a few deep breaths and stood tall. "I can do this. I must do this."

Ewan kissed her cheek. "That's my girl."

A boom hit, scattering rocks. Rocks? Ceallach had the shield up. When he turned, the roof above Evie had broken fully away from an attack from Manix.

At the end, Ainslie bent over the box beneath the window for lust. "My stone doesn't want to come to me!"

Aodhán's voice chased him, rough and cutting like a thrown stone. "Lust seeks another!"

Manix flew overhead, hovering as he sent a mindspeak. *Of course, the gem does. An evil stone knows its master.*

Manix hurled another spell, dark and seething. Aodhán sprang into motion, throwing up a shield over Rannick and Ainslie. *Not in this lifetime or another, Manix.* The vow crackled through the air as Aodhán shifted, his magic arcing wide until the protective sphere fully enclosed the couple. Ceallach couldn't sense what passed within, the spell veiled too tightly—but he trusted their love would hold strong where magic could not.

The black stone flew into Ainslie's hand. "I have the gem!" Aodhán dropped his protection, allowing Ceallach to proceed to the next stage.

Ceallach called out to all, adding magic to be heard. "The shield must position himself behind the maiden, so she faces the center of the chapel." Each couple rotated as every shield held their love and protected her in his arms.

Manix came at Ceallach's shield, but he held the spell hard, feeding off the love between the couples.

As the white dragon flew by again, Manix hit her with his tail. She cried out as she tilted but righted, staying close to the chapel. They needed to hurry. The white dragon could only hold out so long, a fact Manix counted on and used. Ceallach closed his eyes, drawing a steady breath as he reached inward, centering his energy. One by one, he called to the gods—old and forgotten, light and shadow—summoning their strength to stand with him now.

As their powers filled his body, mind and soul, he sent a mind message to Bree, starting the last task the Iona Stones had under the MacDougall guardianship. *Bree, come to the light.* Ceallach called upon the Stone of Destiny, his voice steady but thrumming with power as ancient syllables rolled from his tongue. The moment his hand touched the surface, the stone pulsed beneath his fingers—once, like a heartbeat—and then a shock of energy surged outward.

The power wasn't just light or sound. This energy was *presence*, a raw, living force that radiated from the stone and filled the chapel like a storm turned inward. The floor trembled. Stained-glass windows rattled in their frames. A golden-blue radiance burst from the center, spiraling into the rafters like a column of divine fire.

Every soul present absorbed the force—deep in their bones, in their blood, as if the energy itself rewrote them from the inside out. All in the chapel cried out in a single, instinctive gasp, not from pain but from the overwhelming weight of something sacred, something far greater than any one of them. The air thickened with power, humming with the voices of Fae long gone and destinies yet to come.

Ceallach didn't flinch. He stood rooted, eyes glowing faintly, his body the conduit between earth and legend. The Stone had heard him—and the sacred gem had answered.

Concentrating on the Stone of Destiny, he continued his lifelong duty. *The maiden summoned the stone, and she must take her place.*

Colin called out, the desperation in his voice clear. "Bree?"

She yelled back, firm and sure. "Colin, the stone calls me. I must."

Ceallach opened his eyes as Colin grabbed Bree, and she sidestepped. "I am the maiden of the stones."

Colin bellowed as he reached for her. "No, I cannot protect ye if ye are not in my arms." He strode forward again, intent on protecting his soul mate.

Manix flew overhead, taunting Colin, taking advantage of his anger. "Come, human, come at me for yer love."

Colin's roar tore from his throat, a sound steeped in rage and defiance, aimed squarely at Manix. "I beat Balor. I shall beat ye as well." He stepped farther beneath the shattered roof as his intention to confront Manix came strongly to Ceallach.

No! He had to remain by the window to power the stone, or he'd leave an opening to the stream of power leading directly to the stone maiden, Bree. If Manix hit that, the spell would hit Bree, killing her.

The words burst from Ceallach, hard-edged and

unrelenting. "Colin, control yer anger. Ye must remain by the window for love."

Colin's voice crashed into his like a thrown hammer, thick with defiance. "He will not have my love if I can prevent it!"

Focusing, Ceallach sent him a mind speak. *Colin, remember. Yer anger will be yer undoing.* The stone guardian stopped as Ceallach sensed the memory of Brigid's warning flood Colin's mind.

A rumble came from Colin as he stepped back. "Protect her with yer life!"

Ceallach's mind message replied. *I will.*

The ruined chapel split into three arenas: before the altar, where Bree stood beneath the rose-window cross; the nave, where the six couples formed a ring of power; and the gaping sky-hole, a jagged mouth in the roof that vomited wind and dragons in equal measure.

As Bree stepped into the shaft of energy pulsing from the Stone of Destiny, the wind rose with a howl, circling the chapel like a living force. Magic surged, drawn inward, gathering into a single blazing point. The Stone had been summoned—and now, at last, destiny would answer the call of the good Fae.

Bree clutched the Stone of Love to her chest, the gems glow casting streaks of light along the tear-tracks on her cheeks. Ceallach's chest tightened, but he couldn't spare a glance—couldn't break focus to comfort her.

Manix swooped low, unleashing a spell with deadly precision aimed straight at Bree. Ceallach shifted his stance, hands steady as he channeled power into the shield, forcing the barrier to catch each blow before the hex struck.

Manix snapped, *Damn ye, Fae. The stones are mine. They belong to the Fomoire.*

Above Manix, the white dragon wheeled and struck—her spell landed clean, and for the first time, Manix faltered. He tumbled from the sky like a wounded star, crashing to earth beside the chapel. The impact rocked the ground, tremors rattling through stone and shield alike. Yet every maiden held fast, every barrier stood unbroken.

Overhead, the white dragon circled once more, her low, haunting moan echoing like a lament through the storm-laced sky. She didn't have feelings for Manix, did she?

Ceallach chastised himself. *Focus on the stones; that's all that matters.*

He anchored the shield with unwavering focus as he gave the following directive. "The maidens must offer their stone to the stone's maiden."

As she held the Stone of Doubt to her chest, Evie shouted. "But we will let them go."

Aodhán yelled for all to hear. "Evie, that's the plan." He kissed her cheek and called again. "Trust me." His head came up, and he made eye contact with each shield and maiden. "It's time to let them go."

Marie's voice rang sharply across the space. "I trust in the stones. I have no fear!"

As Moira held the glowing green Stone of Hope, her face lifted. "I hear them! I have hope!"

Lorelei held the blue Stone of Faith towards Bree. "I have faith." She bent over. "Hurry, I can't hold out much longer!"

The stone gleamed as Ainslie pushed her hands out. "I willingly give my stone to the maiden." Five stones streaked from their maidens' hands, converging above Bree in a blaze of color trails matching each stone. The chorus of assent washed over Ceallach, a tide of hope he drew into the shield-spell.

****

Kat's heart raced—the evil Fae King. Wait, Evie said he was dead. Kat's focus rose, stopping on the face of the man who stood before her. *He's not real.*

He chuckled as his voice echoed in her mind. *Hello Kitty.* He folded his arms, taking a casual stance that didn't fool Kat. This man was pure evil. Wickedness dripped from him like rotten sap from a tree. He shifted closer as Kat took a step back. A heady musk scent filled her nose, and she blew out, trying to keep his evil away from her.

He breathed near her, *Mmm, flowers. So sweet an aura ye have, Kitty.* His glare held hers. *I shall enjoy killing ye if ye don't get me my stones.*

Kat blinked, snapping her reply. "Before, it was a riddle. Now it's some damned stones." She bent, locking her eyes on his. "Which is it, goblin?" She smiled, using Laird Mac's term. The insult demeaned the *badman*, as Lorelei called him.

She stood straight, fixing her gaze on the darkened path beside her. "I think ye don't even know." Turning his demands over in her mind, realization dawned on her. The answer to the riddle was her way out.

She inched toward the dark opening as she spoke. "It can't be touched and can't be felt. It can't be seen, heard, or smelled. It lies behind stars and under hills, and any empty hole it fills. It comes early and follows after, ends life, and kills laughter. What is it?"

Kat yelled. "Darkness!" She turned and ran for the

dark pathway, hoping to find her salvation in the answer, in the blackness. She hit a wall and burst through with the force, tumbling head over heels onto dirt and grass. When she stopped, she quickly sat up and turned. She'd come out of the chapel door into the chapel yard. As she stood, all the people she cared for stood inside the now ruined chapel.

Seeing Ceallach, she called for him. "Ceallach!"

****

One by one, the stones floated and absorbed into the Stone of Love Bree held over her head. Ceallach took a deep breath. One stage left, the transfer, and all he'd lived for would be complete, leaving him free to pursue his wishes, his dreams.

His name came on the wind, then firmer. He turned, and the sight that met his eyes rocked his world to pieces. Kat stood outside the chapel door—outside his shield. His heart thumped to his throat. He had no way to protect his love and the stone maiden simultaneously. One of his fears, now faced a potential reality with no solution in sight. Kat as a maiden, a target of the evil Fae. He had to stay the course, focus on his mission, but not his love.

Ceallach called out. "Kat, no!"

She strode toward the chapel door as Manix's mind speak came to Ceallach. *If the shield won't let me have Bree and the stones.* His chuckle filled Ceallach's mind. *I'll take the next best thing—his love.*

Manix swooped overhead, and the spell struck Kat with brutal force. Ceallach's breath caught as her body lifted from the ground and hurled down the path. She hit hard, landing on her back with a sickening thud that echoed in his chest. Ceallach shouted, his voice cutting through the chaos as Marie and John jolted in alarm.

Manix struck again—then again—each blast slamming into Kat. Her body convulsed with every hit, and Ceallach's heart roared with helpless fury.

Aodhán's shout cut through the clamor. "No! We all must remain in position." His mind-speak hit Ceallach. *The new guardian awaits Ceallach. Finish this!*

Ceallach's gaze shot skyward. Hovering above Bree, the white dragon beat her wings in silent vigil. Below her, the stone maiden stood firm, holding the Stone of Love high. Ceallach poured energy into Bree, channeling the spell with all the precision he had left.

A bright oval stone erupted through Bree's aura, shooting upward like a blazing comet. Bree cried out as the light pierced through her—raw, divine, unrelenting. In the rays' wake, a streak of her hair turned white, the mark of something ancient awakened.

Colin went toward her as Aodhán called out. "No, Colin, the maiden must complete the task alone!"

The stone guardian's shout cracked the air. "Bree! The maiden's sacrifice!"

She tossed her words back, sharp and quick. "Colin, I'm fine. The stones protect me!"

Sensing Kat's life force bleeding away, ebbing like a tide with each passing breath. A scream clawed up Ceallach's chest, but he locked his jaw and swallowed the temptation down, refusing to let his focus break free. He could not shift his gaze, not even a flicker. Turning to her to save her would take only a moment, a breath, a single heartbeat. One movement and the power within him could rush to her aid, sever Manix's cruel magic, and call her soul back from the edge. He could feel the path, just there, within reach. But to do so would leave the Stones of Iona unguarded, the maiden vulnerable.

221

A cold wind coiled around him, the telltale shiver of the Fae slithering closer, sensing weakness, waiting for the slip. The air buzzed with ancient tension, with energy barely contained, as though time held a breath.

Ceallach stood unmoving, arms trembling as he held the shimmering shield in place, the glow flickering with strain. The magic surged through him, a conduit of will, binding past and present, the fate of the realms funneling through his bones. This—*this*—was the moment his fate carved for him. He had trained for this, bled for this, and been bound to his purpose by powers older than stone or song. And still, the sound of his love's pain cut through everything.

Each spell Manix hurled at Kat struck not only her, but echoed in Ceallach's soul like shrapnel, tearing through memory and heart. He could hear her—barely—her voice calling his name. Or were her cries only in his mind? A cruel echo from the gods? Tears welled, but he did not blink. His heart cracked with each beat, but he did not move.

"No," he whispered, so low the stones might have been the only ones to hear. "My duty first."

He locked eyes with the ancient monolith, the Stones of Iona inside the Stone of Love now pulsing with eerie, silent light. They *knew* the cost. They *felt* the toll, too. But they did not bend, and neither could he.

Kat's life hung by a thread. His soul frayed with hers. But if the stones fell, if evil took them, that act would mean ruin not just for this world but all realms. Each heartbeat that passed without saving her was a blade to his soul—but still, he stood because he must.

As he ignored his dying love, he took a breath and spoke the stone transfer spell, "I give ye hope that faith is believing without seeing. No doubts. Open yer heart to faith which grows, lusting for love. As ye take these stones, have no fear in their guardianship. They shall guard ye as ye protect them."

The Stone of Love, the red radiant heart gem faded into the off-white glowing stone, which lifted from Bree's hands as she called out. "I feel it. The power, the love." The powerful single stone flew higher. The marble-like jewel struck the dragon's chest—then, as if melting into the beam, the gem dissolved into her, leaving a pulsing light at her breast. The dragon gave a roar that echoed across the land and took off in flight toward Ben Chruchen. At her departure, Manix stopped his attack on Kat and turned, staring after the white dragon as she flew away.

He flew, hovering over the chapel, sending a mind message meant for all to hear. *Ye may have the stones, but I have the female dragon and soon the Stones of Iona.* As he glided over Kat's prone body, he chuckled. *And the life of the shield's soul mate.*

A bellow tore from Manix as he shot skyward, hunting the white dragon with savage speed.

Ceallach lowered his shield. The stones were with the new guardian. The burden was now upon her. A moment of stillness marked the end of a journey, the stone's last duty with the MacDougalls. As if starting from a frozen breath of existence, all around him erupted in chaos. He stilled, and time shifted into slow motion.

Bree sighed and fainted in the chapel. Lorelei cried out when her water broke, and the cycle of a new generation was upon the MacDougalls. Colin rushed to Bree, scooping her in his arms as she stirred. Everyone gathered around Bree while Ewan led Lorelei to the

Loch, as she announced that her son must come into the world in the water as she had.

It all dimmed as Ceallach stood gaping at Kat's prone body. He didn't think, just shifted to her, taking her limp body in his arms. Tears gathered, and he sensed her spirit left her. He drew in the air and blew a healing breath on her face. Nothing. He cried out, pressing his hand to her heart, reaching for the bond—trying to force a heart meld. Nothing came. No spark, no thread of life. Ceallach rocked back and forth, anguish tearing through him as the silence of her stillness screamed louder than any battle cry. Marie and John rushed to kneel beside him.

Marie took Kat's hand, her love feeding his power. "Can ye save her?"

A bellow burst from Ceallach. "I'm trying!"

Aodhán's hand rested on his shoulders. "Ye cannot do a heart meld without the Stone of Love."

Ceallach lifted his head and yelled to the gods. "Why now? Why wait to take her when I don't have the stones to help?" A light wind blew, but no answer came.

Kat's body grew lighter in his arms as Aodhán whispered. "There is only one way to save her."

Ceallach knew what his cousin referred to. He stood shaking everyone off as he lifted and held Kat's limp body close to his. "Aye, between the realms. The Veil where she must make a choice."

His cousin stood back, holding Evie's hand. "It's the only way. Her choice must lie with ye." Aodhán fingered his Fae immortal necklace. The one his wife gifted him at their wedding. A twin to the one he'd given her and his immortality to save her life.

Aodhán's lips twitched, the tease clear before he

even spoke. "If she accepts yer gift, cousin."

A rough sound escaped him, sharp and low, as if daring another word, "Of course, she will accept my gift. She is my soul mate."

He turned, facing Marie and John, certainty thread through his reply. "I will save her, I promise."

With a flick of his shoulders, he transported into the Fae realm, holding the body of his love, his soul mate, with her life held in the balance of her choice.

Chapter 16

Aodhán's gaze tracked the dragons' retreat, a dawning clarity tightening his brow. The Stone of Destiny Fae fable wasn't about anyone there. This was about her, the stone's guardian.

The fable echoed in his mind. "You are the one who sees me for me." With a dragon as the stone's guardian, everything made sense.

Another part echoed through his mind. *The true love of a servant of the stones shall no longer be the maiden's sacrifice for evil. Was happily ever after possible for them all?* He held Evie closer and sensed her love lift his heart.

Marie and John stood holding each other, staring at where Ceallach had just stood, holding their daughter's body in his arms.

Marie choked out, "Please, God, save her soul."

John turned, kissing her head. "I trust Ceallach. His love for our daughter will save her as ours has us." He moved back till they gazed into each other's eyes. "I thank God for our best blessing. Our love."

Colin slipped an arm around Bree's waist, lifting her gently to her feet. "Yer hair, *mo chridhe*. It's part white."

Her hand went to her head as she wobbled. "I do feel different." Bree's focus went to where the dragons flew. "If the black dragon is Manix, who is the white one?" She turned to Aodhán, masking the falter in her knees with a stubborn lift of her chin. "The new guardian? Will she be able to protect the stones?"

Aodhán glanced over the mountain range where the dragons had flown. "Aye. The MacDougalls have completed their duty."

As Evie stepped closer to her parents, Colin's huff sounded loud. "The chapel door, will it still be a portal?

Evie turned, staring at the closed wooden doors as Aodhán spoke. "It will always serve the Fae, even when Bree rebuilds the roof again." His wife shivered in his arms, her skin flickering with faint light before vanishing. Aodhán felt the spark beneath his palms—her Fae magic radiating from her.

Aodhán glanced at the doors, then back at his wife. "What is it?"

She moved stiffly, her expression vacant, lips parted but silent. "The Dunstaffnage ghost has found peace." A smile graced her face. "Now that the stones have left, she can rest eternally." Aodhán caressed her face as a woman's scream pierced the air.

Ewan yelled over the resounding echoes of his wife's cries. "I could use a little help over here. My son is about to enter the world!" Bree jolted out of Colin's arms, stumbling to the loch's shore, followed by the rest of the group. Aodhán stepped aside as Colin shoved forward, and Bree dropped to her knees beside her daughter-in-law, gently taking her hand, while Ewan gathered his wife into his arms. Lorelei grunted, and she clenched her teeth.

Moira knelt on the other side of the soon mother to be. "Breathe, honey, you've got to breathe."

Dominic stood behind her. "Moira, there's more to this than just breathing."

227

His wife rolled her eyes. "Says the man who fainted when our Olivia came into the world."

Rannick held Ainslie as she stood behind her parents. "There's nothing to it. Women do this all the time and have for centuries."

Lorelei growled through clenched teeth. "Ewan, we will never have sex again!" With a loud, long scream from the future mother, the baby popped from her body into the loch's water.

Ewan scooped up the wiggly baby with a fishtail, announcing to all. "It's a boy!"

Colin yelled at the same time. "He's a merman!"

When Ewan lifted the baby from the water, his fish tail wavered, forming two human legs.

Bree gripped Colin's arm. "He's perfect!"

****

Clouds swirled around her ankles, cool mist curling along her skin as she hovered weightless in an endless sky. Her body didn't hurt as she had only moments ago, and the pressure on her head eased. The pain that consumed her earlier had disappeared completely. She turned, searching for something, anything, but met only clouds.

She shook her head, recalling her last memory. The grass prickled against her skin, each breath came easier while shadows of dragons crossed overhead. She'd heard people scream, but the sounds made no sense. Turning again, she caught movement—a white flower drifting through the air toward her. As the bloom neared, the flower was familiar. She'd seen them many times and kept them all in a secret box in her room. The white Camellia floated before her, bringing a smile to her face as each one had before.

Ceallach's voice tickled her ear. "Take it *mo bruadarach.*" Kat's hand rose and cupped the flower now resting in her palm.

The clouds parted with her turn, revealing Ceallach standing firm in the haze, as if he'd always been there. "It *was* ye all along, the flowers." Ceallach grinned.

She pulled the flower to her chest. "Where are we?"

Ceallach brushed his hand on her cheek, the touch fleeting. "The Veil."

Kat lifted her gaze to his eyes. "The Veil?" She tried to reason the scientific explanation of a veil, only thinking of tulle, flowers, and a wedding.

The corner of his mouth lifted, a warm sound slipping free. "Ah, the scientific mind battles the heart. The best way I can explain The Veil is, we float in the thread between our worlds. That of the human and the Fae."

Her body shifted back, uncertainty flooding her mind. "Why are we here?"

Ceallach's focus dropped, and she caught the flicker of thought behind his gaze. "At the end of every narrow road lies redemption. The choice of what redemption it is, is up to ye."

Kat wasn't sure what he meant, and the scientific part of her mind shut down even though she tried to reason what he meant and what had occurred. "I don't understand."

Ceallach floated away from her and took her hand in his. "Every human who serves the Stones of Iona must make a choice. Ye reach salvation still, yet the Fae grant a choice: what shape will yer eternity take? The choice of life in the afterworld as ye know it. Or…"

She floated with him, not needing to take a step as

her desire to be with him came strong. "Or?"

He took her in his arms as comfort washed over her. "I call the choice a Fairy's wish." He brought her hand that held the flower between their faces. "The other part of the choice is living in my world, the Fae realm." The time tale he told flashed in her mind. *Value what time ye are given. Time is a fleeting thing, more precious than ye can ever know.*

He kissed her lightly as his breath brushed them when he spoke. "If ye accept my gift, we shall have eternity here in the Fae realm." Ceallach lifted his head, removed his Fae immortal necklace, and placed the chain on her neck. "I gift ye my immortality." He stopped, not closing the clasp as his eyes met hers. "Do ye accept my gift, Kat?"

Tears gathered. She'd dreamed of his gifting her with his immortal necklace since first meeting him, since learning what the necklaces meant. Her mind turned over the meaning of his gift, his sacrifice.

Her free hand gripped his, stopping his completion. "But doesn't this mean ye will be mortal, like Aodhán?"

He bent, kissing her ear. "Aye, if gifted in the human realm. But here…"

Slowly, he raised his head, locking his gaze with hers. "It makes ye immortal."

Her breath caught, and she had to gasp to speak. "Ye mean forever, as in eternity?"

Ceallach's nod came once, firm. "But ye must accept my gift to make it so."

Kat swallowed as more tears gathered. "Aye, I accept."

He closed the clasp as he whispered. "Forever, my soul is kept in this stone. A part of my blood, a part of my bone. A piece of myself I give to thee. A part of my soul for all eternity."

His head rose, and her breath slipped out. "A fairy's wish." Her wish for them to live together in eternity.

Ceallach touched her cheek. "Aye, with the discovery of true love, its power will give you the desire of your heart and make all your plans succeed."

Kat giggled as lightness filled her body. "What now?"

The moment his hand closed over hers, the air shifted. They rose together, the vast sprawl of the Fae realm unfolding like a living map beneath their feet. "A life together for eternity."

****

Weeks later, Kat walked down the aisle of her wedding in the Fae realm, led by a proud Annie who spread white Camellia petals before her. Kat's da, John, walked beside her as they made their way to the end of the throne room, where Dagda stood ready to preside over her and Ceallach's bonding ceremony in the Fae realm. As her da took small steps, keeping his promise to allow her to savor the moment, they passed people from the Fae. Some of whom she recognized, some not.

When they got closer to the end, where the balcony opened to the cliff off Broemere Castle and the sea beyond, they passed the guests from the human realm. Moira and Dom sat as Moira held a napping Olivia. Next were Ewan and Lorelei, who held their infant son, Percy, whom they'd named after Titan's brother. Evie winked at her when she passed them with a grin. When they reached the end, Evie waved Annie to her. The child ran into her ma's lap, giggling as they sat beside her grandparents, Colin and Bree. Bree still showed some effects of the Iona Stones transfer. There was a white streak in her hair, but there was also a tiredness about her she'd dismissed as age.

When Kat's da passed her off, he didn't say anything. Earlier, she'd met with her parents along with others who had passed and lived in the Fae realm now for the first time since her passage from the human realm to the Fae realm.

As her da kissed her cheek, his declaration rang in her mind. "Kathryn, yer ma and I are so happy ye found love." He huffed. "Even if it is with a Fae boy."

The flush climbed fast, and she looked down, heart knocking harder. "Da, he's a man."

Her da stood tall, pointing a finger at her. "I always warned ye be careful of a bargain with the Fae."

She grabbed the end, saying "Da" again in three syllables.

Her brother Doug had interrupted. "Da, the Fae bargains aren't so bad. The world here is nice."

Granny Mac had chuckled. "It was I who warned yer father about promises made. But, aye, everything all turned out so nice." Douglas MacArthur, her grandfather from the past, with his wife in his arms, had wiggled his bushy eyebrows.

When her da pulled back and winked after kissing her cheek, she knew everything would be okay. Doug, Abigail, and all their children couldn't participate in the ceremony if attendees from the human realm were present. However, they still shared a meaningful moment with the others from the past living in the Fae realm. She smiled as she turned to face Ceallach for their vows of commitment. There would be many more moments with her brother. They both now had eternity.

An animalistic roar sounded throughout the valley below. Kat tilted her head to the side. She'd heard the sound before in this realm as the image of a large greenish-blue dragon flying through the sky flashed in her memory. In the balcony opening, the same blue-green dragon flew past, rocking the room with another rumble. He drifted up, rotated in the air, and flew towards them. Kat stepped back, and Ceallach gripped her hand, keeping her in place. As the dragon flew fast through the balcony opening, the shape twisted and morphed into a man who ran hard at them. He looked much like Ceallach, tall with jet-black hair and built like a bodybuilder. His shirt hugged his muscular build as his kilt swayed as he ran, one in the old highland fashion Kat recognized from the reenactment events at Dunstaffnage Castle.

When the man turned toward Morrigan—standing beside Ceallach—Kat gasped and grabbed Ceallach's arm. When the large man arrived, he swept Morrigan into his arms and kissed her like a man who hadn't seen his love for eons. Their mouths tangled, moving together in a rhythm that blurred time. She barely noticed Dagda's impatient foot tapping until the sound thumped louder, breaking through the haze.

When the man finally lifted his head, Morrigan sighed, speaking breathlessly. "Hello, husband."

As he lowered his head to hers, their brows gently pressed together, the weight of their bond as clear as the sky above. "Greetings, soul mate." Dagda cleared his throat, and the large man holding Morrigan turned to face Dagda and bowed.

He rose and rotated to Ceallach and her. "Son, I am honored to be here for yer vows." With the same cat-like stealth as Ceallach, he tipped forward in a graceful bow, steeped in respect and honor as his gaze never left hers. "Yer soul mate is as beautiful as I knew she would be." When he rose, he winked at an open-mouthed Kat.

Ceallach returned the gesture with similar motions. "Kathryn Marie MacArthur, please meet my da, Eragon." There was a lilt in his voice, light and playful, as if his lips couldn't help but smile. "He spends much time away protecting a glen." Ceallach cleared his throat as his dragon story echoed in her memory. "A promise he made long ago."

When Eragon took his place beside Morrigan, Kat hissed to Ceallach. "Eragon. Ye mean the tale ye told of the dragon is yer da?" As Ceallach turned them to face Dagda, Kat tugged on his arm. "The dragon, can ye do that?"

His shoulders shook just slightly, that familiar warmth of his amusement brushing over her. "Well, my da *is* the dragon from the tale." He turned his head till their eyes met. "While no dragon is inside me, I have dragon powers." He bent, kissing her lips. "And my soul mate."

Dagda let out a mock growl, his expression bright with mischief. "Now that we've addressed that grandson, can we get on with it? There's MacDougall whisky to drink."

Kat turned, breath catching as she faced him—the man who'd given up a piece of himself, surrendering his immortality just to save her life.

Tears stung, but she forced them back when Dagda gathered both their hands in his broad, steady grip. "Flowers represent unending blessings and provisions in our lives." His voice rose, echoing in the grand room overlooking the sea. "The life of mortals is like a flower that flourishes in the field." He glanced at Ceallach, then her. "But ye both, ye are a flower. Ye not only survive the rain but use the darker times to grow." Dagda squeezed their joined hands once. "The flower may wither then fade, but yer love will stand forever." He released their hands. "Now exchange yer vows and rings as sweet Kat wants her human wedding." Dagda held out his finger to her, where, at the end, sat a ring made of Fae crystal. A symbol of their eternal love. She took the ring as Ceallach offered his left hand to her.

As he grinned, she slid the ring to his knuckle. "Ceallach, you are mine, and I am yours. From this day forward, I promise to love you without end." Her voice hitched a bit, but she took a deep breath. "With this ring, I choose you to be my destined partner, whom I will love and cherish for eternity." She pushed the ring over his knuckle. As she pulled away, his other hand rose, and both held hers. He took a breath, huffed, and gazed into her eyes.

Tears gathered in them as he spoke. "Kathryn, you are the most inspiring woman I have ever met." The words didn't waver—his voice clear and resolute, meant only for her. "Your intellect and beauty are far above anything in any realm." Without a word, he lowered his brow to hers, the familiar gesture grounding them both. "On this blessed day, I take you as my wedded wife in this human ceremony." As he twisted his wrists while still holding her hands, she felt a weight on her left finger. Ceallach whispered the last as he kissed her. "With this ring, I profess my love to you for all eternity." She peeked at the band, which was also made of Fae crystal.

Dagda huffed. "Kissing her already? We still have the Fae vows, boy."

Ceallach lifted his head, nodding to his grandda. "Aye, we do."

****

Bree sat next to Colin for the grand Fae wedding. She'd loved weddings all her life. But after hers in the past, each one moved her more. Since the stones transferred, age clung to her—heavy in her joints, sharper in her thoughts, as if the weight of centuries had settled into her bones. Sitting up taller, she chided herself; she wasn't old. Maybe the sensation was more content. Her heart lifted, airy with relief, even as her body sagged under an invisible weight. She huffed—old age.

She caught Colin's glance from her periphery. He'd kept a close eye on her since the incident with the dragons, much as he had when she returned from her captivity with her ex, Tony, whom the evil Fae King, Balor, had possessed in his search for a magic Iona stone. Back then, she'd complained that everyone treated her like an egg. This time, she seemed to need softer care.

Kat's eyes flashed, and Ceallach smiled as they exchanged necklaces, symbolizing a Fae bond. Bree sat recalling her wedding in the eighteenth century when she married Colin. As the two lovers stood before she spoke their vows, hers from so long ago echoed. They'd been so young, each innocent to the ways of life.

Colin had whispered the first part of the vows, love, and promises, but the last part stuck with her forever.

He paused and squeezed her right hand, which held the Iona stone. "I promise to love thee wholly and completely without restraint, in sickness, and in health, in plenty and in poverty, in life *and beyond*, where we shall meet, *remember*, and love again." The memory faded as the couple before her blurred in her tears.

Colin leaned over, now whispering. "Life and beyond where we shall meet, remember, and love again." He kissed her cheek. "I will love ye till eternity, Bree."

She turned, tears in her eyes. "And I, you, Colin."

The crowd erupted in cheers, pulling Bree from her memory. She held Colin's hand hard as she struggled to stand and clap for the couple. Another wedding, another generation grown, time passed, as it should.

****

Tuatha Dé Danann Throne Room — One Month Later

Dawn spilled through cobalt-blue crystal spires, painting the vaulted chamber in restless sapphires and turquoise. Prisms burst across the glossy floor, rippling toward the raised dais where Kat claimed the Queen's seat, a sky-glass throne, whose spare lines disguised the final authority they conferred.

The monarchs advanced along the central aisle, their crowns blazing. The king's star-quartz circlet flared, four wind-points alive with emerald filaments and a south-set garnet that pulsed like a trapped heart; every measured step sent green light skittering through the citadel walls. Beside him, the queen's moon-petal diadem shimmered with seven crystal lilies. Haloed droplets of starlight hovered above each bloom, flushing rose-gold at her smile, while the opal at her brow spun and summoned a low crystalline hum that thrummed through Kat's bones.

Ceallach stationed himself at her right shoulder, fingers curled around the throne's back in a silent vow, danger would reach his soul mate only over his corpse.

His resolve brushed her thoughts; she looked up, found his grin, and answered with a steady smile. Together they faced the gathering Fae Council, hearts in rhythm with the living heartbeat of crystal and crown.

Below, the semicircle of the Fae Council argued like ravens over winter grain. Dagda stood aside, not in a position of power having recently relinquished his crown to his nephew but still stood as advisor being a long-time powerful King. His wife, Tethra, beside him as they held hands.

Scrolls rattled, voices rose, and at the center stepped Councilor Bressal, grey-browed and proud in silver robes. "The law speaks plain," he intoned, striking the floor with an obsidian staff whose echo rang against crystal. "Only Fae blood, or a relic sanctioned by the gods, grants a mortal claim to that seat. What proof has the human?" Dagda stepped forward, but Ceallach's growl held his grandda back.

Kat rose, shoulders back, one hand resting on the new life growing within her. She inhaled cedar smoke from braziers, the far tang of the sea, and Ceallach's quiet, ozone scent. Confidence settled over her like a cloak. They were bound not only by his Fae immortality necklace but also by something stronger. Her memory rang when Ceallach explained the dragon soul mating ritual, as her thoughts echoed in his mind.

"We are soul mates, truly? Not only bound by the Fae necklaces?"

He'd held her tightly. "Aye, the first one was yer scent, which I smelled when we first met at Evie and Aodhán's wedding." She rocked back into his embrace as he spoke. "The next happened when I was in the human realm; yer tear shed on me."

238

Kat hummed. "My tear gems."

Ceallach nodded. "The next was intimacy."

He bent, kissing her ear as she turned in his arms. "Us together?"

He grinned. "Aye, the first of many I've enjoyed."

Kat rested her head on his chest. "Any others?"

His arms tightened around her. "I don't possess full life healing breath, but it's a step from a full-bred dragon."

They stood there for a moment and Kat sighed. "The spell fight between ye and yer cousin, that incantation that hit me. Ye breathed on me waking me that day. Ye healed me."

He nodded once, not wanting to re-live his fear that day. "But the most important one is declaring yer love."

She lifted her face, "I love ye, Ceallach."

He kissed her. "I love ye, too."

Kat's declaration brought him back, the conviction of fate laced through the act. "Ye demand evidence." Her voice carried beneath the crystal vaults. "Very well, behold, the sign logic cannot measure."

She drew a slender chain from beneath her bodice. The pendant shimmered: the eternity knot over fern leaves, crowned by a five-pointed star of clear Fae crystal—the very necklace that holds a Fae's immortality. Months earlier, in the Veil, Ceallach had removed the necklace from his own throat and fastened the chain around hers, gifting her his undying essence and binding their souls for eternity.

A collective breath hissed from the scholars as the jewel pulsed, first blue, then violet, then incandescent white, answering the sunrise with a heartbeat of pure light. Runes flared across the crystal walls, ancient glyphs of bonds and blessings that no council decree could counterfeit.

Kat lifted her chin. "Love offered proof before any of ye asked. The results stand before you, this child, this kingdom, and the life Ceallach not only staked to mine but committed via a bonding of fate, the dragon soul mating ritual."

Ceallach's laughter rolled across the hushed hall, warm and certain. He clasped her free hand, and sparks danced over their fingers and vanished into her skin.

His voice rumbled like velvet over steel. "Ye heard yer Fae queen," he lifted her hand and kissed the back. "Challenge her, and ye challenge *my* immortal pledge and the gods who witnessed it."

Councilor Bressal's staff lowered. Slowly, he and, one by one, the rest knelt on the sapphire floor. There was no fanfare, no trumpets, only the hush of conviction settling like dew.

In the quiet, Ceallach bent to Kat's ear. "Evidence enough, *mo bruadarach*?"

She smiled, tears of sun-lit joy pricking her eyes. "More than logic ever dreamed."

High above, crystal bells chimed the hour, their music tangled with seabirds' cries beyond the balconies. As the council rose in acceptance, petals of star-white camellia, Ceallach's silent courtship gift, spiraled down from unseen ledges, crowning the moment with gentle snow.

Kat closed her fingers around the glowing pendant, the pulse echoing the rhythm of the child beneath her heart. In that moment, she knew—love had rewritten the laws of gods and kings. Eternity now bore her mark. Destiny had not chosen her… she had chosen hers. And never again would the throne of the Tuatha Dé Danann dare question the power of a mortal soul bound in love to a Fae king.

Epilogue

Years later, an older Colin sat in the Chapel in the Woods. He'd left the lights off, preferring the natural sunlight through the stained-glass windows. Days blurred, and somehow his feet always led him back here, like habit turned home. The wind blew around the building, and the new roof held well. Bree had had the chapel rebuilt after the dragons tore the building apart. He chuckled at the image of the wharf guys staring at the carnage as he and Bree explained a storm had taken the roof. Each shook their head in dismay but built the chapel back as Bree requested. *Bree.*

That first day he'd met her in his study returned to him.

His gaze traveled over her body. She wore twill pants, hiking boots, and a button-down shirt that might have been tan if not for the light layer of gray dust. Under that sat a white tank top with a smudge of dirt on the front near her abundant cleavage. His eyes lingered, then continued to her petite features, set perfectly in her heart-shaped face. She wasn't what he expected, far from it.

They were so young then.

He paused and stared at Brielle as she stood there staring at the *Fae Fable Book*, and damn, if she didn't appear like she was his dream girl from the Fae Fable. The one woman he had dreamed of his whole life as his soul mate.

They'd traveled the portal, searching for a magic Iona Stone. He huffed, his hereditary duty. He'd saved her not once but twice. Once in the past, when he sent her to the future instead of him taking the path to purgatory when they recovered The Stone of Love. And again, when she'd nearly given her life in their search for the Stone of Lust.

His breath caught, and his eyes watered. Bree had saved him each time as well. Her love pulled him from purgatory back to her.

The moments after the Iona Stone's transfer came back to him. She'd tried to keep her weakness hidden, standing tall even when her body trembled. But he'd seen her fragility—the way her hands often shook afterward, how she leaned on the counter just a second too long. And that white streak in her hair…the ribbon reminded him every day of what she'd endured. Still, she held strong when she was at her weakest. For him. For the twins. For them all.

His face lifted to the ceiling as he tried to stop the flow of tears recalling her strongest moment. Even weakened by a near mortal injury, she'd given him the Stone of Lust, placing the gem in the Broach of Lorne and combining power with the magic stones Love and Fear so he could cast away Balor, the king of the Evil Fae. He lowered his head, thanking God for all she'd given him: the twins, their life as a loving married couple.

Children's laughter rang from the yard beyond. He puffed at the sound of their grandkids. She had always been there, woven into his days so tightly he couldn't pull the memory of her free. His hand found the MacDougall love stone with ease, like the token always did, the comfort grounding him. Pulling the gem from his pocket, the mate came as well. He held both out as they sat in his palm, nearly together, making a heart.

The night he'd given her half of the stone came to him.

He brought her hand to his lips, kissing the back. As he gazed at her, Colin opened her hand, took her half of the stone, and placed it in her palm, closing his hands around hers.

He squeezed them lightly. "The chapel is very special, Bree. Ye have become even more special to me." She looked at their clasped hands, then back at Colin.

His heart nearly burst, her love for him glowed in her expression. "I wanted ye to know how special ye are to me, Bree. How much ye mean to me."

A tear slid down her cheek, and he wiped the moisture away. "Carry the half of the stone, Bree. Carry my heart with ye always. So, no matter where we are, ye will know I love ye."

The stones blurred in his tears. Maybe now was time he passed them on. Ewan was the future Laird. Colin gripped them tightly, almost sensing Bree's love. He pocketed them, thankful their children had each found their true loves as he and Bree had.

The kid's squeals came again. Maybe he'd spent enough time here, dwelling on the past. He wiped his tears, grabbed his cane, and rose from the pew. Step by uneven step, his cane guiding his balance, he crossed the chapel, drawn to the only place that ever truly belonged to her. Stopping at her sarcophagus, he rested his palm where the chilled cement form of her laid with her hands folded over a necklace pendant shaped like a heart.

Colin leaned over, whispering. "Life and beyond

where we shall meet, remember, and love again." He kissed the cold stone cheek that resembled his loving wife. "I will love ye till eternity, Bree."

He rose and limped down the aisle, imagining his bride was by his side, like they had at their wedding. When he opened the chapel door and the wind blew, he heard her soft reply in the breeze. *And I, you, Colin.*

****

The sky swallowed Colin whole, clouds curling around his legs as he hovered, weightless and unmoored. There was no ground, no horizon—only endless sky stretching in every direction, as if the world itself had forgotten him. His body didn't hurt as he had only moments ago. The weakness and difficulty breathing had fled. He took a deep breath, feeling young. A slow pivot carried him through the haze, but nothing waited—only endless clouds swallowing the sky. Clouds, was he in heaven?

The name tore from his throat, but the fog smothered the sound, leaving only the echo in his own ears. "Bree!" His feet pounded against nothing, chasing a break in the mist, but the clouds only thickened, stretching without end.

He turned as a familiar voice accompanied by tinkling bells drifted to him. "Hello, Colin."

The growl broke out, unbidden, thick with the weight of his rising anger. "No, it can't be ye!"

Brigid, his Fae materialized before him in her impish form, her incandescent wings fluttering fast. "Welcome, Colin Roderick MacDougall."

He folded his arms, flexing them, relishing the youthfulness returned to his body. "Welcome, my ass. Where the hell are we ye gnome!"

She flew over his head, turning a complete somersault as she giggled. "The time between time, human."

As she passed overhead, he swiped at her. "No games and no tricks, Brigid. Where are we?"

She landed before him tall in full human form, the one she used when she spoke of serious matters. "The Veil, Colin, ye are in The Veil between the human and Fae realm."

The retort snapped from his mouth. "Why am I here?"

She lifted her eyebrow. "For a choice human." She waved her hand to the side. "At the end of every narrow road lies redemption. The choice of what redemption it is up to ye."

He stood staring her down. "Redemption?"

She floated again in her impish form. "As a human and a Christian, you have already secured your salvation—your place with God in heaven. But as a human who also serves the magic Stones of Iona, you now face a choice. You can choose life in the afterworld as you have always believed it: with God in heaven. Or…"

The words rumbled low from his chest. "Or?"

She drifted by him. "The other is living in the Fae realm."

His arms dropped from his chest, hands clasping tight as he spoke, each word carried by steady conviction. "I choose Bree."

Brigid stopped mid-summersault. "That isn't a choice available."

He yelled at her upside-down form. "I vowed eternal love. I will always choose Bree."

The damn Fae righted and floated up and down before him. "Bree made her choice. Ye must make yers, Colin."

He reached, grabbing his Fae, yelling as his hand passed through her form. "Bree, I will choose Bree." What end was this? He made Bree a promise, one he would keep.

Brigid flickered as her voice called out. "Yer choice is upon ye, Colin. Ye must choose."

Bree.

He dropped to his knees, stone biting through wool and flesh as clouds puffed. Palms slammed against the rune-scored floor, sending sparks of Fae light skittering across his skin. Bree's name hammered in his chest, fierce as the North Sea surf. Sweat blurred his vision, yet he kept his gaze locked on Brigid, jaw tight, ready to wager every breath for the woman he loved.

The first words came fragile, like he coaxed them from somewhere deep and buried. "I've served the stones as required of me, even in times of strife. At times, at the price of my sanity, or even a greater price, my true love's."

His hands lifted and tightened before him in prayer, a posture between desperation and devotion. "My prayers for salvation fell upon deaf ears as I continued my dedication to the Fae's whim. My fate left in yer hands wishing like no one for yer grace to provide me with hope."

Tears blurred his vision, but still his gaze found his Fae's, shadowed with sorrow. "When hope became lost, I fell upon my faith. When exhausted, I fell upon my true love's conviction that always guided my lost way." He opened his arms. "Yet through all this, her hope, faith, and love saw me through."

Without strain, he stood, his presence filling the space between them. "Happily, I shall travel my last path to the road paved by my love's grace. I shall sing her praises as I pass through the golden gates and find my final salvation through her tenderness, in her arms, her kiss." A fist beat against his chest as he almost yelled. "For her sweet love shall provide me with all I need in this life and the next!" Air filled his lungs in one measured pull, his focus sharpening. "I only desire to be with my true love." He leveled his eyes on his Fae, almost whispering in a plea. "I choose Bree."

Brigid's scrutiny pinned him in place, her glare unblinking. "The only choice ye have is what yer life in the afterworld will be. God and heaven or living in the Fae realm. Bree made her choice. Now ye must make yers."

Warm tracks burned down his cheeks, but he didn't bother to wipe them. Bree had made her stand, her mind set. Still, the question gnawed at him—what would she choose in the end?

A smile tugged at the corners of Brigid's mouth, warmth flickering. "Colin, to live in the Fae realm means living eternally." His memory echoed her last words. *Life and beyond, where we shall meet, remember, and love again.*

He held her withered hand in his as her breathing became labored. "I will love ye till eternity, Bree."

She rasped her reply with her last breath. "And I, you, Colin." *Eternity.* If he'd gone first, he'd choose eternity and wait for her. Had she done the same?

Colin wiped his eyes in one swift motion, chin dipping in a nod that held the weight of certainty. "I have made my choice."

Brigid cut the air with a single sweep, and twin pillars of molten gold erupted before him, forging gates etched in living runes. The hinges groaned open, pouring out a wind that whipped his cloak and thundered in his blood, pulling—commanding—him to cross their blazing threshold. He progressed inside, and the first person he encountered was his ma, Emily MacDougall.

She barely had her arms out before he closed the distance, the years between them slipping away with every step. "Welcome, my son." His head cleared when he took her in her arms, and everything felt right again.

His da came upon them, and he left his ma's arms to become engulfed by his da's strong embrace. "Son, I am so proud of ye."

Colin stepped back, "How?"

A soft smile flickered on his da's face. "All who serve the stones are offered salvation, my son. The choice is yers to make."

Many others gathered around, offering a welcome. Colin's grandparents, then John's parents, followed by a youthful Doug holding the hand of an auburn-haired woman dressed in older clothing he introduced as Abigail. Colin greeted them while many more came forward. Someone tapped his shoulder, and he turned, coming face to face with Archibald MacArthur from the past.

He pulled his old friend into a bear hug. "Archie!" Archie moved back and waved to another man who stepped forward. Colin stood as if facing a mirror—but the man on the other side smirked.

Recognition hit as Colin laughed. "Roderrick!" The man chuckled and hugged Colin, then introduced his petite wife, Mary. Colin glanced around, seeing so many who served the Stones of Iona, his and the MacArthur ancestors together in the Fae realm.

His ma came patting his hand. "Aye, this is overwhelming, son."

From the corner of his eye, her presence pulled his gaze to her face. "Aye, ma, this is." The crowd shifted, but the flash of light brown hair he searched for never appeared—no sign of the woman he sought. Prayed had chosen eternity as well.

A pull on his arm has him turning to his ma's voice. "Ye seek another?"

He took a deep breath and shook his head. "Maybe she isn't here, ma."

Colin's ma turned his body, and the crowd before him parted. As the sun shone behind her, Bree stood in the light blue dress from their wedding, and the sun formed a halo around her head—his dream soulmate. His breath left him, and his ma had to steady him. Bree lifted her gaze to his, and he took one step and then another.

Soon, he lifted her in his arms as she choked with a sob. "I worried you wouldn't come." Colin squeezed her once—their sign that all was okay.

He lowered her till she steadied, and their eyes met. "No one, no Fae or god, shall keep me from ye Bree." He dipped low, capturing her lips in a kiss that chased away the ache of lost time. "Brielle, no matter where I go, no matter if something separates us, ye will always and forever be my true love."

As she gazed into his, a tear traveled down her cheek.

Colin wiped the drop away with his thumb. "Life and beyond where we shall meet, remember, and love again." He kissed her cheek. "I will love ye till eternity, Bree."

She turned tears in her eyes. "And I, you, Colin."

****

Beneath the ghostly glow of the Fae's moon garden, Colin MacDougall sat in breathless stillness, the night heavy with enchantment as he waited for the arrival of his true love, Bree. They had a date scheduled for another tryst in the favored location. A movement came from Colin's periphery, and he turned, expecting Bree, but Dagda emerged from the foliage carrying a glass with amber liquid inside.

Colin settled back, lounging on the hillside overlooking the waterfall. "Dagda. 'Tis nice to see ye, but I expect Bree."

His friend took his seat, moving a little slower now that he'd retired as Fae king, leaving the realm's ruling to his grandson, Ceallach, with his new wife, Kat. Beside him, Colin grinned. The newlyweds were expecting their first child already, and it had only been months since their wedding. He chuckled, thinking of his courtship of Bree.

Dagda's heavy sigh interrupted his thoughts. "I'm still bothered, Colin. The stones. Why the dragon, and why now?"

Colin waved to his longtime friend. "Dagda, leave me in peace. I've served the stones. Bree arrives soon. We plan to take our ease here. Maybe later visit the grandkids in the human realm."

Dagda shook his head. "I should have never shown yer father how the portals work both ways." He shook his finger at Colin. "Time travel was his undoing, ye know."

Colin picked up his whisky glass, sipping some. "We'll be careful. Now leave me in peace."

Dagda sipped his own. "Peace, will there ever be peace? Spells cast in haste leave an echo of a troubled past, paving the way to a disturbed future. When will it all end?"

A part of foliage folded back, revealing Bree, making Colin's heart skip. "Aye, Dagda, let it all end."

Dagda huffed and rose, his silhouette framed by the fading light. At the threshold, he paused, eyes distant. "It's time I look back—back to the moment I hurled the Iona Stones across space and time in reckless haste. The answers lie with the dragons."

A word about the author...

Margaret Izard is a multi-award-winning author of historical fantasy and paranormal romance novels. She spent her early years through college to adulthood dedicated to dance, theater, and performing. Over the years, she developed a love for great storytelling in different mediums. She does not waste a good story, be it movement, the spoken, or the written word. She discovered historical romance novels in middle school, which combined her passion for romance, drama, and fantasy. She writes exciting plot lines, steamy love scenes and always falls for a strong male with a soft heart. She lives in Houston, Texas, with her husband and adult triplets and loves to hear from readers. You can email me at info@margaretizardauthor.com

Thank you for purchasing
this publication of The Wild Rose Press, Inc.

For questions or more information
contact us at
info@thewildrosepress.com.

The Wild Rose Press, Inc.
www.thewildrosepress.com